SHARED

KATE HAWTHORNE

Shared
Kate Hawthorne

Copyright © 2024 Kate Hawthorne

Edited by:
Jordan Buchanan

Cover Design:
Samantha Santana - Amai Designs

"There is no joy in possession without sharing."
- Erasmus

CHAPTER 1
BARCLAY

Val was beautiful when he got off.

Of all the memorable sights I'd seen in my life, and there'd been quite a few, not many things came close to the way his chin quivered on a soft exhale right before he wailed loud enough for the angels to hear. Maybe the first time I'd seen a sunrise in New York City, the way it had felt to be in a city so massive and loud in a small moment of quiet and peace. The awe I felt standing in the middle of an otherwise empty Times Square with a hotel cup of coffee in my hand came very close to the way I *always* felt when I made Val come.

New York had quickly lost its appeal, and the sunset over the Pacific Ocean was beautiful, but routine to me now. Hollywood was filthy and the skyscrapers in downtown were nothing compared to those in New York or Chicago. As a whole, Los Angeles was an unimpressive city full of unimpressive people and things.

But then there was Val.

With his muscles rippling around my cock, I fell forward over him, bracing my hand beside his thrashing head so I could get an up-close-and-personal view of his face was he came. I'd forced so many orgasms out of him, I knew his tells and I knew the signs. I could predict the way the wrinkles around the corners of his eyes would crease and deepen when he slammed his gorgeous green eyes closed before falling over the edge. I had memorized the way his lips turned down, almost into a frown, before his jaw went slack. His nostrils flared, always, before he opened his eyes, those jade orbs searching me out just milliseconds before the first spurt of cum shot out of his dick.

His knees were tucked up almost into my armpits, his lithe body folded in half so I could get as deep into him as physically possible, and still he whined and begged for more. His thighs shook against me and he tried to spread his legs, but I was a man with only so many inches to give him.

"More," he whimpered, cum still leaking from his cock and pooling on his belly. "More. More. More."

It was *more* of the same, with Val.

He was the most reliable and predictable man in my life, and I wasn't enough for him.

Val always wanted more, and it was rare that I had any issues obliging him because Val coming was almost always enough to make *me* come too. Even if he was coming with another man inside of him, but I tried to not stop too long and think about what that meant for me as a person…as a partner.

I rutted deeper into him, like there was anywhere else for me to go. His chanting turned into a staccato moan, and I buried my face into the crook of his neck, kissing my way up to the sensitive spot beneath his ear that always shut him up.

Like clockwork, his whimpers turned into breathy gasps, and I emptied inside of him with a low growl. The orgasm shook through me, starting at the base of my spine and radiating up and out until every nerve in my body was tuned in with his. For better or worse, this was the thing that existed between us. A chain reaction, a domino effect, whatever you wanted to call it. It wasn't anything I'd ever asked for and nothing that I wanted.

But I had Val, just the same.

When there wasn't any cum left inside of me, I pulled out and fell onto the bed beside him, flinging an arm over my face with a groan. Val lay limp next to me, legs still half bent at the knee for how long I'd had him in that position. He turned his head to the side and kissed my elbow with a happy little hum. His desperate moans echoed through my head as I forced myself off the bed and into the bathroom.

More.

I wet a cloth from under the sink and padded back into the bedroom. He'd straightened his legs, but left them open…because he knew me. He knew where I'd go and what I'd do next. I didn't even have to ask. He reached down with his hands and spread his ass apart for me. His rim was pink and swollen, with bubbles of cum and lube leaking out of him. I scooped up what I could catch and pushed it back into him. He was sloppy down there, but far from loose, and his back arched while I fucked him with my fingers. Pushing my cum back into him, I buried my fingers to the last knuckle.

More.

More.

When his voice in my head grew too loud, I pulled them out and used the warm rag to wipe them clean, then I wiped him up with the same level of attention and care as I'd always offered him. I swiped the soft cloth over his hole and his balls, up the length of his cock and around the underside of his bulbous, flared tip. He shivered, and I picked at the cum already drying in the short hairs that trailed from the base of his cock toward his navel.

Without a word, I tended the man who knew my body as well as I knew his, and when I was certain he was clean, I went back to the bathroom. This was more of the routine between us, the expectation. Val would curl onto his side as close to *my* pillow as he could manage without encroaching on my side of the bed, and I would shower alone.

My post-sex showers were a reflection time for me, a few moments of quiet and clarity after the high of sex that always served to bring me back down to earth so I didn't do something regrettable that would ruin this for both of us. It was no secret that

Val wanted more from me than I was willing to give him, but we had an understanding. An agreement. At the very beginning of our—I didn't want to call it a relationship because it wasn't. It never had been and it never would be…but at the beginning of whatever this thing between us was, I'd been clear and he'd signed on willingly.

Val and I were two grown men who liked to fuck and we fucked each other. Often and well. There were no dinner dates or meeting the friends, though the latter had happened over the course of our relations just the same. Because Val didn't just like to fuck me and I didn't care who Val fucked if I wasn't trying to get inside of him.

More.

More.

More.

Val had slept with a handful of my friends. Rather, he'd been fucked by them, and that felt like an important clarification for some reason I couldn't quite put my finger on. He'd been fucked by my friends and his friends and strangers. Sometimes I'd arranged it for him and sometimes he'd done it on his own on nights when I had plans or had told him no. I didn't care. I didn't mind.

Everything Val did was within the rules of our arrangement.

The one thing we hadn't talked about was *dating* other people.

Because I didn't want to date anyone, and Val seemed content to keep things with me—and everyone else—restricted to the bedroom. But he'd been poking around lately, dropping hints that he wanted to date. Not me, of course, but other people. I'd done my best to ignore the comments because I wasn't a stupid man. I couldn't imagine a man, even in the very unique lifestyle we lived, who would be content to date a man like Val while knowing he came over after warming another man's bed. Other men's beds.

Because I wasn't the only one.

I was just the most consistent.

Val dating would undoubtedly put an end to an arrangement

that had lasted and worked for years, and I wasn't ready for that yet. But I wasn't going to compromise either. Not for him, and not for anyone.

I finished my shower and dried off, wrapping the oversize terrycloth towel around my waist. The knot sat low beneath my navel, but even if it fell, who was there to see? Val was already asleep, of that I was certain. Shuffling into the kitchen, I kept the lights off on my way, opting to flip on the light over the stove to keep the house as dark as possible. I didn't need light to find the bottle of scotch or a glass, and I sure as shit didn't need light to drop some ice cubes into the glass, pour two fingers, and drink it down.

I had just poured my second drink when a naked and bleary-eyed Val stumbled into the kitchen, rubbing his eyes with both hands and looking around like it was his first time in my house.

It was far from it. It wasn't even the first time *that week.*

"Go to bed," I told him, shaking the glass so the ice would settle and I could drink it.

"I'm not tired." He yawned.

"Don't lie."

"I don't lie to you," he murmured, closing the space between us.

He didn't ask to take off my towel. His fingers knew the way I tied the knot, knew the tension of the material. The towel was on the floor faster than him, and my cock was in his mouth before I could even think about telling him no.

More.

More.

I tangled my fingers into his hair, guiding him up and down my length slowly because if I didn't, he would choke himself to death on the first swallow. His mouth was as hot and tight as the rest of him, and I groaned as he hummed around my length. I loosened my grip on his hair and Val swallowed me down to the root. The muscles of his throat worked against the still sensitive head of my cock, and I dropped my head back with a groan.

Val knew how to suck me to get me off and he knew how to suck me to drive me mad. He alternated between the two, with long and slow pulls of his mouth from root to tip coupled with short and shallow bobs of his head that barely reached the halfway point of my shaft. I curled my toes into the tile floor, pouring the rest of my drink down my throat before slamming the crystal tumbler onto the counter top.

He grabbed my thighs, fingers splayed as he worked his mouth and throat up and down my cock. He sucked me in the way I liked to be sucked, and I petted the top of his head with a happy sigh. Even though I'd just finished, it wouldn't be long before he sucked another orgasm out of me. He'd had years of practice on my cock specifically, just like I'd had years to learn *his* body. Bringing each other off was like clockwork, but far from boring.

"I'm going to come," I warned him, because I always did when he was on his knees.

He dug his fingers into my skin and relaxed his throat, taking the whole length of me inside his mouth until his lips kissed the hair around the base of me. He flattened his tongue, he worked his muscles, and I spilled into the back of his throat with a grunt. My fingers were still gentle against the top of his head, and my cock thickened against the roof of his mouth as I shot my load onto his waiting tongue.

Val hummed, swallowing happily until he sucked me dry.

It was hard to breathe, hard to stand. He took the towel with him when he stood up, leaning around me and pouring another shot of scotch into my glass. The ice had started to melt, and he pressed the glass back into my hand. He didn't say a word, but his stare danced across my face.

My eyes had adjusted to the dark, even though I didn't need the light to see him. I knew him as well as I knew his body, and worse than that, he knew me. I knew how he made me feel, the way emotions churned and surged in my chest when I made him smile, and how small I felt when I hurt him, even on accident. I knew how Val felt too. I knew what he was trying to say because his eyes screamed it at me even while his mouth stayed closed.

"Go to bed," I told him again, setting the glass on the counter, untouched.

Val licked his lips, and I wanted to kiss him to see if I could taste myself there, but he spoke before I could make a move.

"I am tired," he whispered with a small and sad nod.

And I knew it wasn't a lie.

CHAPTER 2
VAL

THE DINNER TABLE WAS LOUD AS IT ALWAYS WAS, THE CHAIRS SMASHED too close together like they always were. The kitchen counter was smeared with sauce and spilled wine, and my mom hollered at my older sister like we were all still teenagers. Still or again, either way, me and my two sisters hadn't ever grown up in our mother's eyes. Angie was forever fourteen, right on the cusp of her teenage rebellion, and Teresa would always be twelve with a mouthful of braces and a brain full of ideas that didn't align with any of the dreams our parents had ever had for us.

And me...

I was forever the acne-faced thirteen year-old with Coke bottle glasses, not enough friends, and an affinity for math too advanced to ignore. The year I turned thirteen was also the year I got my first kiss, but no one knew about that except for me and Thomas Morello because he was the one I'd kissed and we'd both sworn to take it to the grave. Being forever a teenager in the eyes of my parents also meant that they could pretend I'd never come out to them on my twenty-second birthday.

It wasn't that they had an issue with me being gay. No, nothing as terrible as all that. The issue was, as my mother had explained to me on more than one occasion, how could I make her grandbabies if I was sleeping exclusively with men? I didn't bother trying to explain to her about adoption and surrogacy, let alone the possibility of me ever finding love with a trans man because, as far as she was concerned, two men meant no babies.

Her obsession with procreation had always felt harmless to me. Even more so after Angie got married and had her first son, and even more after Teresa had followed suit and made our mother her first granddaughter. It was just the way of the world. We were Italian and family was everything.

For them, at least.

I loved my family—there was no doubt about that. But they were a lot sometimes. They were a lot *all* the time. There was no shortage of love between us, but I still didn't feel like I could be completely myself around them. But I didn't think that was a problem with them, more so an issue with me. I had spent plenty of nights in my attic bedroom awake and pondering what acceptance would look like for me, and I didn't ever imagine a world where I could come home and talk to my parents about how many men had taken turns coming inside of me the night before.

Not just that I couldn't imagine a safe space to do that, but I couldn't imagine a space where I *wanted* to do that. My sexuality, my dating habits, my love life, it all felt very sacred to me. After watching how my mom and my aunts had meddled their way through my sisters' lives and marriages, I knew I would never want that for myself. Even if I did ever have a serious partner, I wanted to keep them far away from Sunday dinners.

There were ten chairs crammed around the table designed to seat six, and the moral of the story was: once you were in a seat, you sat. There was no other way around it, so I found myself lingering in the corner of the kitchen with a glass of wine in hand while my mom and my sisters argued over how much garlic had made it into the sauce. Their voices got louder, so I snuck out of the kitchen and let myself out onto the back patio. The sliding door rattled on the tracks as I pulled it closed, but no one came after me, so I counted it as a win.

Angie's husband, Marcos, was sitting at the glass top patio

table, and he looked up when I stepped onto the concrete, eyes wide like he'd been caught with his hand in the cookie jar.

"Just me," I murmured.

He huffed out a breath and kicked one of the chairs away from the table. I sat down and shook the tension of the house off my shoulders.

"Where's Andrew?" I asked, noticing my youngest sister's husband was absent from both the patio and the kitchen.

"Talking with your dad somewhere. How's it going inside?"

"The ongoing garlic debate continues. If I would have known you were out here, I would've grabbed the bottle."

I set my wine down on the table and Marcos raised a half-empty beer bottle from beneath the table. Laughing, I leaned back in the plastic chair and closed my eyes. The back yard was as familiar to me as the rest of the house. My parents still lived in Burbank, in the same house all three of us kids had been born and grown up in. They'd done the barest of minimum upgrades over the years, and by bare minimum I meant they'd let me replace their kitchen appliances after I got my first five-figure bonus and they finally redid the kitchen floor after the linoleum had cracked and peeled so badly there was no way around it.

"How's work?" Marcos asked, taking a swig from his beer.

"A lot of the same," I said.

No one in my family cared about my job and that was fine. Rather, they did care; they just didn't understand. No one was good at math the way I was, so there was always going to be a disconnect. My older sister was an English teacher and my younger sister was a veterinarian. My father worked at the truck plant and my mom had always been home. On paper, the Russo family was straightforward and simple, but if anyone were to examine the lineage and look too long and hard at me, they'd find a kink in the chain.

Quite literally.

"And the love life?" he asked.

I raised a brow, rolling my eyes at him. "You too, Brutus?"

Marcos chuckled and shrugged helplessly. "Your sister worries about you."

"Doesn't she have enough to worry about between you and the kids?"

Marcos and Angie had two sons now. My nephews were seven and three, and judging by the state of my parents' living room, they were more than a handful.

"Between me and the kids," he repeated with a laugh. "And your sister and Andrew and the baby, but she finds time."

"She's so much like Mom."

Something crashed inside the house, and I grabbed the arm rests of the chair to stop myself from getting up and going inside to offer help. I knew better.

"Angie just wants to make sure you have someone to take care of you," he said.

I sighed, sucking in a deep breath.

My sister meant well. Her husband meant well. My parents meant well. All of them *meant well*. But there was no world where I could tell them anything about the state of my love life that would make any of them feel better about my situation. It was better the lot of them imagine me single and desperately alone than to know the truth.

Because the reality was much worse.

I'd been sleeping with the same man for the past three years. But I'd also been sleeping with his friends, and their friends, and strangers, and quite literally anyone who was remotely attractive and interested in taking off his pants for me. I wouldn't have gone as far as calling myself a sex addict. It didn't feel that serious to me. It wasn't an addiction. It wasn't a *need*. It was a want, in the most visceral terms.

I loved being fucked.

I craved being used, being passed around…being shared.

And no one fucked me, used me, passed me around better than Perceval Barclay did. But things between me and him were… complicated.

They hadn't always been, but I'd gone into things with him blind and maybe a little naive. I thought the arrangement with him was perfect, and it had been at first. We didn't date. There weren't any emotions or feelings between us. Everything for me and Barclay was completely and purely physical. But maybe it was physiology or who knew…my heart had slowly started to change the game.

For his part, Barclay remained steadfast in line with our original rules.

Sex.

Just sex.

I didn't want to lose the sex, and I didn't want to lose him, so I beat myself up on the nights I spent alone, trying to debate and argue my developing affection for him right out of my system. I'd been met with limited success but managed to convince myself that I could bear the burden of unknown and unrequited love for at least a little while longer.

"Come on, Val. Just go on a date, you know," Marcos said. I didn't know how long he'd been talking for, but I hoped it wasn't long because I hadn't heard a single thing he said. "Even if it doesn't go anywhere, let someone take you out and treat you nice for a bit."

"I can treat myself right," I assured him.

In truth, Barclay could too, but he wouldn't.

In the three years I'd been sleeping with the man, I couldn't remember a time we'd shared anything more than a drink together. It had taken months before he introduced me to his friends, and that had only come to pass because he'd arranged for two of them to fuck me. As time dragged on, I'd become as accepted into their friend group as a boyfriend would have been, even while Barclay insisted on keeping me at arm's length.

"It's not the same," Marcos said softly, but I could tell by his tone he was ready to end the conversation. "You're just like them, you know?"

"Like who?"

I'd been thinking about Barclay and his friends—Archie, Rob, Dalton, and Flynn—and I didn't think I was like any of them. At least not in any material way.

"Your sisters," he said.

I choked on a laugh and grabbed my wine, pushing the chair back and standing. Clearly, the back patio was not going to bring me any respite from the chaos of Sunday night family dinner.

I pushed the chair back in and went for the slider, giving it a rough tug to get it open far enough for my body to fit through.

"Don't tell them where I am," Marcos begged.

I gave him the finger and slammed the door closed. The glass rattled in the frame, and I followed the sound of the chaotic argument between my mom and my sisters until I found the three of them in the kitchen, still over the stove.

"Where's Marcos?" Angie asked. She looked at me, then our mom. "He'll tell you that I don't use too much garlic."

"Haven't seen him," I lied.

"I make it just like you do, Ma," Theresa said, pushing her shoulder against my mom's side.

"Of course you do," Mom said. "You always were the best listener of all my babies."

"I'm right here," I reminded her.

"Good." Angie waved me over with her whole arm. "Come try this sauce and tell me if there's too much garlic in it."

"It's not my recipe," Mom droned on as Angie grabbed me and yanked me toward the stove, shoving a sauce covered wooden spoon toward my mouth. I was fairly certain my dad had swatted us all with that thing at least once in our lives, and I admired the craftsmanship of a multipurpose tool that would no doubt outlive us all.

I tried the sauce.

There wasn't too much garlic in it, but I wasn't ready to meet my maker just yet.

"It's a bit strong, Ange," I said, tearing my arm out of her hold and backpedaling toward the door. I slammed into a body too tall to be my father, and the cologne that wafted around me after the impact confirmed it was Teresa's husband, Andrew.

He caught me and steadied me on my feet at the same time Angie set her sights on her brother-in-law.

"Drew, come try this," she called out.

He'd just saved me from going through a wall, but Sunday dinner was every man for himself. I shouldered my way behind him and gave him a small shove into the kitchen. Grabbing the wine bottle on my way out, I'd bide my time on the porch until dinner was ready, then God help us all.

CHAPTER 3
BARCLAY

From across the table, Dalton eyed me warily. His expression was far removed from the one that had been on his face ever since his husband had relocated from New York to L.A. I hated to think that I was the cause of his dour mood, but such was most likely the case.

It was a Sunday evening and Val always had family dinners on Sunday. I'd never been invited to them, which was just as well because why would you invite the random man you were sleeping with to family dinner in the first place? You wouldn't. So he never had, and I'd never pushed for an invitation. I normally had dinner with Dalton on Sundays, but ever since he'd gotten himself married to Carter Royce IV, or Ivey as he affectionately called the man, the schedule had been lacking.

Recently, Ivey had moved across the country for Dalton, a show of love and devotion that made me happy for my friend, even if the saccharinity of the whole thing made me want to drag my face across a cheese grater.

He'd been giving me a shitty look since we got our drinks, and if this was his new, post-husband attitude, I didn't want any of it. I'd be happy to leave him alone on Sunday nights to do whatever the hell it was the two of them did behind closed doors. Or in the open. Whatever. As long as it didn't involve him looking at me the way he was, I didn't much care.

"What?" I snapped, pushed to the brink of my tolerance.

Even as frustrated as his look had made me, I hadn't intended to come off as harsh as the word sounded to my own ears, but it was already there in the space between us and there was no taking it back.

"Nothing," he said, voice lilting. "Where's Val?"

"Why would I know?"

"Are we still pretending that the two of you aren't in a relationship?" He laughed. My best friend laughed at me. "It's the worst-kept secret in the city."

"We aren't in a relationship," I said.

"Doesn't the lie get exhausting?"

"Coming from the man who was *married* for fifteen years and didn't tell anyone?"

Dalton laughed again, rolling his eyes and leaning back in his seat. "I didn't know I was married," he reminded me.

"And now everyone knows."

Dalton glanced down at the gaudy diamond and blue topaz ring on his finger with a small, secret smile.

"As they should," he said. "Because I love Ivey and I'm not ashamed to admit it. Not how you are about Val."

"I'm not in love with Val," I said.

The protest was almost muscle memory at that point, but the more I said it, the more it tasted like a lie. It didn't matter how I felt about Val, though, because I was no good for him. I could love him and want him until I was blue in the face, but he deserved someone much better than me, and even though I was a selfish prick, I wasn't *that* horrible. I wouldn't saddle him with me and all my doubts and insecurities.

"Okay."

There was a condescending kind of amusement in Dalton's voice that made me want to knock his teeth out.

"How is your husband adjusting to his new life?" I asked, more than ready to change the subject.

"He's happy with me," Dalton said.

I couldn't help but notice how careful the word choice sounded, and I raised a brow in question.

"His friends are a thing," he said.

"In the same way yours are?"

Dalton scoffed, but nodded. "Much the same, but they're…oh, I don't know. They're very protective of him."

"We're protective of each other."

"Possessive, then," he corrected himself.

I sucked in air through my teeth. "Ah."

"Yeah." He finished his gin and tonic and pushed the glass toward the edge of the table.

"How does he deal with that?"

"He loves them, of course. But it's almost like he's a teenager going on a first date, except we're married already and he's never coming home. His four dads are not taking it well."

"Have them come visit," I suggested.

Dalton's eyes went wide and he immediately held up a hand in defeat.

"Why not?" I chuckled. "What could go wrong? Worst case, Grayson talks them to death. Best case, Val fucks them all and they forget Ivey even exists. Everyone goes home happy. Everyone wins."

"Is that really best and worst, or do you have them flipped?"

"I'm not going to have dinner with you if you insist on talking everything around to the way you think I feel about Val."

Dalton exhaled loudly, rubbing at his right eye. "Alright," he conceded.

"Just because the lot of you want to partner up and do all of that, it doesn't mean I do, and it sure as fuck doesn't mean he does," I said.

Dalton swiped his thumb under his eye, lips pursed, but he didn't argue with me again.

"So," he said, giving his shoulders a wiggle. "What's been going on with you?"

There wasn't anything going on with me, at least nothing worth bringing into the conversation. My life was by far the least eventful of my friends, but I liked it that way. Even though Dalton and I had finished school together, I was a couple years older than most of them, except for Rob, who was a dinosaur in comparison.

I lived a quiet life in a condo by the beach. I got up and I went to work, and I spent time with my friends, and then I came home. Sometimes we went out to Rapture and every Thursday we had drinks at Cunningham's. Three years ago, Val fell into the mix and he was an unexpected splash of excitement for me. He was part of the routine now, but that didn't make him any less…well…he was just Val. He was there and he was a part of my life. But not in the way Ivey was for Dalton or Owen was for Archie. It was hard to explain to other people, but it made sense to us.

It worked for us.

Maybe I'd gotten too comfortable in the monotony of my life, because if you would have told me a single cream envelope with a wedding invitation inside would have turned my life upside down, I wouldn't have believed you. But ever since that invitation and the RSVP card showed up at my condo, things were different.

It wasn't every day the love of your life got married to someone who wasn't you.

Finding my name on the invite list at first felt like a slap in the face, an oversight so glaring, I imagined someone would lose their job over it. But the invitation was never recalled, and I quickly realized it wasn't an accident. My name had made the list because Dennis's mom was on three boards with my mom, our fathers had done business together a handful of times, and when you were a millionaire, that's how wedding invitation lists were decided.

I'd spent four years of my life with Dennis. He wasn't my first serious relationship, but he was the *most* serious. Everything with him felt real and tangible…intense. Dennis had shown me a lot of things, some of them sexual and some of them not. Unfortunately, he'd also shown me what it felt like to catch the man you thought you were going to spend the rest of your life with in bed with one of your college professors.

Catching Dennis in the act was beyond horrible.

Finding out that wasn't the first time was earth-shattering.

Realizing that I'd built my future on toothpicks, that I'd been so blind to the infidelity…it had been enough to send me so deep inside myself I had no interest in coming back out.

Ever.

And I wasn't crazy enough to blame Dennis for the whole thing, no.

It was my fault.

I wasn't enough for him, or maybe I'd been too much. I wasn't sure. I'd spent enough nights searching for the answer at the bottom of a bottle, but it wasn't there and eventually I gave up.

Dennis had taught me an important lesson, though.

I wasn't enough.

After things collapsed with him, I didn't swear off men altogether, I swore off falling in love with men. I didn't date—I fucked. And saying that out loud sounded crass, so I never did. But I always made sure the people I got involved with understood they could have me for a good time, not a long time. If they wanted to go out to dinner or go shopping, or any of that shit, I wasn't the one.

The problem, of course, was Dennis wasn't the first person to cheat on me, to break my trust that way. It happened in high school twice, and college once before I met him. Every relationship I'd ever had ended with betrayal, and by the end of it, I was embarrassed it had taken me so many tries to learn the lesson that Brandon Willard had tried to teach me my junior year of high school.

Over time, the edges of my lacking had softened, but they would still cut if I poked at them too long. So, I stopped doing that. My friends used to tease and taunt me over my commitment to not having a commitment, but they'd stopped. Everyone stopped eventually.

Val, though.

He'd just started.

The hints had come on slow at first, but I saw them just the same. He wasn't bold enough to ask me to take him on a date, but I noticed the way he enjoyed being around my friends when we all had our clothes on. The way he'd started showing up to Rapture early, before things really got going. How he would sit on my lap and grind his ass against my cock while talking about work with Archie.

It didn't get past me, but for some reason, I let it slide.

Val acted the same when it was him and me. Sex and aftercare, and whatever it was, but the change was there…It had started after the wedding invitation showed up. Val was there, because of course he was. He'd met me in the lobby after work and I was going to fuck him into oblivion. That was the plan. I checked the mail on our way to the elevator, flipping through the bills and the junk as we rode the elevator up to the top floor of my building. By the time we got into my condo, the wedding invitation was the only thing left in my hand, my thumb pressed hard against the last names on the top left corner.

Val was the one who'd called my friends.

Val was the one who'd sucked my cock while I cried over it.

Val was there.

Val was always there.

I recovered from the shock and rallied, like always. But that night had been a change for us, and as the days drifted on, I wasn't sure it was a change for the better. Val was getting grabby, and I didn't want to lose the one person who actually meant something to me.

I didn't love him, not like my friends accused, but I'd gotten accustomed to his presence in my life. I didn't want to lose that by changing things between us. That was a risk I wasn't willing to take.

He meant too much.

But I wouldn't ever tell him that.

"Earth to Perceval Barclay." Dalton waved his hand in front of my face and I startled, smacking him away.

"Get your hand out of my face," I grumbled.

"Where the fuck did you just go?" he asked.

"I was thinking."

"About nuclear physics?" He scoffed. "You totally zoned out, glassy eyes and all."

"I was thinking about Dennis," I said.

It wasn't a lie. I had been thinking about Dennis, but I'd been thinking more about Val.

"You should…not do that."

"Your fault. You asked what had been going on, and his wedding is very much what's going on."

"Well, it's not like you're going," he said, eyes widening when I didn't immediately agree with him. "You're not going, are you?"

"My parents already told his that I am."

"Don't get me started on parents, and considering what Ivey and I just went through, let me remind you that you're a whole adult man and you don't have to do what your parents tell you to. Not anymore."

"I want to go," I lied.

"No, you don't."

"I want him to see that I don't care about him anymore," I said, which wasn't a lie. "I want him to know that he doesn't mean anything."

"Barclay." Dalton's voice was soft with tenderness and I hated him for it.

He knew just how much Dennis had meant, how much he still did.

"It was college," I said with a shrug. "A long time ago."

"You don't need to prove anything to anyone."

"If I don't go, he'll think it's because I'm still heartbroken over what he did to me, and I'm not." I smoothed my napkin over my lap, ignoring the way my fingers trembled. Pretending my palms weren't clammy at the thought of seeing Dennis again.

"Barclay," he said again, the same tone, the same concern.

I worked my jaw back and forth, grinding my molars until they hurt. "What, *Dalton*?"

"You don't have to do this."

"I know," I said through gritted teeth, napkin fisted in my hand. "But I'm going to."

CHAPTER 4
VAL

Thursdays were always my day.

Barclay had a standing date with his friends and I generally worked late, grabbed take-out on the way home, and binged a show. This week, work had kept me later than I'd planned, so it was careening toward eight by the time I made it to the elevator. The last thing I expected when the doors slid open was to find company inside. The other occupant of the car looked just as startled as I must have, his eyes going wide before he huffed out a breath.

"You scared me," he said.

The doors slid the rest of the way open and I stepped in, turning and leaning against the wall beside him. My leather laptop bag was slung over my shoulder, and I slid it around to the front of me so I could rest against the railing. He stood much the same, his tie already loose and his blazer draped over one of his forearms. He was an objectively handsome man. Older than me and taller than me, closer to Barclay's build more than my own.

"Working late?" I asked, reaching to loosen the knot on my own tie.

"Had some late calls with Australia," he said.

The elevator doors were polished steel, so clear I could see the way his eyes trailed over the shape of my body in the reflection ahead of us. I licked my lips, the irony of feeling nervous under his appraisal not lost on me. I'd gotten naked for men after from much less attention.

"I don't think I've seen you in the building before," I said, trying to make conversation because anything was better than the silence of the ride down to the lobby.

"I got hired on a couple of weeks ago." He plucked at a corporate badge on an elastic cord clipped to his belt. The plastic card jostled and settled, and I tried to not look because it was treacherously close to his cock and I was dangerously horny for no good reason at all beyond the fact that I was almost always horny.

"Bridgehouse and Waters," I read out the name of the company on his badge, a name I recognized as the company occupying the upper floors of the building my office was in.

"Guilty." The man let out a deep laugh that rumbled the entire elevator, reaching for a handshake. "My name's Jason. And you are?"

"Valentin," I answered softly, sliding my hand into his.

Another rumble that definitely wasn't a laugh. The elevator lurched, fell, and then jammed to a stop. The fall hadn't been far, couldn't have been more than a few feet, but it was enough for both of us to lose our footing. Jason staggered into the corner and my feet came out from under me entirely. If not for his tight grip around my hand, I would have ended up on my ass.

"Are you okay?" Jason's blazer was on the floor and his other hand curled around my forearm as he helped me to straighten up.

The lights in the car flickered and went out.

"I'm fine. Thank you for catching me." I slid my bag off my shoulder, discarding it at our feet beside his blazer. "You good?"

"Bit claustrophobic," he admitted, "but I'm good for now."

I pushed to the other side of the elevator and pressed the emergency call button. A dim red light flickered to life, casting an unsettling glow over the small space.

Of course, nothing happened.

I pressed it again, harder. "Piece of shit elevator." I fished my cell phone out of my pocket.

I had one bar.

"Are we going to die in here?" Jason asked.

I glanced over my shoulder and watched him slide down onto his ass, legs bent at the knee. He dropped his head in the gap between his knees and his chest, arms stretched straight. I patted the back of his head and chuckled.

"We aren't going to die in here," I assured him.

The single bar on my phone meant I was able to get a call through to building security, their voicemail very helpfully telling me I was calling after hours but to leave a message because the box was monitored once an hour. I didn't see the need in telling Jason that, so I left a message and delivered as much relevant information as I could manage, praying the service held and the words were clear on the other end.

"Is someone coming?" Jason asked, keeping his face between his legs.

"Uhm...yep." I pushed the emergency button once more for good measure, then joined him on the floor. "But it might be a bit."

"Figured as much." He sighed and shifted, dropping his head against the wall and staring up at the roof. "I'm real sorry, I missed your name in the commotion."

"Val," I said. "Valentin."

"Which do you prefer?"

"Either, honestly."

My family were the only ones who called me Valentin, but I'd never hated my name. I'd gotten teased a bit for it in school, but as I got older, it was impossible to hear someone call me by my full name without hearing it in my mother's voice, and that was like a warm blanket most of the time. It didn't bother me, but I didn't have a preference either.

"Valentin is unique. Nothing like Jason."

"But your name comes with 100% more serial killer jokes than mine." We were on separate sides of the elevator, but the toes of his shoes pointed toward my thighs, and I gave him a soft bump.

He scoffed, but nodded in agreement.

"Tell me something about yourself," he said, stare still cast skyward. "Distract me."

"I'm a middle child," I said, holding up one finger, then another and another while I counted off all the boring facts I could think of. "I was born and raised in Burbank. I love Thai food. My favorite color is orange."

"Orange?"

"Orange," I repeated.

"I don't think I've ever met someone whose favorite color was orange."

"Well, now you have." I smiled, and he dropped his chin down, smiling back at me… and I was done for.

Immediately.

Jason's smile was soft and gentle, but unrestrained and bright. It relaxed his whole face, his shoulders, his arms. The tension even leaked out his fingers, and he gave them a little shake.

"What about you?" I asked.

"Only child," he answered. "From Bakersfield. I've never had Thai, and my favorite color is blue."

"You've never had Thai?"

"I'm not really an adventurous eater." Jason's cheeks darkened. "More a steak and potatoes kind of guy."

"You'll have to try it sometime," I said, swallowing.

My spit lodged in my throat, and was it getting hot in here or was it just me?

I popped open the top button on my shirt and rubbed my fingers against the dip of my throat. Jason let out a rough groan, looking at the far side of the elevator, his hand pressed to his throat in a mirrored version of mine.

"Maybe you can tell me what's good." He was staring at me in the reflection of the mirrored wall, and I caught his gaze and held it, my fingers slowly falling away from my throat.

"Like a date?"

Jason opened and closed his mouth a couple of times like a fish, sounds and syllables garbling together on his tongue but none of them truly making sense. It was adorable in an innocent way, and it had been so long since I'd been around anyone like him. I didn't know how to handle it. I was so used to men like me, like Barclay and his friends. Confident in our sexuality and our wants because of how important it was to give voice to them.

"Was I being presumptuous?" I asked, patting his forearm in what I hoped was a reassuring way. "I didn't mean to make things weird."

"No!" he almost shouted the answer at me, twisting his mouth into a grimace and turning his attention back toward the roof. "No, it's not that."

"Okay."

I wasn't going to press him.

"I like Tom Kha Gai," I said with a shrug. "It's a coconut soup with lemongrass and chicken."

"That's not what I meant."

"I thought you wanted to know what to order."

"I did. I do. I...I did mean a date, but I don't even know you and as soon as I said it, it sounded too bold." His cheeks went red again, and sweat beaded against his temples.

It really was getting hot inside this damn elevator.

"Okay," I said quietly, realizing my hand was still on his forearm. I gave him a gentle squeeze before pulling it back.

"Okay?"

I hadn't dated anyone in three years.

From the very first time Barclay and I had fallen into bed together, I knew he was it for me. But three years on and he didn't feel the same about me. He'd made it clear a hundred different times and a thousand different ways. Our relationship was sex. Whether it was sex between the two of us or sex between the two of us and others, it was sex.

Sex.

Not dating.

No feelings.

Definitely not love, even though…

It may have been too late for me there, but I'd held out hope that after time, Barclay would come around. He'd see what was right in front of him. He would see *me*, and it had been a long time since I'd given up wondering if he ignored me deliberately or otherwise.

Part of me had thought the invitation to Dennis's wedding would be the catalyst for us to take things to the next level, but it had the opposite effect. Since Barclay found out his ex was getting married, things between us had gotten *worse*. Whereas before he had corners that softened for me, there were now new walls and dangerous traps that I hadn't even been aware of before. Like Dennis's engagement had stripped away the defenses I'd spent years wearing down, only to reveal an entire new level of protection.

Whether I'd wanted to admit it or not, things between Barclay and me were heading for an end. It didn't matter that I didn't want things to end, because I couldn't make him want to be with me. I couldn't carry a relationship for both of us. So it was time for us to have a conversation that I didn't think either of us really wanted.

In theory, I supposed we didn't need to have it.

Our relationship was physical. He'd never promised me an emotional tie, let alone a commitment.

There was never an agreement that I wouldn't date other people, just like there wasn't an issue if I slept with other people. Of course, he was the person I slept with the most. The person I wanted above all others, but he wasn't the only.

No matter how much I wanted that, in the ways I could…

My feelings for Barclay were beyond complicated because I wanted him and I wanted to love him loudly and in the open. I wanted that back from him, but I didn't want the sexual dynamic between us to change. I loved the use, the sharing…I just wanted *more*.

That was my own fault.

"That's the point of a date," I told Jason. "That's when you get to know someone, so you weren't out of line with the ask."

He looked at me again, the intensity of his dark stare almost taking my breath away. I'd not had a chance to note the color of his eyes before the lights in the elevator had blinked out, and while I could tell they were brown, I wasn't sure of the shade.

"So…" Jason's mouth twitched in the corner. "It's a date?"

The elevator jostled with another loud groan and the lights flashed back to life. It was such a jarring change from the darkness that I covered my eyes and cursed under my breath.

"Oh, thank God."

The speaker beneath the buttons crackled, and I couldn't make any sense of what was being said, but less than ten minutes later the doors were pried open and four firefighters helped Jason and me climb out. I let him go first, on account of the claustrophobia, and once we were both free of the temporary prison, I realized his eyes were amber, like the scotch Barclay and his friends spent so much time drinking.

My heart skittered around my chest, and I couldn't fight my way past the feeling that saying yes to dinner with Jason was somehow cheating on Barclay. Even as my brain screamed at me, reminding me of all the times Barclay had told me it was just sex, the ways he'd reminded me.

"So."

In the light of the lobby, I got my first real look at Jason beyond my initial observation of him being tall and handsome. He was both of those things, but his shyness etched across the tired lines beneath his eyes, and he was just the opposite of everything I'd ever wanted for myself.

Maybe that wasn't such a bad thing.

"So," I repeated, hoisting my bag back over my shoulder.

Jason's hands fluttered around a little before he reached into his pocket and pulled out his wallet and produced a business card from the billfold.

"My cellphone number is on here," he said, handing it to me. "You can call or text and we can…"

He had slender hands and long fingers, and it was beyond adorable the way he couldn't formulate a whole sentence to save his life. I was so out of my depth with this situation, with this man. I needed to be honest with Barclay, honest with him.

I needed to be honest with myself.

"It was a pleasure being temporarily trapped in an elevator with you," I said, taking the card and sliding it into my pocket. "Can't wait to do it again soon."

CHAPTER 5
BARCLAY

THREE DRINKS IN ON A THURSDAY NIGHT AND I WAS FEELING AS normal as I ever did.

Perfectly content to lean back and listen to my friends banter and bitch back and forth during our weekly meetup, I sipped at whatever top shelf scotch Rob had ordered for everyone, trying to stay out of my head, but failing.

It had been almost a week since I last saw Val, which wasn't unusual in and of itself, but I'd been restless and the days apart felt like months, felt like years. It didn't help that the wedding invitation was burning a hole in my kitchen counter, smoldering hotter every day that inched closer to the date.

"You're thinking about the wedding," Rob said beside me, his voice louder in my ear than the chatter from the rest of our friends.

"No," I lied.

"Thinking about Val, then," he said.

Was I so fucking predictable?

"I'm fine," I assured him, taking another swallow of scotch.

"Yeah." He chuckled. "You look it."

"What?" I rolled my eyes, annoyed at the implication I was lying, even though I was. "I am."

"Are you taking Val to the wedding?" he asked.

It would have been a lie to say the idea hadn't crossed my mind, but that wasn't who Val and I were to each other. Asking Val to come to the wedding with me would have been a step into the territory we'd both agreed not to tread near.

"Why would I?"

Rob made a frustrated noise, the same sound I often heard him make around his boyfriend, Grayson. "Because you're a couple, whether you like it or not, and that's what couples do."

"We are not a couple." The word tasted funny in my mouth, bitter and tart against my tongue.

"I thought Grayson was stubborn, but you put him to shame."

"Val and I have an understanding," I said, repeating the same fact I told myself at least once a day.

"You know as well as the rest of us that anything can be renegotiated." He clinked the edge of his glass against mine, then flagged down the waiter to get a fresh round.

I passed off my empty glass, debating whether a fourth was advisable, but not quite caring enough to stop. I could get a ride home and deal with my car in the morning.

"I like how things are." There was that bitterness again.

I dragged my tongue across the front of my teeth.

It didn't matter whether I liked how things were or not. Things were tolerable as they were on a bad day, a dream come true on the best. If Val and I renegotiated or reevaluated…if I let him slip from casual into serious…

I would lose him.

And that wasn't an exaggeration or an unnecessary worry. I had a track record to prove it, starting in high school and continuing right up until the first time I sank my dick into Val's mouth. He was the longest-running anything I'd ever had, and I was sure as shit not going to fuck that up by trying to change what worked for us both.

"Does he?" Rob asked.

The waiter came and handed us fresh drinks, and my stomach

roiled at the smell of the scotch. Maybe four was a bad idea, but lots of things in my life were bad ideas, like the conversation he and I were currently having.

"He hasn't complained yet," I said.

"Is he allowed to?"

I inhaled an irritated breath, shooting daggers in Rob's direction while I waited for my heart to kick back into its usual pattern.

"I don't treat him the way the rest of you treat your men," I said under my breath.

Rob grinned, head bobbling side to side in amusement. "With respect?"

"Fuck you."

"I don't know what you think you're after with the dig," he went on, unfazed. "But you're falling short of whatever insult you were after."

"You were the one trying to insult me."

"Far from it." He took a sip of his scotch, eyes dancing. "I let Grayson tie me up sometimes because it makes him happy, because making him happy makes me happy. Archie doesn't let Owen come for weeks sometimes because that's what they're into."

"I would die," I interjected.

Rob laughed and shrugged, ignoring me. "Rose lets Flynn spend money on him because it's the easiest way for Flynn to love him."

"And Dalton?" I asked.

At the sound of his name, Dalton glanced up from the other end of the cluster of chairs, but Rob waved dismissively, and he went back to his conversation with Flynn and Archie.

"Dalton lets Ivey take care of him."

"That doesn't feel like a compromise," I murmured. "Or a loss."

"It isn't for any of us, because the needs and wants align."

I raised a brow. "You want to be tied up?"

"I want Grayson," he said simply. "And that's the cost."

"I'm still missing your point."

If this conversation kept up, I would need a fifth and maybe a sixth drink to get through it.

"What are your needs? What about Val?"

"Val needs to get fucked as hard and as often as I can manage, and honestly even more than that."

"And you?" Rob cocked his head to the side. "What do you need?"

I needed Val to not leave.

"Not a thing," I said, clearing my throat and angling away from him. The conversation was going nowhere fast and I wanted to be done with it.

"Barclay."

"Not a thing," I repeated, pulling my phone out of my pocket. It was quarter to nine and I was already done with the whole lot of them.

Normally, I didn't bother Val on Thursdays. It was his night to do whatever he did with whoever he wanted, but the conversation with Rob and my lingering thoughts about the wedding had me feeling itchy. I was too close to drunk for anyone's good, but I texted him anyway.

Me: Do you want to come over later?

He didn't answer, the check mark on the message staying gray for so long I got tired of looking at it. I turned the screen upside down, resting it against the top of my thigh and tapping my fingers against the back case.

"What do you think, Barclay?" Archie asked, and I was happy for the distraction.

The knot in my chest loosened, and I pasted mock interest on my face. "What's the question?"

"Pineapple on pizza or not," Dalton said.

The bitter taste was back in my mouth. "Obviously not."

Archie barked out a sharp laugh and smacked Dalton's arm.

"That wasn't the question," he said. "We were debating the merits of marriage."

"I'm not the one to ask." I turned my attention toward my scotch, even though there wasn't enough liquor in the bar to get me out of the conversation now. I would have been better off under Rob's singular scrutiny, and the laugh he let out beside me confirmed he knew the same thing to be true.

"All the better reason to ask you," Archie said.

"I think marriage is a scam," I said, raising my glass to Dalton. "No offense."

"None taken."

"Why, though?"

"Why are you asking?" I countered. "Is Owen pressing you to put a ring on it now that he's seen a band around Ivey's finger?"

"It's Dalton's ring that has him seeing stars," Archie said. "But he'd move back to Brixton if I ever dared to spend that much money on him."

"He has to get used to it," Flynn said. "There's compromise from both sides."

"A sixty grand wedding ring is not a compromise for anyone," Dalton said.

I choked on my drink, covering my mouth with my hand before it dribbled down my chin and over my shirt. "Sixty grand?"

Dalton rolled his eyes like it was pennies.

"You're getting off topic," Archie whined, fluttering his hands around to bring the attention back to him. "But I take your answer to mean you're never getting married?"

"I don't see the point," I said. "If something is working, don't change it."

Like Val and me.

Things with us were working, and I wanted them to keep working. Any change would introduce new variables, and that was when things could go wrong.

I thought back to college with Dennis, wondering what if I had changed or done something different. I'd had the same thought process for years over it, and the only new variable that had been introduced there was the cock of my constitutional law professor right into his mouth.

That was a hard lesson, but I'd learned it well.

People lied and people left.

"It's like the next step," Archie explained. "You date, and then you commit, and then you fall in love—"

"Or whatever order works," Dalton interrupted.

"Obviously," Flynn said.

"You do the things and then it's just the next thing," Archie finished.

"Relationships aren't a checklist," Rob said, leaning forward, elbows braced on his knees.

Archie said something that I didn't hear because the conversation did what it always did, moved on without me. I wasn't mad about it, though. I was quite content to lean back away from the microscope of their scrutiny and enjoy the last of my scotch while the four of them continued the discussion.

There had been a time when I wanted to get married. I couldn't have been older than ten when I sat on the couch and watched a movie with a big wedding in it. I'd imagined what it would be like to have a beautiful woman walking down the aisle toward me, massive bouquet of white flowers clutched in her hands. As I imagined it, though, I was my ten year-old self and she was her ten year-old self—Julia Martin, the daughter of my father's best friend —because we'd been raised with the idea we were already betrothed.

Never mind I'd already started to wonder about boys more than girls.

Marriage in our world had never been for love, only for advantage, so my outlook on that step of a relationship was different from that of my friends. Getting married didn't have anything to do with love. It had to do with contracts and bank accounts and family names, which felt so archaic to me, even as a kid.

Julia was sent to boarding school at thirteen and I never saw her again. I rarely thought of her, except for a fleeting vision of our wedding going up in a fireball when I kissed my first boy. My parents would never arrange that kind of marriage for me. There was nothing anyone else could have or offer as leverage that would balance their gender, so I shoved the idea out of my head.

By the time I graduated high school, it became apparent to me that my parents didn't care if I ever got married, which was as much of a relief as Julia getting sent to boarding school had been. They were content to let me focus on undergrad and then it was internships and job opportunities, and life was upon me.

I finished the rest of my scotch, listening to my four closest friends snap back and forth at each other, all in good fun, all good natured. An hour and one more round later, my phone finally buzzed against my palm. I startled, having forgotten I even held it. I had zoned out, thinking about another wedding altogether, which was enough to sour my mood beyond repair.

At least, until I saw Val's name on my screen. A soft smile pulled at the corner of my mouth when I read his reply.

Val: Always.

I swiped a quick reply to him.

Me: I'm still at Cunningham's.
Me: Maybe drank more than I should have.
Val: What's new?

I groaned at the implication, then finished the last of my scotch and stood up.

"I'm taking off," I announced, setting my empty glass on the table beside me.

"Off to fuck Val, no doubt," Archie sing-songed, raising his glass to me.

"So what if I am?" I asked. "He's better company than you assholes. He's never once talked about getting married."

"Not with you, he hasn't."

My breath caught in my throat, a tight ball blocking my ability to suck in any more air. Archie noticed it, a smirk flickering across his face. I knew Archie and Val had developed some kind of friendship, but I didn't think…

"What are you saying?" I asked.

My voice sounded like it had been through a food processor.

I cleared my throat, and Archie shrugged, but the look on his face made it *very* clear to me that he and Val had talked about me and our relationship on more than one occasion. It made me feel like a fool. Because here I was always saying how things were… saying we were both happy with how things were.

Well, maybe happy was an overstatement, but we were used to how things were. Accustomed to the status quo. Which…made it sound like a business relationship, not a sexual one, but…

Fuck, I hated this.

Hated the way Dennis had surged back into my life and fucked everything up to for me. I swallowed past a sharp and uncomfortable feeling in my chest that threatened to explode and slice me to pieces if it was poked too hard. Rubbing my sternum, I held Archie's penetrating stare.

He knew.

My phone vibrated again, shocking me back to the present, and I looked down to find another message from Val on my screen.

Val: That was rhetorical. I'll be there in half an hour.

I clutched my phone in my fist, hating how much comfort his words brought me. But it was fine.

I was fine.

Some fresh air and space from my friends would clear my mind enough and get the talk of marriage and commitment out of my head, then I could go home and fuck the rest of my sanity away. Maybe when I woke up, Dennis wouldn't be getting married and I wouldn't have to go, and Val would be happy with me as the man I was, not the man he wanted me to be.

It wasn't a solid plan, but it was the only one I had.

CHAPTER 6
VAL

It was muscle memory.

Cleaning out and prepping, getting dressed, getting the car, driving across town…the relief in my chest when Barclay always opened the door and smiled at the sight of me.

I was such a fool.

He'd definitely had more to drink than usual with his friends. I could tell by the way he leaned against the door after he opened it. The way he leveraged his weight on the knob when he stepped aside to let me in. I knew him too well to ignore the signs and I knew myself too well to care.

"I've been drinking," he said, the words right on the cusp of a slur.

"I know."

I pried his fingers off the door handle and closed it behind me. Locked it.

"I shouldn't have texted."

"Why not?" I asked, toeing off my shoes and peeling off my socks. I left it all by the door, giving him a gentle push toward the living room.

"They were being jerks," he murmured.

"How so?"

We rounded the corner into his bedroom and he shuffled

toward the edge of the bed. He was barely dressed, already undone from drinks in a pair of black slacks and a half-buttoned black shirt. Tufts of golden-brown chest hair peeked out from above the buttons like a frosting on his bronzed skin.

"They want more from us than we are," he said, fidgeting with his belt.

"It's not for them to decide," I reminded him.

It wasn't the first time he and I had talked about what his friends thought we should be in comparison to what we actually were. It didn't matter that as the years had drawn on, I'd started to agree with his friends more than with him. Something was better than nothing, and I liked being able to fuck him bare whenever I wanted. For the time being, the pain of my heart and the pleasure of my body were in enough of a balance to carry on.

Barclay sat down on the edge of the bed and I straddled him, working open the buttons he hadn't yet managed to get undone. I pushed the shirt open, letting my fingers dance across his warm and broad chest before easing it off his shoulders and down his arms. His body was so predictable.

So familiar.

Getting his shirt off snapped him out of his head, because he moved surprisingly quickly after that. Tugging my shirt over my head, he had me on my back before the soft cotton had made its way down the length of my arms. He used a knee between my legs to spread me apart, and then his hands were on my fly and my zipper. My pants came off, my underwear followed, and he was still in his slacks on top of me.

He pulled his cock out of his underwear and slicked it with lube, teasing it around my crack. His pants were still on, the wool soft and somehow scratchy against the backs of my thighs. I couldn't get my shirt off my wrists, and he pinned them to the bed, stretched above my head. With his face buried in the crook of my neck, he thrust into me with so much force I couldn't help but arch off the mattress.

His fingers around my wrists tightened, keeping me pinned

like a bow, and then he was all the way inside of me and everything was good in the world. Everything was soft and quiet and perfect. Barclay's lips were against the side of my neck and his nipples rubbed over mine as he pulled out and pumped back in.

"It's not for them to decide," I repeated, hoping he heard me. Hoping that he agreed.

I needed him to agree because I didn't want to lose this.

But for as settled as sharp snaps of his hips made my brain, there was an intrusion in the corner of my periphery that I couldn't quite blink out of focus. It was tall and slim, shy and nervous. It was shaped like a man with claustrophobia named Jason who had handed me a business card instead of a phone number, and I couldn't stop thinking about him.

"They don't know," Barclay murmured, dragging his lips up my jaw to my ear. He sank his teeth into my lobe, and I spread my legs wider for him. His grip on my wrists was punishing and I loved it because it felt like home. I could pretend that Barclay knew about Jason and he'd pinned me to the bed to fuck and remind me who we were, what we did.

He didn't know about Jason, though.

But if I was going to go through with a date, he needed to know.

"I want to feel you come," he groaned into my ear, and I wiggled my hands beneath his hold.

"I can't if you don't let go of me."

"You've done it before," he said.

He wasn't wrong.

I'd long ago lost count of the times Barclay had made me come hands free, but he'd been far more sober and I'd been much less distracted.

"You're sloppy," I told him.

He took it as a challenge, pulling out and hauling me onto all fours. He pumped back into me from behind, fingers digging bruises into my hips. Barclay set a punishing pace, determined to rub my prostate into submission. Burying my face in his sheets, I arched, giving him a sharper angle and a better chance. I closed my eyes and sighed, content to listen to the harsh pant of his breaths as he fucked me, shivering as his sweat splattered and fell against my spine.

The orgasm was a slow build. Tingles in the base of my spine that spread up and out every time he bottomed out, balls slapping against mine. Fisting the sheets, I held on for dear life as the force of his thrusts had fucked me halfway across the bed and I was quickly sliding toward the far edge. He was still half-dressed, I realized, my brain zeroing in on the contrast of his skin against the abrasion from his slacks.

"More," I demanded, my body eager to comply with the orgasm he'd demanded, even if it was still barely out of reach.

Barclay grunted, and I heard the lube open. It was a messy pour, leaking down the crack of my ass, my balls, and my thighs. But then the burning ache, the stretch as he hooked both of his thumbs into my hole alongside his already thick shaft.

"Oh, fuck," he groaned, hips skittering. "I love your tight ass. Love your…"

He trailed off, and I balled up the sheets and shoved them into my mouth to muffle anything that I would have said in response to that.

His cock and his thumbs inside of me felt amazing, but I wanted more. I wanted another cock, a fist, anything that would stretch my body wide enough that my mind could just shut the fuck up for long enough so the orgasm could crest, crash, and sweep me under.

His thumbs were gone, and then it was a new sensation inside of me, tight enough to send a tremor through my whole body from my toes to the top of my head.

"You like that." It wasn't quite a question.

I moaned around the self-made gag, arching into him to take his cock deeper.

"My thumb and two fingers around my cock," Barclay explained, my rim popping around his knuckles as he fucked into me. "If you were looser and wetter, I could get my hand inside of you. I could jack off inside your ass while I fuck you."

The thought of it.

Just the thought and it was over.

I cried out, choking on the sheets, choking on my spit. My muscles convulsed, clamping down around his fingers and his cock as I spilled all over my stomach. Barclay grunted, fingers of his left hand curling around my shoulder as he hauled me back onto him. He lifted me—him going back onto his knees and me shifting onto his lap. Gravity did the rest and there was so much of him inside of me…

I was helpless.

It was perfect.

My mind went blank and everything I'd been worrying about was gone. The expectations of his friends, my own feelings for him…and Jason…all of it was just…

Gone.

I came to with his face between my cheeks, hot mouth licking up the cum that had started to spill out of my body. I'd done that, my subconscious reminded me. I'd made him come. I'd made him so crazy for it that he was eating his spend out of my ass because he was so horny for me.

I'd done that.

No one else before me and no one else after.

How could I even think about another man when we had this…

This magic.

"I'm still hard for you," he mouthed against my well-fucked rim.

I lifted one of my legs higher. An invitation.

Barclay rolled me onto my side and situated himself behind me. He pushed his cock inside of me, the cum and lube from our first round slicking his way. I wouldn't have called him hard, but he wasn't soft, and I loved how he felt inside of me. With my head against his shoulder, his arms wrapped around me, fingers spread across my chest as he set a slower, softer pace.

If my body's reactions to him were anything to go off, I hadn't ever stopped coming from the first time. My fingers still tingled, and I could still feel my pulse in my balls. I shook and twitched against him, head falling forward. I wasn't trying to get away from him, but I was in sensory overload, and when he pressed his lips against the back of my neck, cum leaked out of my cock.

He murmured against my sweaty nape, words muffled beyond comprehension. I screwed my eyes closed, the sensations threatening to overwhelm and undo me. My brain had turned back on, ideas again racing, and I cursed under my breath. All I wanted was to get lost in him.

In us.

"Fuck."

He bit the back of my neck and went still. His cock throbbed and pulsed inside of me, and his body gave one last valiant shake before he went boneless behind me. I curled my hand around my dick, squeezing and stroking until the last bits of cum squirted out of my tip.

I love you.

The death sentence was right there on the tip of my tongue, so I bit myself until I bled. The hot taste of iron flooded my mouth and I sighed, closing my eyes. Barclay's hand reached down between us, his fingertips tracing over the place where our bodies were joined. He said something unintelligible, then with the utmost care, eased his way out of me.

I hated that part.

Hated the gaping absence of him that lingered in more places than just between my legs. With his cock out of me, though, he petted his fingers over my hole until it was too much for me to take anymore. I pulled away, but rolled over so I faced him. He brought his arms around me again and I kissed the spot on his chest that I knew shielded his heart. He tasted like soap and sweat, and I pressed my forehead against him with a tired whimper.

"Did I hurt you?" he asked against the top of my head.

I'd never outright lied to Barclay, and I didn't want to start. He hadn't hurt me physically, and maybe he wasn't even the one hurting me emotionally. I was doing that to myself by staying silent about my feelings, but...

"You were perfect," I said, "as always."

Another kiss against the top of my head, and he untangled himself from me, leaving me cold, wet, and bereft on top of sweaty and cum-soaked sheets. But he stood and reached for me, hauling me to my feet.

"It's late," I reminded him.

"Are you staying the night?" he asked.

"I don't have clothes for work," I said.

Three years of this, and I didn't have more than a toothbrush here, which was more than he had at my place. But we sure had rules. Enough rules to last a lifetime.

His mouth quirked into a frown, and he shoved his damp hair back from his face. "Do you want to shower before you go?"

There was cum on my stomach, my balls, lube dried and crackling against the sensitive creases of my thighs.

And Jason was there again in the back of my mind. Seriously, what were the odds of us meeting? Getting trapped in that elevator together on a Thursday night...

"What time is it?" I asked.

Barclay huffed out a soft laugh. "I honestly have no idea."

This was how I liked him the most. When he wasn't pretending to be anything more than he was. These moments when he was quiet and cute, almost vulnerable. When I could pretend we were different people, at least for a moment.

"Quick shower," I agreed, letting him pull me into the bathroom. "But there's something I need to tell you first."

CHAPTER 7

BARCLAY

I IGNORED HIM.

I ignored him because I had to. Because if I didn't, I wouldn't have been able to get us to the bathroom, wouldn't have been able to check the temperature of the water, make sure there were clean towels out, usher him under the spray. I didn't bother turning the lights on. Even though I didn't know what time it was, I knew it was late. The nightlight on the vanity was enough, casting long and golden shadows across the glass doors.

Val stepped under the spray and tipped his head back, working the water through his hair with steady hands. I lingered against the far wall of the shower, cold and shaking, but too scared to get close because, even though I wanted to pretend otherwise, I knew what he was going to say.

He was going to leave me.

They always left me.

He shampooed his hair, washed his body and rinsed, then he reached for me with his eyes closed and pulled me under the water. His body aligned with mine in all my favorite ways, and I knew him with my eyes closed. I knew him by touch, by taste, by smell...knew him by the way he made me feel.

When the water had rinsed him clean, he started in on me,

washing my fingers one by one, my wrists, my forearms, the crease in my elbows.

"What do you need to tell me?" I forced out the question, even though I didn't want the answer. I'd known all along this was where we'd end up.

My fears were too much for me to overcome to change the outcome of things between us. There wasn't anything I could do or say that would make me enough for him, and he was destined to leave me, just like the rest of them had. He'd be better in the end for it.

Val washed my armpits, my shoulders. He dug his fingers around the curve of my clavicle then worked his way up the side of my neck. I tilted my head back and closed my eyes, trying to focus on the feel of his hands and not the emotions rolling off of him like lava.

"I…" He trailed off, dragging his tongue across the front of his teeth.

He cleaned my throat, my sternum, my stomach, and lower still. My cock, my balls, my thighs and the backs of my knees. He didn't say another word until he reached my feet and told me to turn around. I did, feet sticking to the tile for how hard I'd been digging in to hold myself up. With my back to Val, I rested my head against the wall of the shower and he worked his way back up.

The crack of my ass, the small of my back, and then it was finished.

He was finished.

"I want more," he said.

I turned toward him, studying the way water beaded on his eyelashes, hanging on tight even as he blinked up at me. He wrapped his fingers around my wrists loosely, like he was using me for support, not comfort. I hadn't known until that moment there was a difference, but I could feel it in his hands. The way he touched me without holding me.

I fucking hated it.

"That's not—"

"It's not what we agreed," he interrupted me before I could finish. "I know. But three years seems like enough time to renegotiate a contract, doesn't it?"

He let go of me and turned off the water.

"We don't have a contract," I said.

He pushed open the door and grabbed a towel for me and one for himself. He stepped onto the bath mat to dry off, then left the towel on the floor. I watched him walk naked out of the bathroom, and I wrapped my towel around my waist and followed behind. Back in the humid warmth of my bedroom, he pulled his underwear and jeans back on, then held his shirt in his hand. He sat down on the edge of the bed, looking weary and beaten down.

Looking how I felt.

"We don't have much," he said, swallowing and sucking in a breath big enough to raise his shoulders. "But that's what I'm asking you for."

"This was just sex, Val."

I hated myself.

Hated my shortcomings.

Hated the crestfallen look on his face.

"This *is* just sex," I corrected.

He clenched his jaw and dragged his stare across my face with such an intensity I could feel it against my skin. I tightened the knot in my towel, clutching the wet terrycloth. Water trickled off my hair and fell down the back of my neck, racing down my spine and farther down to the floor.

"That's what it has been, and I'm telling you that I want more from you."

"I can't give you more," I pleaded with him, ready to fall to my knees at his feet and beg him to understand that he had more of me than any man ever had, ever would. He had the most I could give, the most anyone else would ever take.

"Is that because of Dennis?" he asked.

The sound of Dennis's name had one of my knees buckling, but I used the momentum to push me forward. Instead of falling at his feet, I managed to land my ass on the bed, right beside him. The juxtaposition from earlier wasn't lost on me. I'd fucked him half-dressed and now he was breaking up with me half-dressed. Though, he wasn't really breaking up with me, was he? We weren't even together.

Right?

"Because of the wedding," he pressed when I didn't answer. "Are you still in love with him?"

"What?" Something almost like relief flooded my chest. "You think I'm still in love with Dennis?"

"I don't know what to think." Val wrung his shirt in his hands, leaving deep and sweaty wrinkles in the fabric as he worked it back and forth between his fingers. "You don't ever talk to me about him."

"He's no one."

"Obviously not." He raised his voice. Not a yell, but definitely an admonishment that landed as intended.

I dug my nails into the towel and my toes into the floor. "Dennis was a lesson," I said carefully. "One of many."

"And what was the lesson?"

He was really going to force the ugly truth out of me, but if he was leaving me, if everything had come full circle, I wanted him to at least understand. I needed him to know it wasn't him —it was me. It was my brokenness, my shortfalls that had brought us here. He'd been nothing less than perfect. The most wonderful gift I could have ever been given. Far more than I deserved.

"That I don't get to have good things for myself, Val. That they all leave in the end."

"I'm right here, you piece of shit." He slapped his hand against the front of his chest, shifting so our knees pressed together and his eyes caught mine like a tractor beam.

"And you're leaving, aren't you?" I swatted his hand away from his heart. "You're trying to tell me you're leaving."

"I'm trying to tell you I don't want to leave, but..." His exhale turned into a grunt, and he smacked my arm away from him. Both our hands fell into our laps, and my breath trembled when I saw the way he'd abandoned his shirt to pick at the skin beside his thumbnail.

"But I don't want things to stay the same."

I scrubbed a hand down my face, and then I did something new.

I reached for him, threading our fingers together and clamping down so tight around his hand he would have to fight me to get free.

"No," he said quickly, trying to get away.

I held him tighter, yanking him to face me more fully. His stare flickered from our hands to my face and back to our hands. He shook his head, flexing his fingers against mine.

"I'm not good for you," I said. "But I'm selfish and that's what brought us here, and I won't let you walk away from me."

"Do you even hear yourself?" He stretched his fingers straight before giving up and curling them around the top of my hand. "You're not even listening to me."

"I'm saying that I can't let you go."

"And I'm saying I don't *want* to go...but I can't pretend that I'm not—"

I cut him off before he went too far. Before he said something he couldn't take back. "I can't give you what you want. It's not... it's not fair."

"*This* isn't fair." He was loud again, palm clammy against mine.

"You said it was time to renegotiate," I said.

"And you said this wasn't a contract."

I ignored his barb. "What are your terms?"

"Let go of me."

Val shook his hand out of mine, and with all of the reluctance that had ever existed in my body, I let him go. As soon as he was free of my hold, he was off the bed and across the room, back pressed against the window and arms folded in front of his still bare chest. His shirt was on the floor at my feet, and I reached for it, smoothing out the twisted wrinkles because I didn't know what else to do.

The fear was beyond paralyzing, wrapped around another feeling in my chest that I didn't dare give a voice to. I was a selfish hypocrite, but if I wouldn't let him admit he had feelings for me, I wouldn't let myself do it either. Because the feelings were the problem. The feelings were what I'd tried for so long to avoid. Falling in love meant letting your guard down, and I didn't have it in me anymore to do that.

Not even for him.

Not even for the love of my life.

"What are the terms?"

"Are you really sitting here and telling me that this is all it's going to be between us?" Val dropped his arms at his sides. Helpless. Defeated. "Just sex for the rest of time."

"That's what I need it to be," I choked the words out, hating them as much as I hated myself.

"I won't ask you to tell me that you don't have feelings for me because I know you'll lie. I see right through you, Percy."

His use of my first name was like a bucket of cold water on my face. My eyes burned, and I blinked quickly, ignoring the moisture that pooled against the corners of my lashes.

"I deserve to be loved, don't I?" he asked.

I swallowed and managed a nod.

"But not by you?"

I wanted to tell him no. I needed to tell him no, because everything would get so complicated if I said anything different.

If I admitted…

Even though he was across the room, it was my back against the wall, the anticipation and terror coiled so tight in the pit of my stomach I worried I was going to be sick all over myself. The scotch had long since settled and fled, leaving me to face the reality of the situation I'd constructed with no buffer between us.

"I need you to trust me when I tell you I can't."

"I deserve it, though," he repeated. "Right?"

I bit the inside of my cheek and gave him another nod.

"Then I'm going to go find it," he said.

"I can't." I was off the bed before I realized my legs had moved. The towel fell away and I was on him, against him, one arm against the window over his head, the other around his waist. I pressed my body against his and his body against the window, our noses brushing together and our lips so fucking close I could kiss him.

I should kiss him.

When was the last time I kissed him?

"I can't lose you. Lose this." I swore against his lips, unable to look him in the eye.

I was being beyond selfish. The worst of the worst, but I was a rich man, a greedy man, and I would not give up the only shred of happiness in my life without a fight. I didn't expect him to understand the why of it. I didn't even want him to understand it. I wanted him to accept me as I was, the parts of him he could get his hands on, and I wanted that to be enough because if I let go of the whole of me…

He would find me lacking. And then it would be over for good.

"I'm not trying to take it from you," he said softly.

Val snaked his hand between us, pressing his palm against my chest, over my heart. I was impressed the organ hadn't beat its way out of my body for how hard and frantic it slammed against my ribs. But I went weak at his touch, a trembling breath ghosting over his lips when he touched me.

"Thank you."

"This…this is whatever it is, but…" He made a frustrated, pained sound in the back of his throat. "I deserve to be loved. Loudly and openly. And if you won't do it, I want to find someone who can."

Any protest died in my mouth, in my chest.

I loved him.

I loved him so much, but the words were a thorny mess in my throat and a death knell if I ever dared to utter them.

"I know what our arrangement has been," Val said, clearing his throat. "And as much as this hurts me, I don't want to lose you either. I can't walk away from you because I—"

"Don't," I murmured.

Another frustrated noise, and his fingernails in my chest, like he wanted to dig in and tear my heart out with his bare hands.

"You're the fucking worst man I've ever met," he said.

"I know."

That was what I'd been telling him all along. That was why I'd tried to protect him from the disappointment of *me*.

"I met someone tonight."

I didn't think I'd heard him right, but I must have. I knew the words, but in that order, in that sentence…in his voice. The floor fell out from beneath me finally and I went to my knees. My hold on his hip so strong I took him with me. We crashed together against the floor, his back against the window and my body between his legs. He cursed under his breath, and that was when I realized his cheeks were tracked with tears.

Like mine.

"What's his name?" I croaked.

"It doesn't matter." He shook his head and swiped at his lower lashes. "You can't have it both ways."

"I know," I murmured, following the path across his cheekbone where his tears kept falling.

"It'll be just like it has been between us," he promised. "You and me, and…this. And I've always slept with other people."

"I know."

"Now maybe I'll just…date them too."

My chin trembled at the statement, at the expression on his face. His lashes were clumped together, his lips parted, the lower one quivering. It looked like he was breaking up with me. It *felt* like he was breaking up with me, but…

It was just a concession.

A change in the terms.

"If that's what you want."

"It's not," he snapped, shoving off of me.

I'd made him angry because of course I had. I ruined good things because I wasn't good enough to hold on to them. I knew this was how it would end.

"It's not what I want." He stood up, gesturing with his hands and talking down at me.

I didn't think I'd ever be able to get off the floor again.

"I want you. I want to fuck you and whoever you bring home, and I want to date you and go to dinner with you and have clothes here so I could spend the night if I wanted. I want all of that with *you*, but you refuse. You fucking *refuse* me."

I raised my hands, fingers splayed and tapping madly against the bridge of my nose. There was no hiding my tears now, hiding my failures. Everything I said made it worse, and I couldn't lose him. I knew I would eventually, but this could at least buy me a little more time. Another few months with him before he got tired of me and left for good…

"It's what I have to do," he said, tone deathly calm. He smeared his fingers across his cheeks and inhaled a sloppy breath through his nose. "It's survival, Percy. It's the best I can do until you're willing to hear me when I say that I—"

"Fine." I almost yelled the concession, sliding across the floor and pressing my back against the window. I was naked and exposed, my most vulnerable in more ways than one. Bending my legs at the knee, I propped my elbows on top of them and managed to look up at him.

"Fine," I said again. "Date whoever you want and you and me…"

He sucked in a tired and watery breath, shaking his head.

I bit my lip until fresh tears poured over my lower lashes. Val held his hand out for me and helped me to my feet, taking a step away before I could reach for him. He stepped back again, again, then grabbed his shirt off the bed and pulled it over his head.

"I fucking hate you, Percy. I hate how much I need you. Hate the way I…" He trailed off on his own.

"Not more than I hate myself," I admitted, no longer able to look him in the eye.

It hurt to admit, but it was the most honest thing I'd ever said to him.

CHAPTER 8
VAL

THE NEXT DAY, I CUT OUT EARLY FOR LUNCH AND WALKED THE FEW blocks to Archie's office. I wouldn't say that he and I were friends, but I'd spent the most time—dressed—with him out of the rest of Barclay's friend group, and I needed to talk to someone. When I arrived at his office, he looked beyond surprised to see me, but ushered me in and closed the door, requesting his secretary to hold his calls.

"You look like shit," he said as I sank into one of the guest chairs in front of his desk. "Did Barclay do something?"

A knot tightened in my chest at his concern. "No, but…kind of. I do want to talk to you about him, so if you don't feel comfortable with that, just tell me and I'll go."

"Are you here to gossip?" He arched a brow. "Because you and I don't have that kind of relationship."

"Not gossip," I said, shaking my head.

Archie worked his jaw and tilted his head to the side in question.

I sucked in as much of a breath as I could manage, wringing my hands together in my lap. For as much as I didn't want Archie's judgement, I didn't want my worry for Barclay to get lost in the mess of whatever I was about to say.

"You know that Barclay and I...we just...it's casual between us," I started.

"It's not casual," Archie said. "But the two of you insist on pretending it is."

The knot squeezed itself around my heart, around my ribs, making it impossible to breathe. I forced myself to untangle my fingers, wiping them dry on the tops of my thighs. I couldn't get Barclay's face out of my mind, the pain in his voice from the night before as we'd torn down the only good thing we had.

And for what?

Was it worth it?

Losing him to go on a date with a stranger that I didn't even know anything about?

Stop.

It was more than that. In reality, it didn't have anything to do with Jason. What it had to do with was the fact I was in love with Perceval Barclay and he was too dense to let me love him. He dug his heels in, doubled down, and shoved me back into the box he wanted me in, and I deserved more than that. I needed more than that.

"It's supposed to be." I shrugged, hands again falling in my lap. "But I have feelings for him. That wasn't part of our arrangement, but..."

"He loves you too," Archie said.

I bit the inside of my cheek like the pain would hold back my tears.

"No." I cleared my throat. "He doesn't want things between us to change and I...I can't let them stay the same."

"Because you love him too."

"There is no *too* about it," I snapped, scrubbing a hand down my face. Why was I shaking? What was I scared of? This was Archie Davidson; he wasn't anyone important to me. He was the best friend of the man I loved, and I wasn't here to confess the deepest secrets of my heart to him. All I wanted was for him to keep an eye on Barclay for me. I wanted him to make sure Barclay was okay…

Archie sighed, loosening the knot of his tie. "He's really gone and fucked this up, hasn't he?"

"Depends on your perspective. He would say I was the one who ruined it by asking for more than he was willing to give."

"What happened?" he finally asked, leaning back in his chair and folding his arms in front of his chest. His shoulders looked weighed down, almost slumped. He'd known Barclay for years, I reminded myself. There was no way I was his first—or last—rodeo. Barclay had a type, and he had rules, and…

Why had I thought I was special?

Blinking back tears, I shrugged, because the words were a fog in my throat, real and fake at the same time and stuck there either way.

"Did he hurt you?" Archie asked.

"No," I croaked. "I hurt him, I think."

"If you hurt him, Val, it's practically self-inflicted because he's too stubborn to avoid it."

"Is that supposed to make me feel better?"

Archie chuckled, scratching his eyebrow. "Did it?"

"No."

He huffed and leaned forward, folding his arms again, but this time across the surface of his desk, bringing us closer together.

"It's taken an embarrassingly long time," I murmured, not able to keep my eyes on his face. I had a hangnail on my thumb, and I picked at it until it bled. Cursing under my breath, I sat on my hand.

For his part, Archie sat quietly, not prompting or pushing, just waiting for me to put it together. I appreciated the stoicism, even though the words were razor blades and I would have preferred he piece it together for me so I didn't have to say it out loud.

"I want more than just sex," I said.

"You've been perfectly happy with the way things have been," he said. "The sex and the half-friendship. Whatever it is between the two of you."

My cheeks flushed because I would never *not* be okay with sex, but I wanted more than the physical. I could get the sex anywhere with anyone. I wanted to feel special. Important.

Irreplaceable.

"I know," I said.

"But now you want dinner and dates and all of that? You want a relationship out of him?"

"Yeah."

He exhaled loudly, a knowing look flashing across his face. "How did that go?"

"Not well." A garbled laugh caught in my throat. "He says he can't. We can't. I don't know. I met someone."

Archie raised a hand, eyes going wide at my confession. "You what?"

"I met someone," I repeated. "He's honestly nobody important, but the way he looked at me…"

His voice went low, the words measured and gentle. "Have you not seen how Barclay looks at you?"

I did see how he looked at me.

I'd spent three years seeing how he looked at me. *Feeling* how he looked at me. But his eyes and his heart weren't in agreement, and that was the crux of the problem.

"The way he looks at me doesn't match up with the things he says."

Archie answered that with a slow nod, eyes tracking across the wall behind my head like the truth was written there. I had to straighten my neck to stop myself from turning to look. I'd been enough of a fool with these men.

"I love him and he might love me, but he'll never admit it. I'm happy being with him physically. More than happy. I like that part of the relationship, but I want the rest of it. I've been watching you and Rob, Flynn…Fuck, the whole lot of you. I want that." I pressed my hand against my chest, heart battering against my sternum. "I deserve that."

"And you met someone," he said, expression unreadable.

I managed a nod.

"Someone who wants to do the dinner and dating stuff you want."

I nodded again, swallowing down a mouthful of bile.

"Because that's what you want."

His tone was so flat, his face completely blank.

"Yes," I rasped.

Archie dragged his tongue across the front of his teeth, fiddling again with the knot on his tie.

"Do you want it with someone else or do you want it with Barclay?"

"I want it with Barclay." The answer came as easily as my next breath, and nothing had ever been closer to the truth. "Of course I want it with him, but he won't give it to me."

"So, second best then," Archie supplied.

I was tired of shrugging, tired of feeling lost and helpless about my own life, but I shrugged at him because I didn't know what else to do. The whole thing felt so messy and unfair to everyone. Unfair to me and Barclay, and mostly to Jason because how could I date someone while I was in love with someone else? Date Jason and be in love with Barclay, still sleeping with Barclay…

I didn't want to give him up entirely, but I wasn't sure I could have both.

Fuck Barclay.

Fuck him for being arrogant and stubborn and perfect.

Fuck him for making me fall in love with him and his bread crumbs.

"What would you have me do, Archie?" I asked quietly.

"It does feel like a lose-lose," he said. "And I know how much it sucks to love someone who won't admit they love you back."

"He doesn't love me."

"He loves you beyond measure," he said quickly, eyes dark and serious. "He loves you beyond reason."

"Well, he sure has a way of showing it."

"We talked last night. Or…whatever it was. It was horrible, and I wasn't coming here to gossip, I just…you're his friend and I want to make sure he's okay because I don't think he is. He hides from me, you know."

Archie nodded, brows knit together in understanding. "I hear you."

"I love him," I said again, like if I said it enough times or to enough people it would change anything between us.

"I hear you," he said again. "So, tell me about this other man."

"He's…I don't know much about him. I didn't come here to talk about him."

"Is he inconsequential?" Archie asked.

"He's not Barclay," I said simply.

"That doesn't sound fair to any of you."

"Life isn't fair."

Archie's cell phone started to vibrate its way across his desk and he reached for it, lips twisting into a frown. He angled the screen toward me, revealing Barclay's name on the screen. It rang and rang, then went to voicemail. Archie dropped the device back onto his desk and turned his attention back to me. The phone vibrated again, a quicker beat and not a ringtone.

A voicemail.

"To make sure I understand this all right," he started, tapping his finger against the black screen of his phone. "You and Barclay are in love with each other, but he won't admit it. He doesn't want to treat you like the boyfriend that you very much are, so you've told him you want to find someone who will. But you don't plan on ending things with him?"

"It sounds horrible when you say it like that," I grumbled.

"It sounds the way it is," he said. "It *is* horrible. For both of you. The three of you."

I covered my face with my hands, ready to scream. "I don't know what else to do."

"I don't have any advice on that front, beyond fighting for him until you can't anymore."

"Do you think I'm giving up on him?"

"I think you've fought harder for him than most people would," Archie said. "And we all see that, for what it's worth."

I grunted, dropping my head back and looking up at the blinding fluorescent lights in the ceiling of his office. Had I really, though? I'd let him have his way with me because, for so long, our wants and needs had aligned. I was the one who had tried to change the game, and I'd been stupid for that. For reading into the way he looked at me sometimes, the way he touched me.

Barclay was unlike any man I'd ever met before, and when he and I had gotten together, it was great. At the time, I hadn't been looking to date at all. It wasn't like I'd tried to bait and switch or trap him, or anything like that. Our relationship started as sex and it had been so good. It still was good, better than good. Barclay was the best lover I'd ever had, and I didn't want to lose that.

I wanted more of it.

More of him.

Because if he was that good to me in bed, I knew he'd be amazing in all the other ways too. I wanted more. It was perfectly normal and okay to outgrow situations and people, but I hadn't. At least, not entirely.

"He sees it too," Archie added. "He's just...scared."

"He hasn't been himself since the wedding invitation showed up," I shared.

The invitation from Dennis had been a sore subject since it showed up. Barclay hadn't said much to me about it and I didn't think he'd talked to his friends either. But it was impossible, after all, to talk about the situation with Barclay without addressing the elephant in the room.

The day the invitation arrived, he'd gone into a spiral like I'd never seen before, coming at me with some of the most primal and emotional sex we'd ever had. He'd fucked me until I wasn't sure if he was sweating or crying over the top of me, then we'd gone to Rapture with his friends and he'd done it all over again. The sex had felt like a punishment, but I was already in love with him, so carrying the weight of it was easy if it helped ease the pain he was feeling.

And that was the last night he'd talked about Dennis or the wedding, even though the invitation stayed on the counter in his kitchen, right beside the fruit bowl.

"Dalton knew him best back then. Have you talked to him about it?"

"No." The idea was absurd. "I'm not gossiping about him."

"No. But you are trying to help him," Archie said gently. "Because you love him."

"Can you stop reminding me?"

He responded to that with a noise that sounded so sad and pitiful I had to fist my hands at my sides to stop from flipping his desk over on top of him. I didn't want pity, and I didn't want Barclay's friends to look at me any differently than they already did.

I was the man who'd let himself get slotted into a box it was impossible to get out of. I was the one who'd made my own bed and now that I was lying in it, there was no way out.

Clearing my throat, I stood up, smoothing my hand down the front of my shirt, over my tie.

"I only came because I wanted to ask you to please make sure he's okay. He's closer with you than me," I said.

"Is he?"

I wasn't interested in entertaining the suggestion that, at some time over the last three years, I'd usurped his friends. Barclay didn't tell me anything beyond what position he wanted me in.

"Give me a break, Archie," I choked out. "This is fucking killing me, okay?"

His expression sobered, and he tweaked the knot on his tie back into place.

"If you need anything, and I mean *anything*, Val, you know where we are."

We.

"I know," I said, rubbing my eyes to make sure the sudden blurriness wasn't from unshed tears. "I just want to make sure he's happy."

"Don't let yourself get lost in the middle of that," Archie said.

His phone vibrated again, the same pattern as when Barclay had called him the first time. Archie checked the screen, lips tilting down into a frown.

"I should get this," he said, tone making it clear we both knew who was on the other end.

I nodded and went to the door. "Thank you, Archie."

I didn't mean for the talk, either. I meant for answering the call.

CHAPTER 9
BARCLAY

ARCHIE ANSWERED THE SECOND TIME I CALLED.

"What are you doing?" I asked after he said hello, not waiting for an answer. "Are you free for lunch?"

"Jesus." He let out a quiet laugh. "The two of you are exhausting."

"Two of who?"

"Nothing. Yes, I can get lunch."

I exhaled a worried breath. "I can meet you. Just tell me where."

"Are you buying?" he asked.

"Fine."

"The Palm in twenty," he said. "Did you want to call me a car too, so I don't have to drive?"

"Fuck off. I'll meet you there."

I hung up on him and grabbed my keys, wallet, and phone. He worked ten minutes from The Palm and I was at home because pulling myself out of bed and getting dressed after my night with Val had taken all the strength I could muster. I was worn down in a way I didn't have words for, but I knew myself well enough to know not to be alone.

I met Archie twenty-two minutes later, and he was already at a table with drinks for us both. He gave me a sad look as I slumped into the seat across from him, then sighed loudly.

"Do you want me to hear your side of it or do you just want me to give you my opinion?" he asked.

"My side of what?"

"The disaster you've made of your relationship with Val," he said.

"I don't have a relationship with Val," I muttered.

"You do and you know it. You have a relationship with me, you have a relationship with Grayson. You have relationships with people, whether you like that or not."

"He's not a boyfriend, I meant." I smacked my tongue against the roof of my mouth, absolutely disgusted with the taste of that confession.

"He's still a relationship," Archie said, tone thick with a warning that made me shiver. "But if you don't get your head out of your ass, he won't be for long."

Realization dawned that Val had somehow gotten to Archie before I did. I knew they'd gotten close, at least more than casual acquaintances, but knowing Val had gone and sought him out...it was just another layer of misery and confusion on top of the rest.

"You talked to Val," I said.

"I did." Archie leaned toward the center of the table, cupping his left hand around the side of his mouth and dramatically whisper-yelling, "And what the *fuck* is wrong with you, Perceval?"

"You know I hate being called Perceval," I grumbled.

But I didn't hate when Val called me Percy.

"I hate watching my friends ruin their lives for no good reason at all," he said, gesturing wildly with his hand, almost smacking our waiter in the face. "Are you trying to send yourself into the kind of spiral that involves eating nothing but canned spray cheese while you contemplate your life choices? Because it's not a good place to land."

"Can I...take your order?"

The waiter looked extremely perplexed, but I ordered water

and a club sandwich just the same. Archie got a salad and another drink, even though neither of us had touched the first round.

"I don't think I've ever eaten spray cheese, and I'm not going to start now," I said. "That's more your speed."

"I almost lost Owen," he said, fingers pulled together. He tapped his fingertips against his chest, eyes earnest and wide. "Like, I almost lost him for good. I thought I had."

"You were kids."

"And you're a fucking adult, so what's your excuse?"

He leaned back and I sucked in a breath, rolling my eyes at him.

"Why are you suddenly so passionate about my *relationship*, Archie?" I threw up air quotes as I repeated his own word usage back to him.

"Because I don't want you to make a mistake," he answered quickly. "Because I've known Val as long as you have and he's never once showed up at my office unannounced."

"What did he have to say?" I asked, even though I wasn't sure I wanted to know the answer.

Even though we had reached an agreement, we hadn't parted on the best terms. Everything between us felt sticky and prickly, painful and raw. I couldn't blame him for it…for the things he said or the things he wanted. But I could—and I would—hold on to him as long as he allowed me to. I'd known all along Val wouldn't be a forever thing for me. Not for lack of wanting. Just on account of my state of existence. It wasn't a lie for me to say "it's not you. it's me."

At least, not when it came to him.

Archie twisted his mouth into a half-frown, giving me a look that dripped with disdain. He picked up his drink and took a sip like the whiskey would wash his opinion of me from his mouth.

"He's worried about you."

Every nerve in my body sparked an alarm, muscles going rigid and tense at the thought. "Why?"

"Because you're a stupid piece of shit."

"Is that what he said?"

Archie laughed, situating himself in his seat, elbow propped up and his drink still in hand. "Would he have been right in the assessment if he had?"

I pinched the bridge of my nose, doing everything I could to stop myself from imagining what Val and Archie's conversation had covered. Val would have been within his rights to say a thousand horrible things about me and they would have mostly all been true. I knew what I said the night before had hurt him, but one day he would thank me. One day...he would understand I'd done him a favor by denying him the one thing he swore he wanted the most.

"He's always known what we were to each other," I said, almost under my breath. "Time hasn't changed that."

Archie shook his head. "Time changes everything."

"Me and Val are not you and Owen," I reminded him.

"Owen and I both had at least a morsel of common sense between us." Archie raised his finger and thumb, pressed so tight together they were almost touching. "Even if it took us ten years to find it."

"By all accounts then, I have seven years to go."

"You'd be lucky to get seven days." Archie took another swallow of his whiskey and then set the glass down on the table.

The waiter chose that moment to appear, setting our plates and fresh drinks down without so much as a word. He left, Archie's warning hovering in the air between us.

"We agreed that...agreed things would stay the same."

"He's in love with you, yeah? Nothing is the same."

"Did he say that?" I croaked.

I loved him too, maybe. In the only ways I knew how, but that still wasn't enough to change things. And the look Archie gave me confirmed the truth of that.

I gestured madly at him, dropping my voice to a hushed whisper. "You're coming at me like this is what I *want*."

My appetite was gone, and I shoved the uneaten sandwich

toward the center of the table, reaching instead for one of the two glasses of whiskey in front of me. I took a drink, and then another, but it wasn't enough to dry my clammy palms or settle the tremor in my hands. This was a disaster of my own making.

Seven days, Archie had said. That wasn't nearly enough time.

"When is the wedding?" Archie asked, the question such a sharp change of direction it almost gave me whiplash.

"Why does it matter?"

"You're the one who called me, wanting to get lunch. Was there something else you wanted to talk about besides the only two men you've ever loved or did I misconstrue your intent?" Archie stabbed his fork into the middle of his salad, filling his mouth with sufficient lettuce to hopefully shut him up long enough for me to get my head screwed back on.

"I don't want to lose him," I finally admitted, barely loud enough for me to hear over the heavy thud of my own heartbeat in my ears.

Archie shoved a couple more forkfuls of salad into his mouth, then dropped his fork onto his plate. He chewed. Swallowed. Rinsed it all back with a healthy drink of whiskey, then folded his arms in front of his chest and gave me the most exasperated look I'd ever seen on his face.

I held his stare for as long as I could before finally looking away from him. Across the room, at the condensation on my glass, before finally landing in my lap. I wrung the napkin together under the table, hating myself as much as he did.

As much as Val did.

"Are you really going to dig your heels in over this?" he asked. "Over this antiquated and misplaced idea that you're no good for him. Or worse, that it's up to you to decide what's best for him?"

"Isn't that my job? My responsibility as the dominant partner?" I asked.

"You're not his Dom."

"I'm trying to save him from being hurt later," I protested.

"By hurting him now."

It was a good thing for all of us that Archie hadn't gone to law school, because he was too sharp-tongued and quick on his feet. He would have made mincemeat of any opposing counsel, regardless of what side of the bench he sat on.

"What are you going to do when he goes through with this date?" Archie asked. "And don't tell me you're going to drink yourself unconscious or go find someone to fuck while he's gone because we both know neither of them are the truth."

I was going to sit at home.

Alone.

I was probably going to cry.

But I absolutely would not admit the last one to Archie or any of the rest of them.

"They both sound like viable options."

"I'm being serious." Archie pursed his lips. "What are you going to do?"

I didn't have a real answer for him because I hadn't thought that hard about it. In a perfect world, Val could go out on his date and come home to me. He could get his attention and his meal, and then I could fill him up with cum and tuck him into bed. That was what I did best, after all. Some of the only things I was good for, whether he was willing to admit that or not.

"I don't know, Archie."

"Do you know what he's going to do?" Archie asked.

"Hopefully meet a nice man and fall in love," I grunted.

"He's already in love," he reminded me. "Though you are far from nice. To the point, he's going to hate himself the whole time."

"Then he should just not go," I suggested.

"You can't have it both ways."

It was the second time in as many days someone had told me that.

Archie pushed his chair back and stood up from the table. He dropped his napkin onto his chair and shook his head, disdain for me rolling off of him in waves. "You are going to lose him if you don't get it together, and I was mistaken in thinking that meant something to you."

"He means…"

Everything.

"I'm telling you this with as much love and respect as I can muster for you right now." He tweaked the knot on his tie. "Get your act together, you absolute fuckup of a man. Thanks for lunch."

And with that, he turned on his heel and stalked off.

Nothing he had said to me was wrong, and more than anything I wanted to be the man Val thought I was. Wanted to be the man Archie was accusing me of being. I didn't know how. I didn't see the way there. Not with the wedding invitation and the proof of my past hanging over my head the way it did.

But Archie was right. I had to do *something*.

I pulled my phone out of my pocket and called Val. He answered quickly, voice sounding confused as he greeted me.

"Hello?"

"Hi," I said softly. "It's me."

"I know it's you," he said. "What do you need?"

His tone was frosty at best, and I deserved that.

"I wanted to see if we could get together tomorrow night."

"I honestly don't know, Percy." His voice cracked, and I knew what was coming before he said it.

"Okay." I hoped it would stop him, but the words came out his mouth anyway.

"I have a date."

CHAPTER 10
VAL

IT HAD BEEN SO LONG SINCE I'D GONE ON A DATE, I WASN'T SURE what to do…how to act, what to say. For his part, Jason looked just as nervous, which made me feel somewhat human even though I knew I was going to make things worse when I came clean about my relationship with Barclay.

Jason had picked a restaurant by the beach for dinner. It was cute and cozy with checkered tablecloths and taper candles in straw-wrapped Chianti bottles. There were baskets of bread on the tables and little trays of olive oil. The whole thing was positively romantic, but I couldn't shake the unease of being there with him and not Barclay.

It wasn't a Jason problem.

It was a me problem.

My brain was so hard-wired to revolve around Barclay that the merest thought of being with another person short-circuited my thought process completely. I knew that was something I would have to get over, though. Because things were not going to change. Not in any tangible way.

"You look like you want to be anywhere but here," Jason said quietly, a soft and sad smile fluttering across his face.

He was so handsome. So kind.

"It's not that," I said quickly, reaching across the table and patting his hand. My palm was sweaty, and I pulled back quickly so he didn't realize. "I haven't been on a date in a while."

"No?"

"It's something I actually need to talk to you about."

He paled, brows lifting toward his hairline. "You don't have a boyfriend, do you?"

It was impossible to not laugh at the thought. "No boyfriend."

The wine at this place was delicious, fruity and rich while still managing to be dry. I reached for my glass and took a drink, hoping the alcohol would warm my blood enough for me to get the confession out. It wasn't anything I'd had to tell anyone else about before. Barclay's friends knew what we were, my family didn't know about him at all, and I'd never bothered to even mention his name to *my* friends. I didn't expect any of them to understand why I settled for half a man.

"There is someone, though," I admitted, mouth twisted into a pained smile. "But it's kind of complicated."

With that, Jason let out a rough-sounding laugh of his own. "I bet my complicated is more complicated than yours."

I choked on my next drink, using the tips of my fingers to swipe the dribbled wine away from my bottom lip.

"I find that unlikely, but mine is the kind that we need to get out of the way." I gave him what I hoped was an apologetic look. "I probably should have brought it up to you before I agreed to this date."

"I mean...same."

I didn't know what Jason could have in the vault of his life that was worse or harder to understand than what Barclay and I had, but the threat of his confession made me feel a little less insane for what I was getting ready to tell him.

"You go first," he offered, raising his glass to toast me. "We can compare notes."

His tone shifted from nervous to a soft kind of ease, and it immediately relaxed the tension that had spent the past hour tangling and wrapping its way around my spine. I didn't know how the conversation was going to go, but I was infinitely less scared of it than I had been when we first sat down.

"I don't have a boyfriend," I started, still not certain how to piece the words together. "But there is a man I've been…sleeping with. Uhm, pretty consistently for the past three years."

Jason let out a low whistle and heat flooded my cheeks.

"It's just meant to be sex with him, but I'm in love with him." I swallowed, chin angled toward my chest. Daring a glance up through my lashes, Jason didn't look upset. He watched me carefully, thoughtfully.

He was an open book. Even if I couldn't make out the emotions that flashed across his face, I could see him thinking, calculating.

"Does he love you?" Jason asked.

"He says no."

"That does feel slightly complicated," he said. "For you."

"It's just gotten complicated recently. I've been pushing him for more, and he's said no."

"Did he call things off with you?"

I scoffed. "No. He…we agreed things would stay the same, but he knows I'm dating other people now."

"Does he know about me?"

"In concept," I said. "Not in name."

"So, you're saying that you want to date other people…have relationships with other people, but still sleep with this man?"

When he said it like that, so straightforward and concise, it sounded so much worse than it felt. So unfair for everyone involved.

"Essentially," I admitted softly.

I finished off my wine, and Jason was quick to refill my glass.

"I…" I covered my face with my hands and let loose an awkward and high-pitched laugh. "I don't know how to say the next part without sounding wretched."

"There's more?" Jason leaned back in his seat, eyes twinkling with amusement.

"It's the least of it," I said. "It works with him because I have a very…voracious sexual appetite."

Now it was time for Jason's cheeks to flush. "Is he your only sexual partner?" he asked.

I shook my head.

"So you want to date people, and sleep with those people, but also sleep with other people? Sleep with this man you're in love with?"

He summarized it all together again, doing nothing for the guilt I felt. Maybe Barclay was right. Maybe I was selfish.

"Essentially," I admitted. "Now, you go."

"I'm not sure I can top that," he said, huffing out a laugh. He took a drink of his wine, the same familiar fortifying move I'd just done myself.

"Have at it."

"This whole date is a ruse." The corner of his mouth twitched. "And I feel less bad telling you that than I normally do."

"Why?" I asked, curious as to where he was going with his confession.

"I don't want to date," he said. "At least, not in the conventional sense. Not in the way you're looking to date."

"Is it because of…" I gestured with my hand, like the train of men I'd slept with were standing and observing just to the side of the table.

"No." He shook his head, his lip twitching into a full smile.

God, he was handsome.

"It doesn't have anything to do with you, but it has a lot to do with me."

"Jesus." I groaned. "I've heard enough of that to last me a lifetime."

"I'm aromantic," he blurted, shoulders lifting into a shrug. "I don't…I'm not…"

"You don't want to have a romantic relationship with anyone," I said, hoping my very basic understanding of the identity was close enough to not be offensive.

"I go into things with the whole premise of dating partly

because that's what people expect. It's what they want. But also because I think it's kind of fun sometimes."

I was more than familiar with doing things because it was what was expected, and I almost instantly saw myself in Jason, even if we were on opposite sides of whatever this spectrum was.

"I don't feel romantic feelings for people," he went on. "And before you ask, I've tried. I've spent my whole life trying."

"It's okay to not be what people think you should be."

"Easier said than done." He took another drink of his wine. "It gets lonely sometimes, but just because people don't get it. They are either turned away that I can't love them…that I don't want them to love me, or they're convinced that being friends with me means I think we're together and that's not how any of it works."

"I see how that can be isolating," I said softly.

He cleared his throat. "So, who do you think wins the complicated contest?"

I laughed at that, feeling comfortable with the situation for the first time all night. Jason wasn't going to be my next great love, and I found relief in that. Because no matter how much I wanted to love and be loved, it still tasted like infidelity to me. I worried that I wouldn't be able to find that happiness for myself until I was completely free of Barclay, but the thought of that was enough to send tears pricking at the corners of my eyes.

"They feel like different kinds of complicated," I said. "I have to ask, though. If you don't care to have romantic relationships or feelings, why bother asking me on a date?"

"To grease the wheels?" He raised his left shoulder and gave me a cockeyed smile that only made him more attractive. His honesty was really hot, but I didn't want to get ahead of myself.

It was still a refreshing change in his composure, I noted. Like all the nerves from the elevator and the phone call to set up the date, and even the start of the date itself were gone. With his truth out in the open, Jason was a changed man. And I had to admit, speaking about the situation with Barclay did make me feel somewhat lighter. I still felt like I was committing some horrible kind of adultery, but I didn't feel like I was pretending to be someone besides myself. And it was clearly the same with Jason, like he'd spoken magic words and transformed into the most authentic version of himself.

Jason presented as a man who was comfortable with himself and uncaring what other people thought of him. If they were not for him, he didn't strike me as the type to hold a grudge or burn a bridge.

"It's a habit at this point," he went on, smile still soft on his face. "Like a foot in the door before I drop the bomb."

I chuckled. "That's more than I've ever gotten."

"You really haven't dated anyone since you started sleeping with this man?" he asked.

"Three years."

"What's his name?" Jason asked, the question so comparable to when Barclay had asked the same of me.

"Does it matter?"

"He matters to you, so…yes."

"Barclay," I said. "It's his last name, but that's what he goes by."

"Valentin and Barclay," Jason murmured. "Tell me about him?"

"We don't need to talk about him."

"You're right," he agreed. "But we can. If you want."

"He's handsome, but he's impenetrable."

"Is he good in bed?"

Jason's question caught me so off-guard, I choked on my wine, spewing it out and down my face. He barked out a laugh at that, taking my glass out of my hand while I reached for my napkin. I dried my face as best I could, beyond mortified at the drops of wine on the tablecloth and the white plate in front of me. Some of the bread had turned polka dotted, the alcohol seeping into the dough and rushing toward the crusts like the tide.

He watched me steadily, that self-assurance and knowing clear as day on his face. He wasn't just comfortable with himself, he was comfortable with his sexuality too.

But more than that…he was comfortable with mine.

"Was that too much?" he asked. "I'm sorry. I just assumed it was okay to ask since there's clearly nothing here for us besides friendship."

"It's fine." I patted my lips again, then returned my napkin to my lap. He'd put the friend label on us, and that took away so much of the pressure. "It's fine. I just didn't expect it."

"You don't have to answer."

"He's the best lover I've ever had," I said.

Jason's eyes darkened, and he tilted his head to the side, eyeing me like a predator. "Sounds like challenge," he rasped.

"Oh, lord." I covered my face with my hands, tapping my fingertips against my forehead until I was sure I could open my mouth without laughing, crying, or saying something irreparably stupid.

"Did I misunderstand the arrangement you and Barclay have? You said you slept with him and other people. And honestly, Valentin…I would love to be one of those other people."

"A week ago…" I cleared my throat. "Immediate yes. I would have had you in the bathroom or the car, with a proposition like that."

"But now?"

"Everything feels…I don't know."

Fuck Perceval Barclay for ruining everything for me.

Fuck him for making me fall in love with him, because I was so consumed by the way my traitorous heart beat for him that I couldn't even get my head around the idea of taking someone else to bed. Fucking had always been okay, within bounds. Whether he arranged it or I found a partner on my own, sex hadn't ever been a limit, but now that…

Shit.

It wasn't him—it was me.

It was since I'd admitted my feelings for him that everything got harder for me.

It felt like cheating because, to my heart…now it was.

"I think you win the complicated contest." Jason raised his glass, and with a self-deprecating groan, I clinked the rims of our glasses together. He held my stare while we both drank, eyes alight with something playful and troublesome at the same time.

"I'm not sure it's a trophy I'm after." I grumbled.

"Does he know you're out with me?" Jason finally asked.

"He knows I'm out with someone," I said. "I didn't give him the details."

"What does he think about it?"

I replayed the conversation from the day before in my mind. The absolutely crestfallen slide his voice had taken when I'd told him I had plans. When I told him I had a date. And the way he'd gotten his shit together and rallied, pretending it was business as usual before asking me to come over when I was finished.

"He's not thrilled."

"Because he loves you too?" Jason arched a brow.

"Depends on who you ask." I tipped the rest of the wine into his glass. "He wants me to come over when we're done."

"To fuck?"

The word itself was enough to send a rush of heat between my legs, and I shifted in my seat, already thinking about what it would be like when I sent Jason on his way and went to Barclay's. Because I always went to Barclay's.

"That's the plan."

"What if I'd gotten lucky?" he asked. "What if our date went really well and I wanted to fuck you at the end of the night?"

"I'd still go after," I said, directing my voice into my lap for how shameful the thought of it was.

Jason let out something that sounded almost like a growl, mirroring the shift in his weight that I'd just done to alleviate the ache in my balls and my cock.

"Do you ever…" He trailed off, licking his lips. "You said you fucked him and other people. Did you ever do that at the same time?"

CHAPTER 11
BARCLAY

VAL WAS ON A DATE, AND I WANTED TO PEEL MY SKIN OFF.

I'd come so close to fucking it all up and asking him on a date the last time we talked. It was on the tip of my tongue, and that's when I knew I was crazy. I'd been willing to do literally anything to keep him close.

Even that.

But he'd beaten me to it, dropping the bomb that he was going out with that man whose name he refused to tell me. At his confession, the words had crumbled to dust on my tongue and I'd settled for second best, instead asking him to come over after. The least I could do was fuck his date right out of his memory.

Remind him how good we had things together.

I avoided drinking a bottle of whiskey, which felt like a win, and when Val called me just shy of nine, I answered on the first ring.

"Hello?" My voice cracked and I hated it.

"Hey." I could hear the smile in the single word, and I collapsed onto the floor, back against the wall.

I was so relieved to hear his voice…

"Are you done on your date?" I asked.

He laughed softly. "Kind of."

"What does that mean?"

"Things with…things with Jason aren't going to go anywhere. At least not romantically." Val paused, a small inhale of breath. "I like him as a friend."

I swallowed down the bile that threatened to rise up my throat and spew out of my mouth.

"I'm sorry it didn't work out for you."

He chuckled louder. "Are you really?"

"No."

Val made a thoughtful sound that almost felt like agreement. Like understanding.

"Jason wants to come over," Val said.

"He wants to…"

"Fuck."

In three years together, I'd never told Val no, at least not about anything related to sex, and I wasn't going to start now. But knowing that this man, at some point, had romantic intentions toward him had me more on guard than I wanted to be.

"Are you there?" he asked.

"I'm here."

"Can I bring him over?"

"Yeah. Yes." I cleared my throat. "Of course."

"Alright." Val didn't sound sure. "We'll be there in a bit."

"Okay. I'll be waiting."

The call disconnected and I dropped my phone on the floor, burying my face into my hands and letting out a garbled scream into my palms.

What the fuck had my life become?

That train of thought would have to wait until later because Val was coming over and he was bringing company. I shoved my phone across the floor, pleased to watch it slide across the living room before coming to stop in front of my bedroom door. That was close enough. Groaning, I rolled onto my knees and pushed up onto my feet. I didn't have to worry about cleaning up or anything, but I needed to get my head on straight before Val and…*Jason*… showed up.

I had twenty minutes before they were knocking at my door, and it took every ounce of control in my body to remain calm when I opened it. When Val saw me, his face softened like he was relieved, and that immediately untangled the knot that had taken up residence in the pit of my stomach.

Jason, on the other hand, looked a bit like a skittish raccoon caught in a garden where he didn't belong. He was objectively a handsome man. About my height, but not nearly as broad, with dark hair and golden eyes.

I saw what Val saw in him.

And I saw what he saw in Val because it was all the same things I saw.

"Come in," I said, stepping out of the way.

The two of them followed me inside, Val closing the door behind him and latching the deadbolt.

"This is Jason," he said, resting his hand on the small of Jason's back.

"Valentin has told me so much about you," Jason said, shaking my hand.

"Valentin," I murmured.

Val rolled his eyes and brushed past me, heading right into the bedroom, muttering about pissing and posturing under his breath. I gave Jason a quick onceover, gesturing for him to follow after Val.

"Enough with the formalities then?" he said with a laugh.

"We aren't going to fall in love, Jason."

"No. *We* aren't."

We joined Val in my bedroom and I found him sitting on the edge of the bed, his shoes already off and the top button of his shirt open.

"Are you two acquainted?" he asked.

"Enough," I said, turning to Jason. "No kissing."

"You or him?"

I traced my tongue across the front of my teeth, wondering if I had underestimated the man I was about to allow into my bed. We'd shared about as much pleasantries as I ever did with a potential partner, but there was something about Jason's cool arrogance that had me second-guessing if his intention to be just friends with Val was sincere or manufactured.

"Me."

"Can I kiss you?" he asked, glancing at Val.

"Well and often," Val said.

"Val and I don't use condoms," I said, interrupting their moment. Jason's mouth twitched in the corner and he looked back to me.

"Of course, you don't."

"You will." Val leaned over and pulled open the drawer in my bedside table that held the condoms, lube, poppers, and other toys we liked to have readily accessible. He dropped a condom and the lube onto the bed beside him, fingers hovering over the small brown bottle before flittering away.

"Of course," he agreed. "Is there anything else I need to know?"

"Val likes cock," I said, beginning the work of opening the buttons on my shirt. Val mirrored me, undoing the rest of his before shrugging out of his shirt and throwing it behind him. "The more of it the better."

"I like to suck cock too," Val added, beckoning Jason closer with a playful waggle of his fingers.

Jason eyed me warily, but eventually gave in.

I couldn't blame him.

Val was a fucking siren.

Of all the times Val and I had taken another person—or other people—to bed, I'd felt in control of the situation. There was a hierarchy in my bedroom and that had always been respected. Jason, though… he was like a weight on the wrong side of the scale. For the first time, Val had the upper hand on me and I wasn't sure what to do about it. I was fighting so hard against the voices in the back of my head that were yelling about what a horrible idea it was to keep sharing the man I was undoubtedly in love with. So hard, I almost missed Val's fingers doing their dance in my direction.

His cheeks were hollow, Jason's cock already out of his pants and down his throat, and Val called me closer until he got his fingers around my belt loop. Jason and I bumped together and he groaned, hand hovering over Val's head before settling softly on top of his hair. He let Val set the pace, like he was perfectly content to be a bystander, not an active participant, and somehow that alleviated some of the stress the situation had me feeling.

Val's fingers around my cock finished the job, and then his mouth was around my length, the familiar wet heat of his tongue doing its part to erase everything out of my brain that didn't revolve around him. As if there was ever a time when he wasn't my absolute everything.

Even if he didn't know it.

"Face each other," Val murmured, turning Jason and me by our cocks so the tips pressed together. He walked us in until we were almost toe to toe, then he mouthed both of our lengths at the same time, using his hands and his mouth to work us into a frenzy like no other.

Jason was more dressed than both of us, and I reached forward, tugging at the soft cotton of his t-shirt until he took over and pulled it over his head and off. He had dark hair on his chest and a tattoo on his ribs, a coarse trail of curls heading down behind the waistband of his boxers.

Val started to whimper and moan between us, his kisses getting sloppy and frantic. Precum leaked out of my cock, smearing against the tip of Jason's already wet dick and I couldn't lie. It felt *good*.

"You need to get fucked." I threaded my fingers through Val's hair and pulling him off our cocks. "Don't you?"

"Yes, please," he whined, fighting against my hand and flinging himself back on the bed. He made quick work of his pants, spreading his legs and making sure we both got a front row seat as he swirled his finger around his asshole.

"Do you want both?" I asked.

It pained me to admit Jason's cock was thicker than mine, but at least it was shorter. Val had taken more than him, more than me and him put together, but I still wanted to be sure. Because Val liked to be shared, but he liked to be involved too. Though…he did make a great fuck toy when the mood was right.

The mood was not right tonight. Not for me.

"Not yet," he said.

"What do you want, Val?" I rasped, closing my eyes with the ask.

Beside me, Jason made a choked-off sound, and after that…I could have heard a pin drop. I knew what Val wanted, and it seemed Jason did too.

"I want your cock inside me," he murmured, reaching down between his legs. "Here."

"And Jason?"

Val licked his lips.

"It's a good start," I said. "Get on your back."

Val lay on his back, head cushioned on the pillows, and I grabbed his ankle before he could settle, giving him a sharp tug until he was sideways, his head hanging off the edge of the bed. Clearly, Jason knew what to do because his cock was back in Val's mouth before I'd managed to get the lube open.

This was fine.

Better than fine.

This was the best case scenario, I told myself as I climbed onto the far edge of the bed. Val spread his legs for me, bending at the knees. He cupped his cock and balls in his hand, lifting them up so I could see his hole, already twitching and ready. I needed to get inside of him, needed to claim him, to know he was still mine.

I lubed my cock, pouring enough over my fingers to prep him, but when I teased around his rim with the tip of my finger, he grunted and smacked my hand away. Jason's hand was around Val's throat, lifting and falling with every thrust of his cock. His eyes, though… Jason's eyes were transfixed on *my* cock, and I watched the way his nostrils flared as I pressed my way into Val's body. Watched the way Jason's hips stuttered when Val moaned around him at my intrusion.

I eased into him slowly, not wanting to hurt him even though I knew he liked the burn of unprepped entry. His body stretched around me and I touched the place where he made room for me, the place we were connected. Jason stilled until I was all the way inside, and Val choked around the length in his mouth and throat. His muscles twitched and convulsed, grabbing and sucking at my cock, and I could have come just like that. Still inside of him and relishing the way his body reacted to being stuffed with two cocks, one from each end.

Jason's eyes rolled back and stared up at the ceiling, muttering something under his breath that I couldn't make out over Val's moans and protests at our stillness.

"You want more, don't you?" I petted my hands down Val's stomach, his muscles strained even as his hips bucked off the bed, trying to get more of my cock inside of him.

It was the second question I'd asked that had a double meaning, but Val and Jason were already so gone with lust that neither of them made mention about it. Instead, Jason stepped back, his cock sliding out of Val's mouth. There were trails of spit connecting them together, and Jason tore open the condom with record speed.

"How does this work?" he asked, nostrils again flaring as he shifted his attention toward where I was already inside of Val. "I've never done this before."

I managed to keep my dick inside of Val as I moved onto my back, taking him with me until he was straddled over me, ass up in the air.

"Like this." I stroked my fingers over the round globes of Val's ass before spreading him open. "Start with your fingers while I fuck him."

Jason climbed onto the bed between my legs and touched Val's ass with lube-slick hands. His touch was hard, but not aggressive, and I shivered, groaning at how it felt to have my cock touched by two men at the same time. And then one of Jason's fingers slid inside, along the length of my dick. Val shivered above me, hips circling down against me as Jason was quick to add a second finger.

Sweat beaded on Val's temple, and he stared down at me, eyes almost frenzied if not for the sadness in the depths of them that I knew was only there because of me.

"Look at you," I whispered, brushing his hair back from his face as Jason dragged his fingers against my cock, fucking them in and out of Val's body. "Look at you getting ready to swallow up two cocks."

I set an easy pace, pulling in and out of Val alongside Jason's fingers, and I wanted to know what it would feel like to have his fingers curled around my cock. Wondered if he'd be able to get his hand inside of Val's ass and what it would feel like to fuck his fist and spill inside of Val's body like that.

A shiver ripped through me and Val moaned, muscles holding hard against my dick and Jason's fingers. Jason cursed, withdrawing completely.

I felt the loss.

"You almost broke my fingers," he said, stroking his hands over Val's waist until he steadied and stilled.

"Want more," Val moaned, already lost in the way he loved the most.

"I know."

Val dropped his forehead against my shoulder, and over his back, Jason caught my stare. He was sweating too, cheeks flushed and the hair matted against his chest. I couldn't see much beyond his arm stretched down, and then the latex covered tip of his cock pushed against mine. On a pull out, he aligned our shafts as much as he could and then Val cried out.

I wrapped my arms around him, holding him against my chest. Gooseflesh broke out, racing up his legs and arms, the back of his neck, and Jason went slower and slower until we were both inside of him as far as we could reach.

"There you go." I kissed the side of his head. "Is that enough for you?"

"Move," he groaned against my shoulder.

It was hard from my angle, but Jason heard him and pulled out slowly before pushing back in. Val's body was tight with one cock inside of him. With two, it was nearly unbearable, even for me. Jason's cock was heavy and hot against mine, and it didn't take more than a few minutes of the tense slide for Val to spill all over my stomach.

He was a quivering mess, muscles gripping and grabbing around the base of my cock as he came, and then Jason went still, collapsing over the top of Val's back. I could feel him coming, cock pulsing and throbbing against mine as he spilled into the condom. It was undeservedly hot, and it only took a few upward strokes for me to chase after the two of them.

My mind went blank when I came.

I was only aware of Val's body against mine, his heart, his mouth. And there was Jason's cock against mine, the condom sagging against the tip of my dick, filled with his cum.

"Holy shit," Jason murmured.

He pulled out and Val's hole gaped before sealing tight around my softening cock. I grimaced, lifting Val off of me and rolling out from beneath him. With Jason on one side of my bed and Val in the middle, I sat on the edge, my back to them both. Val scooted closer to me, his fingertips grazing over the small of my back and the outside of my thigh.

"You're perfect," I assured him. "I'll get you cleaned up. Don't move."

He hummed, eyes closed.

"I should go," Jason said softly, leaning down and leaving a kiss against Val's temple. Val turned half onto his back, mouth chasing after Jason's. I watched the whole thing, watched Val search him out, watched Jason's stare flicker up to catch mine in the millisecond before their lips connected. Jason's lashes fluttered and he kissed Val, ending it sooner than I would have.

Val's face was soft and relaxed at the end of it. He'd never opened his eyes, never moved save for to angle himself for the kiss.

"That was amazing," Jason whispered against the corner of his mouth. "You are amazing."

He looked up at me, then slid off the bed.

Val's fingers were still on me, and I pressed my hand against his.

"I'll be right back," I promised him.

I didn't bother waiting for Jason and I sure as fuck didn't bother getting dressed. I went into the bathroom to get a warm washcloth, then went into the kitchen to get a bottle of water. I met Jason in front of the door as he finished tying the laces of his sneakers. There was an imbalance between us, even though I felt as in control as the situation allowed. Naked in front of him, I gave him a wary look, unsure of what to say.

"That was really something," he said, rubbing the back of his neck and looking down. His shirt was plastered against his chest. I should have at least offered to let him shower, but he hadn't given me a chance. Val was always my first concern after sex, and I hadn't tended him yet.

"You want to do it again."

"Are you asking?" He arched a brow.

"Val would want to do it again," I said instead of answering him.

Jason sighed, checking his pockets. "Val and I are only ever going to be friends," he said. "We don't want the same things."

"What do you want?" I asked.

"Ask me the more important question." He squared his shoulders, facing me head on and fully dressed. "You don't need to ask it, though, do you? You know the answer."

"There's plenty about me and Val that you don't know," I warned.

"And there's plenty about me that you don't know." He tapped his thumb against his fingers, one by one. "Plenty about me and Val you don't know. But I know he loves you. I know that man loves you more than I thought anyone could love another person."

I licked my lips, my throat parched. They'd been on one date. How did he know? What had Val said? What had been given away? I opened my mouth to ask, even though it didn't matter. It wouldn't change the truth.

From the bedroom, Val called out for me.

"You would be an idiot to lose him," Jason said, stare flickering toward the bedroom.

"I know," I said softly. "I know."

"Then don't." He opened the front door, one foot outside on the mat. "Because if you do, that's it. He'll be gone forever."

"I know," I said again, the words like barbed wire in my throat as I forced them out.

Jason wasn't telling me anything that I didn't already know, and I'd been so close to giving Val everything he wanted when Jason came into the picture in the first place. His arrival had been a wrench, but I couldn't let it be a roadblock. For some reason, I believed him when he said he was only interested in Val for friend-ship, and obviously also for sex, but if it wasn't him, it would be someone else.

Val was perfect in a million different ways, and if he wasn't with me, he'd be with someone else. The thought of it made me feel physically ill, a painful churn in my stomach that made me feel like throwing up.

"I liked that for more than Val, by the way." Jason's voice snapped me out of my head and I blinked at him, the words not quite making sense until I saw the hint of a smirk pulling at the corner of his mouth.

"Same," I said, barely louder than a breath.

What the fuck had my life become?

This wasn't new, but it was different at the same time, and I had no fucking idea what was going to happen next.

Val padded out from the bedroom, barefoot and sweaty, cum smeared across his stomach. He walked right to me and pressed himself against my side, kissing the shell of my ear with a tired sigh.

"What's taking so long?" he murmured.

"We were just saying goodnight," Jason said, not looking away from me. "I was telling Barclay how lucky he is to have you."

Val hummed against my ear and I slid my arm around his shoulder. I twisted the cap off the water and pressed the bottle into Val's hand.

"Let's get you sorted out," I said. The thought of another man being the one to clean Val up after sex was enough to put my entire body into a state of red alert. I could feel the heat of Jason's eyes on me and my cock remembered the swell of his cock when he came. I gave Val a gentle push back to the bedroom in time to catch the knowing look Jason gave me as he reached to pull the door closed.

"Goodnight, Barclay," he said.

"Goodnight, Jason."

CHAPTER 12
VAL

IT WAS THE SUN THAT WOKE ME UP FIRST, THEN THE OPPRESSIVE HEAT that radiated off Barclay like he had morphed into a furnace overnight. Sweat raced down my spine, and I tried to wiggle out from beneath his arm, but he was stocky and strong, holding me in place.

"You're killing me," I said, voice hoarse with sleep.

"I don't want you to go." He tightened his hold on me.

The sheets were wet beneath me from the sweat. I closed my eyes and relaxed against him, and he rewarded the concession with a kiss against the back of my head.

After Jason left the night before, Barclay had cleaned me up with the washcloth and his mouth. He'd rinsed me and dried me and tucked me into bed with a bottle of water on the bedside table. It was the same level of care and attention he always gave me after I'd been fucked to within an inch of my life, but even in my half-delirious state, it felt different.

I was far too tired to try and articulate the how and why of it, but in the light of day, his arm pulled tight around my chest, the answer was as bright as the sun streaming in through his window.

He was scared.

It might have been wrong to admit that his fear gave me some sick sense of satisfaction, but it was true. His nerves and his unease made me feel like there was still hope for us, for things to be different than he insisted they needed to be.

At dinner, when Jason had proposed the idea of a threesome, I'd almost jumped across the table and kissed him on the mouth. He'd given me a date, which he didn't want…and I'd thought I did, and even though there was no future in it for him and me, he presented me with another option that would work better for us both.

For all three of us, maybe.

And in any other part of my life, any other day, it would have been business as usual. Jason wasn't the first threesome Barclay and I had shared, and I doubted it would be the last. At least, I hoped it wouldn't be the last. Everything had been so volatile since I'd pressed him for more, since that stupid wedding invitation had arrived.

"You're just burning me to death," I grumbled, using my shoulder to try and shove his arm off of me. "And the sheets are wet."

"You've never cared about wet sheets before."

"Let me up," I said again. "I'm not leaving. I just need to breathe."

"I'll let you up if you let me take you out to breakfast."

The words were a dusting of air against the back of my neck and I went still beneath him. He huffed out something that was not quite a laugh, his body just as tense as mine.

"Say that again." I pushed at his shoulder a second time, rolling in place and bringing us face to face.

Barclay's eyes were sleepy, a stark contrast to the tight knit of his brows and the frown pulling at his mouth.

"Let me take you to breakfast," he said again.

"Don't look so miserable about it." I pressed the tips of my fingers against his bottom lip, and he kissed them.

"I don't want you to say no," he whispered. "I'm worried it's too late."

"Who are you?" I asked, my own mouth pulling up into a smile. "What have you done to Perceval Barclay?"

He closed his eyes, the furrow between his brows *almost* going soft. "I should ask you the same thing."

"This feels like a one-eighty from the last time we had this conversation," I said, still not sure if he was asking me what I thought he was asking me.

"It is."

"Is this because of Jason?" I asked, trailing my fingers from his mouth to the stubble-covered line of his jaw.

"Indirectly."

"Explain."

"Can I explain over breakfast?" he asked.

"I haven't decided if I'm telling you yes yet," I said.

He swallowed, and I slid my hands to his throat, feeling the swell of his Adam's apple.

"My life…" he trailed off, closing his eyes on a tired-sounding exhale.

Barclay was a vault of a man, and it had taken me all three years of our *relationship* to learn even the smallest things about him. Sure, I knew the TV he liked, the brands of whiskey he preferred, I knew how to make him come with my mouth and my hands, and I knew that he only snored when he was too tired to stand. There were plenty of things I knew about him and still so many that I didn't, but one thing I did know, with certainty, was that I loved him.

I also knew not to prompt him.

I burrowed as close to him as I could, tucking my face into the crook of his neck. Flinging one leg over his, I hooked it around his waist and hauled our bodies as close together as I could manage. The sheets were still wet, but I suddenly didn't care. I kissed his collarbone and waited for him to find the words to continue. Because if there was anything besides my body that I'd ever reliably given him, it was patience.

"Maybe another time with that part," he said, arms wrapped

around me once again like the vise grip from his sleep. "But…you are important, Val. You're important to me."

"In bed."

"Not just in bed," he admitted.

His heart slammed against his chest, slammed against my chest.

"You can explain over breakfast," I said.

The breath rushed out of him and he kissed the top of my head. Over and over and over, and I unwrapped my leg from around him and pushed him to the other side of the bed. It was impossible to breathe, hard to move, and I pressed my hand against my sternum to make sure my heart hadn't stopped beating.

"I want to be clear, though." I sat up, the sheets pooled around my waist. Barclay shifted onto his side, arm bent in half and his head cradled against his palm. "This is a date?"

There was that knot between his brows again, the worry in his eyes. "If…if that's what you want," he murmured.

I let out a loud and frustrated noise. Shoving his chest, he rolled onto his back and I climbed over him to get out of bed. He scrambled out of the sheets to chase after me, the duvet wrapping around his leg and almost taking him down to his knees. He cursed under his breath, and I ignored him. My clothes were behind the bed and I picked everything up piece by piece—shirt, pants, underwear, one sock.

"Val, wait," he begged. "What did I do wrong? I thought…I thought that's what you wanted."

I stepped into my underwear and my pants, yanking them up so I wasn't facing him absolutely bare-ass naked. "What I want hasn't ever been the problem here."

I pulled my shirt on, but my fingers were shaking too violently to make any sense of the buttons. Barclay took a step toward me, and I took a step back. He raised his hands in surrender, then took another step toward me. My back was already almost against the wall, so I didn't have anywhere to go. He closed the space between us, his fingers somehow steadier than mine as he started at the bottom and worked his way toward my throat.

"If I didn't want to have breakfast with you, I wouldn't have asked," he said.

"As a date."

He clenched his jaw. "I meant it as a date, yes."

"Because it's what I want or what you want?" I asked.

His fingers were warm against the bottom of my throat, sliding along the wrinkled collar of my shirt, just barely dusting across my skin.

"Does it matter?"

"Very much, unfortunately."

"It's not something I've ever wanted for myself." Barclay's eyes scanned my face, fear and uncertainty telegraphing across his features like he'd been painted with it. Some of the fight went out of me, but not the whole of it. "But I want *you*. And I think I'm willing to do things for you that I wouldn't do for other people."

I thought about Jason's fingers in my ass, around Barclay's cock, and scoffed, but the earnestness in his expression zapped the rest of the fight out of me.

"Okay," I said, grabbing his wrists and holding him steady. "Alright. Let's go get breakfast."

I hated the way it felt like a concession instead of a victory, but I wasn't a hypocrite. This is what I told him I wanted, what I'd been asking for, and there was no reasonable way I could turn around and tell him no. It wasn't as if things with Jason had been love at first sight, but I did see the potential to have a friendship with him, maybe a friendship with more benefits, but none of that mattered. Really, the only thing that mattered was Barclay asking me on a date.

Three fucking years.

"Let's shower then," I suggested. I'd dressed because I planned on going home, but if we were going out to eat, I didn't want to smell like stale sweat and cum.

Barclay turned his attention back to the buttons on my shirt, undoing them one by one before sliding it off my shoulders. His fingers dragged down my arms, chasing after the fabric, and when he reached my elbows, he backed me against the wall and slanted our mouths together.

To call the kiss unexpected would have been an understatement. It wasn't something we did often. But he took my face into his hands, changed the angle of my mouth then slipped his tongue past my teeth with the happiest little sigh I'd ever heard come out of his mouth. I slid my hands around his waist, steadying myself as he deepened the kiss. He pressed our bodies together, our lips, our cocks, until I understood with absolute and unwavering certainty just how much *he* wanted this too.

I leaned into him, pulling away from the wall.

I wasn't ready to end the kiss, but I was more than ready for him to take me on a date, so I kissed him and walked him into the bathroom. He chuckled against my mouth, finally breaking away long enough to turn the shower on. Ushering me into the glass stall, Barclay didn't take his eyes or hands off me, not even for a second. He touched me while he washed the both of us, rinsed us, dried us…dried himself.

Putting on dirty clothes didn't feel great, but it was all I could do. My slacks had held up, but the shirt had seen better days, the wrinkles from being cast aside all night deep and severe across the material.

"Here," Barclay said softly, handing me one of his white undershirts and a white button-up.

"You're bigger than me," I reminded him.

"It's just for now," he said.

I pulled the soft and worn shirt over my head and tucked it in, then did my best with the button-up, which hung a little too low on my shoulders, but was passable enough for a breakfast date.

A date.

In all the scenarios where I'd imagined Barclay taking me on a date, never did I imagine it would be a breakfast date, never did I imagine it would be with me in clothes that didn't fit me because he'd woken up after a threesome and realized just how bad things had gotten between us. But when it came to him, I was a beggar.

"This looks horrible." I tried to smooth the excess fabric flat against my stomach.

"No." He shook his head, stare unwavering. "It looks perfect."

CHAPTER 13
BARCLAY

SITTING ACROSS FROM ME AT BREAKFAST, VAL LOOKED LIKE HE WANTED to crawl out of his skin. He'd ordered a Bloody Mary as soon as we sat down, then turned his attention to combing through the menu with more attention to detail than I'd ever seen him give anything else. I was going to get eggs Benedict, and I'd quickly abandoned my menu in favor of studying him.

His fingertips tapped against the back side of the menu and his eyes were narrowed into a squint. He reached blindly for his drink before dropping the menu in front of him with a soft huff of breath.

"What's on your mind?" I asked.

He pursed his lips, chin toward his chest as he glanced up at me through the fan of his lashes. "Are you being serious right now?"

"Yes?"

If this was dating, I had no idea why it was so important to him. This was near excruciating, and Val knew more about me than almost anyone else alive. I had always understood the point of dating to revolve around getting to know someone and establishing sexual compatibility. I knew Val, and to call us sexually compatible was an understatement. I also knew, though, that dating went from that to some unspoken system of weights and measures that were half-likely to end in a separation and half in marriage.

I didn't believe in marriage, didn't want a thing to do with it, and I didn't want to lose Val so I'd never even wanted to get on a road that headed toward those statistics. It didn't stop there, because if you made it to the marriage side, if you stayed together, you were met with a new probability. Fifty percent chance of divorce, one hundred percent chance of death ending it all if you beat the first set of odds.

Val was a numbers guy, and the despite the statistical likelihood of failure with all of those options, this was still what he wanted.

"I'm just trying to wrap my head around your change of heart," he said. "Wondering if you're going to walk it back as soon as you realize Jason isn't a threat."

I'd never really thought Jason was the threat, but that didn't mean the next man wouldn't be.

"I meant what I said earlier," I reminded him. "I want you."

"Want me how?" Val arched a brow, mouth twisted into a tight frown.

"In every way."

"Why now?"

I inhaled sharply, scratching at the stubble on my chin. A year or two ago, it had started to grow in patches of gray that showed my age. I hated the contrast against the rest of my hair, but Val had ridden me to orgasm with his fingers dancing across the lightening strands and I'd started to care about them less.

Val had always been there for me from the start of things, and I imagined he'd be there until the end. At least, I had until recently. The end was looking a lot closer than I ever though it would be, and I wasn't too arrogant to admit that my fear of that loss outweighed the ways I hated myself.

"You have positioned yourself." I walked my fingers across the table before lifting them into the air between us.

"You make it sound manipulative."

"I don't think it was your intent."

"And yet," he whispered.

"You've made yourself...I don't know how to explain it," I said.

Val cleared his throat, angling his head and leveling a tense look at me from the other side of the table. "Try harder."

"Everyone I've ever been involved with...they've all been like Dennis or worse than Dennis," I said, hating the memories. "I've been lied to, cheated on, abandoned. I've spent my entire life being less than the better option for the people I loved."

His jaw ticked, just below his ear.

"You know this about me," I reminded. "This isn't a revelation."

"I've pieced my understanding of you together from three years of half-sentences and closed doors, Percy."

"And I love you for that," I blurted.

He swallowed, nostrils flaring.

"You don't love me," he said.

"You think I don't?" It was all on the table now, and I realized that the only way to not lose out was to keep stripping myself bare until Val had heard enough of the truth. And it was the truth. Every word, even the parts of it that I would have preferred to keep to myself.

I loved Val, but I'd never wanted to tell him that.

Because loving people was a death sentence.

"You're as much a part of my life as I am, and I can't fathom losing that. Can't imagine losing you."

"That's not love."

"Look me in the eyes and tell me that I don't love you." I slammed my hands down on the table and leaned forward over it, chest heaving. Val avoided my stare until he realized I wasn't going to look away, then finally met my gaze with more reluctance than I'd ever seen.

It seemed unfair to me that I was offering him the one thing he swore he wanted above all else, and now he was questioning my sincerity. He was rejecting my honesty, and I fought tooth and nail against the horrible unease that began its slow weave and creep up my spine. Kept my eyes open against the visions of catching Dennis in bed with my teacher, of all the other wrongs I'd lived through. Kept my eyes on Val until he believed my confession.

"Okay," he finally said.

I collapsed back in my chair, breathing for the first time in what felt like an hour.

"Okay," I said back.

Rubbing at the cuticle on my thumb with the edge of my pointer finger, I had to look away because Val and I had done a lot of things together, but I'd never had him strip me naked in the middle of a restaurant with just his eyes before. And whether I loved him or not, I never wanted him to do it again.

"You have to promise you won't hold it against me when this goes to shit."

"The odds are against that."

"They're really not." A low and self-deprecating laugh died in the back of my throat. "And you want this anyway."

"I want you," he said simply.

"And I want you," I whispered. "I need you."

Val smiled, but it quickly fell away. "I know you do."

"I don't want anything to change."

"This changes everything."

"I mean, I get that." Steepling my fingers together in front of my nose, I groaned, knowing that I was so out of practice at this whole thing and also garbage at explaining my emotions to anything besides the bottom of a whiskey bottle. "But the way it's been…"

"I can date you and love you, and still fuck strangers." The smile that flitted across his face stuck a little longer than the last one, and I counted that as a win.

"I sure hope so."

"That's what you meant then?" he asked. "That part of things stay the same."

"Right."

"But now we have this part?" Val gestured to the restaurant, and I answered him with a nod.

"As long as you're patient with me," I said, even though I could have gone without. There was no one more patient with me than Valentin Russo.

"I think I have that one covered," he teased.

A petite waitress with a white-blonde pixie cut stepped up to the table, and I ordered for both of us. Getting Val another drink and getting a mimosa for myself. After I passed her the menus and she walked away, Val arched a brow, giving me a wary look.

"What?" I asked. "Have I already fucked up?"

"You didn't even ask what I wanted to eat," he said. "You just ordered for me."

"Just because we've never gone out to breakfast doesn't mean I don't know the things you like," I told him. "You don't like eggs, but you love cake. Pancakes and bacon felt like a reasonable guess."

Suddenly, I doubted myself. "I can call her back if you want something different. Maybe I shouldn't have. If you don't want me to…"

Val lifted his hand and I bit my lips to stop myself from talking. It was just like me to slide back into my old habits of ruining things, and I hadn't even made it through the first half of our first date.

"Pancakes are perfect," he said softly, brow pinched together in the center. He cocked his head to the side like he was studying me, but didn't say anything else.

"What?" I rasped.

He shook his head, expression turning almost sad.

"Nothing," he promised.

I tried to give him a smile, but it didn't feel sincere so I let it fall away. "I meant what I said before."

"Which part?"

"All of it." I chuckled. "But I meant it when I said I love you."

"Why didn't you tell me before?"

Val was always going to cut me straight to the quick. Dating wasn't easy, but dating him was going to be near impossible.

"I need you to understand that I'm older than you and I've spent a long time being the way I am."

"You're not that much older than me." He rolled his eyes. "This isn't like a Grayson and Rob scenario over here."

"Flynn and Rose," I murmured.

Val gave that one an honest laugh, and the crawling vine of discomfort that had been working its way up my spine slowed down. It didn't stop and it didn't get better, but it didn't get worse. I could breathe, I could feel my heart beat, I could see the man I loved.

Shit.

I was so gone for him and I'd known it all along.

"Are you going to tell them about us?" he asked, swirling a skewer of olives and bacon around his drink.

Ice clinked against the glass and he took a sip of the tomato vodka cocktail, eyeing me from behind the leafy spruce of the celery stalk.

"Yes."

"I've wondered for a long time if they have a bet running on this thing between us," he said conversationally. "How long it would take. Who would cave first. Something like that."

"This isn't a concession," I said.

"Isn't it?"

"It's a lifesaving measure," I assured him.

Val traced his tongue across the front of his teeth, shaking his head. "I should have dated someone else sooner."

"It doesn't have anything to do with Jason," I said.

"I think that's the first lie you've ever told me."

"We had really hot sex last night, Val. Maybe you forgot that he almost had his hand wrapped around my cock—" I leaned over the table and lowered my voice so only he could hear. "Inside of you."

His cheeks flushed as dark as his drink.

I leaned back, smoothing my hand down the front of my shirt, allowing myself to appreciate the look of him in my clothes for the first time since he'd put my shirt on.

"If anything, you dating other people would have been like kindling on our sex life," I said.

"Until it was a bucket of water."

"Either way."

"Either way," he agreed, even though his face looked like he didn't quite buy it.

Convincing Val of my dedication and seriousness over the new stage in our relationship was going to be an uphill battle, but it was still one I would have to fight. He truly had dug in and buried himself into the foundation of my life. Loving him didn't mean I expected the outcome of our relationship to be any different. The fear of failure and separation was an ever-present thought in the very front of my mind. This shift in our agreement would only prolong the inevitable, but I was greedy and selfish, and I would take however many days it would buy me.

"Do you believe that I love you?" I asked, stretching my arm across the table, palm up.

Val studied my upturned palm before sliding his against mine.

"Yes," he whispered. "I believed you earlier. This is just a change for me too."

"But it's a change you wanted."

"I wanted you." He tried to take his hand away, but I tangled our fingers together and held him there. "You were so insistent in telling me no..."

The feeling between us in that exact moment was *my* understanding of love. It was contentious and it was bitter. It was resentful. All things I never wanted to feel toward Val, and yet it rolled off of him in waves. The uncertainty, the trepidation.

He'd given me three years of patience, though. The least I could do was wait him out in return. As for what would happen after that? Eventually, I'd be nothing more than a lesson learned, and that was the best case scenario.

CHAPTER 14
VAL

Another Sunday night.

Another Sunday night dinner.

"You look like the cat that ate the canary," Teresa said, collapsing next to me on the couch in the living room of our parents' house.

"Do I?"

My stomach still churned with pancakes and vodka from the morning, sated but also unsettled. I flexed my hand into a fist, skin still tingling from the weight of Barclay's fingers around mine after he'd confessed his feelings for me over breakfast.

At first, I didn't believe him. Everything felt too contrived, too convenient, too much to his gain. But after taking the time to study his face, to stare into his eyes, and the depths of emotion and need had taken my breath away.

He did love me, but his fear was louder, his doubt even bigger than the first two emotions put together. He doubted himself, doubted me—doubted the whole of it—and still he'd taken a chance. That had to count for something. He saw enough importance in the half-relationship that we'd spent the past three years building to throw some much-needed life into the connection.

I needed to meet him halfway, which was proving harder than I'd ever expected it to be. There he was, practically handing me the thing I wanted most on a silver platter, and my first instinct was to turn him down. Not because I didn't want it, but because, for the first time, I was aware of the cost. It was painted in every worried crease around his eyes and the tight unease in the set of his mouth.

I didn't want him to feel *bad* about being with me.

Ever.

Whether it was sex or more, the thing between us was born from a place of seeking pleasure and he looked like he was feeling anything but.

Yet we'd finished breakfast and made less confrontational conversation, and then he'd kissed me goodbye like he *meant it*, and sent me home with his shirt on my back and his spit in my mouth.

I'd spent the entire day replaying everything. From my failed date with Jason, to his proposition to take us both to bed, to what it had been like to take the both of them at the same time. Then the morning when Barclay had held me until I said yes, and then our very first date.

The whole chain of events felt like a dream, but the ache in my ass was a painful reminder that less than twenty-four hours earlier, I'd had both of their cocks inside of me.

"There it is again," she said, pinching my cheeks. "And you're blushing."

I smacked her hand away, making a frustrated sound. "You're too involved," I told her.

"You can tell me, or I'll go get Angie."

"For being the youngest, you're such a bully."

"I had to be to keep up with the two of you." She pinched my cheek again, but anticipated my reaching for it and she tightened her fingers on my skin, nails digging in hard enough to leave a bruise.

"You're such a bitch," I whisper-yelled, yanking us both off the couch and kicking her in the back of the knee.

She yelped, which sent her husband running in from the kitchen.

"Nope," Drew said, holding up his hands.

"Help me, you traitor," she cried out at him, but I had her on her stomach, face smashed into the carpet before she could get the entire plea out.

"You deserve this," I said, using her shoulders to push myself back onto my feet. "The older you get, the more you turn into Angie."

"I heard that!" our older sister shouted from the kitchen.

"She's coming with the spoon," Drew warned.

"She's the one turning into *Ma*." Teresa flopped onto her back and kicked her leg out, smashing me in the ankle with the heel of her boot.

"Teresa, don't kick your brother," Angie chided.

"He started it!"

"I did not." I brushed my hands down the front of my shirt, straightening it out.

I'd changed out of Barclay's after breakfast, not wanting to risk drawing attention to myself with my sisters or spilling something on it. The shirts were a small thing, but I didn't have clothes at his house. Three years in, but we were nowhere near the clothes-sharing stage. There were no old USC sweatshirts stolen from him in the bottom of any drawers in my closet.

But now…

"Dinner's ready," Angie said. "Ma says for one of you to set the table." With that, she went back into the kitchen.

Teresa scrambled to her feet, shoving me in the middle of my chest.

"Go set the table," I told her.

"You do it."

"Teresa."

"If you don't do it, I'll tell her you're seeing someone."

The flush she'd recently called me out on washed out of my face and my breath lodged in my throat.

"How do you know that?" I asked, stare darting madly from her back toward the kitchen.

Teresa gave me a proud smile, looking more like me than either of our parents. "I didn't. But thanks for confirming."

She patted the place on my chest where she'd just pushed me. "So go set the table like a good boy, Valentin."

"I hate you," I grumbled, shuffling into the kitchen.

I didn't hate her.

I loved both of my sisters more than anything, but I wasn't ready to tell anyone about Barclay yet. Not because I didn't trust him, but because I didn't trust the longevity of it. They would be so excited, especially Angie, especially our mother.

I squeezed past my sister and my mom to get to the silverware drawer, taking the entire plastic caddy out instead of trying to gather everything needed into my hands. That earned me a slap against the back of my head from my mom, but Angie laughed and so did her husband, Marcos, when I reached the table and dropped it in front of him.

He was there and ready to go, flanked by Drew and my dad. The three of them were undoubtedly talking about sports or something I didn't care about, and the one thing I loved about Sunday night dinners was I never got pressured into conversation I didn't know anything about. I moved around them, dropping forks, spoons, and knives onto the table, pushing them into place over white, patterned paper napkins. I set all the places and poured some wine into an empty glass, then settled into my seat.

Drew gave a worried look to the silverware caddy, but Teresa walked into the dining room and I threw it at her with a quick "heads up." She impressively managed to catch it, calling me something I couldn't make out for how shrill her voice was.

My father frowned at me, but didn't chide me, and when Teresa came to sit down, she smacked me in the same spot my mother had nailed earlier.

She and my sisters were really three peas in a pod.

Angie and our mom came out with the food and as soon as everyone had gotten seated and served, Teresa opened her mouth.

"Valentin is dating someone," she said proudly.

Eight sets of eyes landed on me, including my niece and nephew who were too young to even know what dating was, let alone why it deserved so much attention.

I kicked her under the table and she grunted, returning the favor. Her pointed boots delivered far more of an impact than my sneakers did, so I committed the sin to memory and promised I'd pay her back later.

"You have a girlfriend?" Angie asked.

"Boyfriend," I corrected.

My father murmured something, looking down at his lasagna. He didn't care, he just…

He was my dad.

"What's his name?" Ma asked.

"Barclay."

"What kind of name is Barclay?" Teresa asked.

"What kind of name is Teresa?" I snapped, kicking her again, consequences be damned.

My mom threw her hands up the air. "Angela, change seats with your brother."

"What?" Angie scoffed.

"That's ridiculous, Ma," I said.

She flicked her wrist between me and Angie without a word, and we both sighed at the same time. Picking up our plates and wine, Angie and I crossed paths behind my father and I sat down next to her husband and she sat down next to our sister.

"I hope you're happy," Angie said.

"Peachy." I stabbed my fork into the piece of lasagna I'd cut right before my sister outed me to the whole family.

"So." My mom sounded like she had solved world peace and was ready to move on to the next item on her to-do list. "Barclay."

"It's just what he goes by," I grumbled.

"Where did you meet him?" she asked.

"A club."

The less information I could get away with giving them, the better, for more than one reason.

"When?" Angie asked.

"A few years ago."

"And you're just now dating?"

"We've been friends," I said, which was the truth. As much the truth as it could be, I supposed.

"Why more now?" my father asked.

I scratched behind my ear, glancing to his spot at the end of the table. The answer to that was going to give too much away, so I shrugged.

"And he's a boy," my father said.

"A man."

He bobbled his head to the side, then said something to Marcos about the baseball game. I exhaled, shifting my attention back toward the side of the table that held my three inquisitors.

"Do you have a picture of him?" Ma asked.

I did, but…

"No."

"Where did he take you?" Angie asked.

"Who said he was the one taking me?"

"Where did he take you?" Teresa repeated my sister's question, like it was a foregone conclusion that I was the damsel in my relationship.

"The Penthouse," I said.

"He took you to his house?"

"It's a restaurant at a hotel," I explained. "In Santa Monica."

"Sounds expensive," Drew murmured to my left.

I wanted to kick him too.

"Very nice," Ma said. "When do we meet him?"

I barked out a laugh, choking on my dinner. I rinsed the cheese and noodles down with some wine, and after I'd regained my composure, I realized she was serious.

"Oh, really?" I asked.

"Really, Valentin."

"It's new, Ma," I explained. "I want to make sure it's going to work out before I bring him around."

"Three years old," she said. "That doesn't sound new."

"It's different now than it has been."

"Soon, then," Angie said.

"Eventually," I offered.

"I knew you were keeping a secret," Teresa grumbled.

"Work has been going great." I cleared my throat and pasted a smile on my face. "Thank you for asking, Teresa. How's it going shoving thermometers up cats' assholes?"

"Valentin!" my mom yelled at me over the conversation at the table, and I dropped my fork onto my plate.

I was used to fighting with my sisters. It was normally harmless and playful, but the shift in things with Barclay clearly had me on edge.

"I need some air," I said, shoving my chair away from the table.

No one argued when I slipped into the back yard, my only regret that I hadn't brought my wine with me. I hated feeling the way I was, the awkward uncertainty, the nerves, the expectations —all of it was making me miserable. It was the complete opposite of what I thought would happen.

Pulling my phone out of my pocket, I fired off a quick text to Archie because I didn't want to bother explaining the nightmare to Barclay.

Me: How do you deal with intrusive family?

He answered quickly.

Archie: I don't know because I'm only an intrusive friend.
Archie: What's up?
Me: My sisters are being annoying.

My phone rang two seconds later, Archie's name flashing on the screen.

"Hello?" I answered.

"Always happy to chat, Val," he said instead of hello. "But we've never had that kind of relationship before."

"I know." I sighed. "I've always just been that guy your friend is fucking."

"That guy we were all fucking," he said. "Though you've never just been that guy for him."

"I shouldn't have bothered you. I'm sorry."

"It's not a bother. It just feels like a change from how things have always been."

"Yeah." I banged my face down onto the table, cradling the phone against my ear with my shoulder. "That's been going around."

"Did you go on that date?" he asked.

"Yes."

"How did it end?"

"Do you want the long story or the short one?" I asked.

"Owen is waiting for me, so short."

"It ended with breakfast with Barclay," I said, lifting my head and dropping it back onto the glass.

I heard a rustle on the other end of the call and then something that sounded like Archie was trying to talk, but not quite able to find words.

"What's the long story?"

"I went out on the date and then we both ended up in bed with Barclay at the end of the night—"

"Happens to the best of us," Archie murmured.

"And then the next morning, he had a crisis of conscience. I don't know. He asked me on a date and then took me to breakfast."

"Barclay took you on a date," he repeated.

I hummed my agreement.

"Perceval Barclay took you on a date?"

"Yes," I croaked.

"I fucking knew it." Another rustle and a lingering silence, then Archie was back in my ear. "Are you dating now?"

"That's the rumor."

Another silence.

"Are you there?" I asked.

"Yeah. Yep. Just…hold on…just had to fire off a text real fast."

Apparently Barclay hadn't told his friends about us yet.

"It was only a matter of time," Archie said. "I'm glad you waited him out."

"I'm still getting used to the idea," I admitted.

"And judging by the intent of this call, your sisters know now?"

I righted myself, rubbing the dirt from the table off with my fingers. "My younger sister tricked the truth out of me."

"I'm told that's sometimes how it goes."

"I shouldn't have bothered you with it," I said again, another half-apology. "Dinner was just overwhelming and I had to come outside to get some air."

"You don't have to apologize."

The slider behind me creaked open, and Teresa peeked her head out. "Val?"

"Hold on," I said into the phone, giving her a wary look. "What do you want, Teresa?"

"I wanted to apologize," she said, sounding achingly sincere.

"You don't have to apologize." I repeated to her what Archie had just said to me.

"I'll let you go," Archie said. "But anytime you need to talk, you know where to find me."

"Thanks, Archie." I hung up the phone, eyes still on my sister.

"I'm sorry," she said again. "I was just trying to poke fun. We've been waiting so long for you to meet someone. I didn't mean to make you upset."

"Do you mean that, or did Ma make you come say it all?"

I stood up and slid my phone back into my pocket.

"Yes," Teresa answered.

I reached her and looped my arm around her shoulders, pulling her in for a hug. Her defenses were down, and I yanked her off balance, grinding my knuckles into the top of her head until she cried out and slapped me.

I shoved her off, grinning while she tried to straighten herself back out. I shouldered past her, heading back to my lasagna.

"Apology accepted, Teresa."

CHAPTER 15

BARCLAY

It had been a very long time since I was in a relationship, even though my friends often argued that's exactly what Val and I already were. But after going on an actual date with him, I knew they couldn't have been more wrong. Everything was different now, from the way he looked at me to the way my chest felt when I looked back at him.

Confessing my feelings for him had been easier than taking him out for a meal which, in my head, should have been a compliment. Loving Val was like breathing; it was second nature. The wining and dining…all of that came secondary. That was what needed learning and training.

He went home after breakfast, taking my clothes with him, which I hadn't minded at all. I liked the look of him in them. The way my shirt hung an inch too low on his shoulders filled my chest with a completely new kind of proprietary ownership around him. Not that I'd ever felt like I had a claim on him…

Quite the opposite.

Val had always been open with himself, his body, his love.

But now he was mine to keep. Mine to share. That was special.

But standing at my kitchen counter with that thick off-white envelope in my hand, it didn't feel special. It felt fragile and scary, like vines of thorns wrapped around the tender love that had lived in my chest for him for so long already.

My phone ringing was a welcome enough distraction from the train my thoughts had decided to take.

"Hey," I said, answering it on speaker phone when Flynn's name flashed on my screen.

"Is for horses," he said back.

"I thought I was the old one here."

"That's Rob." He laughed. "Speaking of, can you swing over to his house?"

"Rob's?" I dropped the envelope on the counter with a frown. "Why? What's up?"

"Grayson and Rob…" Flynn trailed off.

"Yeah." I didn't need to hear anything else. "I'll be there."

I was nervous the whole drive over to Rob's house, worrying about whatever Grayson had done, whatever Rob had done. Of all my friends who'd fallen curse to the couple trap over the past year, Rob was the first to go and I'd always wondered about the compatibility between him and Grayson. Not that I had anything against his younger employee, but Grayson was more like us than we were sometimes, arrogant and dominant in the most stubborn kinds of ways, and that had to be a breeding ground for conflict.

Everyone's cars were already in Rob's long driveway when I got there, and I knew the front door would be unlocked. I let myself in and followed the sound of their conversation right into Rob's well-appointed and overstuffed library. Five sets of eyes turned on me when I stepped over the threshold—Rob, Flynn, Dalton, Archie, and Grayson.

I hadn't expected to see Grayson considering what Flynn had said on the phone, but…

Wait.

What had Flynn said on the phone?

"What's going on?" I asked warily

Flynn gave me what would have passed as an apologetic expression if I wasn't looking too hard at him, scratching the back of his neck and looking away when he said, "Grayson and Rob volunteered."

"For what?"

"Grayson volunteered," Rob corrected, his face matching Flynn's.

"For what?" I asked again.

"A meeting space," Flynn said. "Just like old times."

"We did most of our meeting upstairs."

"My favorite place," Grayson murmured. "But I think Archie has other plans and you know how he is."

Archie scoffed, rolling his eyes. "Don't act like you weren't eager to get him here."

"What's going on?" I asked again.

"Consider this an intervention," Archie said, clasping his hands together in front of him.

One perk, I supposed, of finally dating Val officially was that they could no longer harass me about not dating Val and I was about to tell them as much, but Archie kept talking.

"Because I thought we were your best friends."

"You are," I said.

"So why did we find out that you and Val are dating from Val instead of you?"

"Wait. What?"

"To be fair," Flynn said, turning to Archie. "I found out Val and Barclay were dating from you."

"So did I," Rob said.

I glanced at Dalton, who shrugged one shoulder toward his ear.

"How did you find out?" I asked.

"He called me," Archie said, standing up and gesturing toward his vacated seat. "Why don't you sit down and we can talk?"

"Why did he call you?" I sat down and narrowed my eyes at him.

"That doesn't matter."

"What changed?" Grayson asked.

I think I'd secretly known all along this was how it was going to go. Whether they found out from me or from him, the questions would come one way or another. It wasn't one of the reasons that I'd avoided dating Val, or anyone for that matter, but it wasn't something I'd been particularly looking forward to. For as much as Val and I were open with everyone else regarding how things had been, I wanted to keep this new piece more private between us. Partially to feed my selfish urges, but also partially because if things—when things—went south, I didn't want any of them to know how truly bad that would be for me.

I didn't want them to know that I loved him.

"He went on a date," Archie said.

"If you don't need me here for this, I can go," I snapped.

"Sorry." Archie poured me a drink. "What changed?"

"Nothing has changed," I said. "I'm not happy about this."

"Don't tell him that," Dalton muttered under his breath.

"It's a concession I had to make so I didn't lose him."

Dalton rolled his eyes. "Don't tell him *that* either."

"I don't know what you want me to say. It wasn't some epiphany where I realized the only thing missing from my life was a dinner date with Val."

"The only thing missing was him," Archie said.

"Has Owen made you soft?"

"Owen made me remember what I'd been missing my whole life," he said earnestly. "I'd always known I loved him, but I hadn't realized how much I needed him to love me back until he came into my life again."

"He came into something alright," Grayson said under his breath.

"But it doesn't matter." Archie rubbed under his nose with the side of his thumb, squaring his shoulders. "We aren't here to talk about me. We're here to talk about you and Val."

"You've been accusing me of being in love with him for years," I reminded.

"And are you?"

I took a healthy drink of Rob's obscenely pricey whiskey.

"That's a yes," Rob said.

"Don't act so surprised."

"It's the least surprising thing about you."

I finished off the whiskey and set the glass down on his side table, a little harder than necessary.

"Well, if that's all then." I stood up and smoothed my hand down the front of my shirt. "I don't see why there's any need for me to be here."

"What do you mean?" Flynn asked with a laugh. He leaned back against the corner of Rob's couch and stretched his legs out in front of him, crossing them at the ankle.

"The group of you seem to already have the answers to the questions."

"You're not wrong," Archie teased. "You're the one who took forever to come around to the idea of dating the man you're in love with."

"I'm not in love with him," I said quickly, half out of reflex and half because I wanted it to be true.

It was one thing to love Val, another to be in love with him. I wasn't sure where the distinction lay, but I didn't think that was what I meant when I told Val I loved him. But, with a slow blink, I recalled the feelings that had churned in my stomach when I'd begged him to see that I loved him back…

"I am in love with him," I corrected myself with a sigh.

My friends let out a collective cheer, coming together and clanking their glasses. Whiskey sloshed over Dalton's fingers and he flung his arm around my shoulder, whispering into my ear, "It's not a curse."

"What do you know about it?" I muttered.

He wiggled his left hand, that ostentatious wedding ring of his flashing under the light.

"Don't say it like it's a bad thing," Grayson said.

It was a bad thing, though.

It was the beginning of the end.

I could love him and want him, and still know that I'd put an expiration date on our relationship. I'd lean into it, though. Because he deserved it. I'd do all of the things to make him happy…

I would be a good boyfriend to him until he got tired of me.

"Are you going to take him to the wedding?" Rob asked.

The happy chatter between the rest of them died down, and their eyes were all on me again, waiting for an answer.

"Absolutely not."

"Why not?"

"That's…something different entirely."

I didn't want Val to come to the wedding because I didn't want him to meet my family under those circumstances. I didn't want him to meet Dennis…I didn't know how I would handle seeing him again, let alone with Val by my side?

"He would be good support," Flynn suggested. "Since we can't go."

"Actually." Dalton cleared his throat, giving me a quick look before he turned his attention to his lap. "I was invited."

Of course Dalton was invited. His family had more money than anyone I knew, my family included, and that was the way of it. Invitations based on social status and last name, not proximity to the couple.

"Why didn't you say anything?"

"Because I wasn't going to go."

"Yes, you are," Grayson said.

Dalton sighed. "We'll talk about it later."

"It doesn't matter," Grayson went on. "You should still take Val with you."

"I don't want to," I said simply.

"You didn't want to date him either," Flynn offered.

"Are you my friends or are you here for Val?" I asked, nerves vibrating just beneath the skin like they were all working to come together and explode, shattering me into a million pieces at their feet.

I'd had enough.

Standing up, I waved off their moans and groans of protest.

"Things with Val are new," I explained.

"Not really," Archie countered.

"They're new and they're between him and me."

"Also not really," he said.

"If Val comes to the wedding, that's a choice that he and I are going to make, not me and the bunch of you assholes."

"At least you've got that part right," Flynn teased. "Well on your way to being a good boyfriend."

I shook my head, pointing at Archie. "I don't care if you and Val are best buddies now or not, but whatever goes on between him and me has nothing to do with you," I warned.

Archie leaned back and rolled his eyes, shoulder to shoulder on one of the couches. "He called me, Perceval."

"Don't call me that."

"He called *me*," he stressed again. "For once, I'm not meddling."

"Then what's this?" Grayson asked, gesturing to the group of us.

"It's a problem." I checked my pocket for my phone and my wallet and keys. "You're a problem of fucking doms with too much time on your hands and not enough sense."

"And what about you?" Grayson persisted. "I'm not in the group chat. You are."

"You can take my place," I told him.

He pressed a hand against his chest, expression twisted into something that felt like a taunt. "I'm not a trophy dom."

"Do you really believe that lie?"

Grayson's cheeks darkened, and I pointed at Archie once more. "Don't fuck this up for me."

It sounded more desperate than I'd intended, and he picked up on the tone, mouth twitching up in the corner, even as my own lips tipped into a scowl.

"Don't fuck it up for yourself," he said.

I glanced at Dalton. "We'll talk about this later."

All I got from that was an apologetic nod.

I walked away from all of them, feeling less certain of my decision to give Val more than I had since I made it. I didn't want him to come to the wedding, and I didn't think that us being in some kind of formal relationship should change that. More so, I didn't think Val would even want to come to the wedding. It was a man he didn't know, a man I didn't even know anymore. The invitation was a burn that had made me more upset than I was proud of, but I knew that even though the return address had Dennis's information on it, he didn't want me there either.

I'd spent enough time thinking about Dennis to last a lifetime, and as I climbed back into my car, Archie's comment about Val poked at me in a way I couldn't quite make sense of. I still didn't know what they'd talked about, and I had even less of an idea as to why Val called him in the first place. I didn't want Val talking to my friends about things that happened privately between us.

Sex had always been one thing, but this was different and it was more. It was what he'd wanted. And if he was already calling *my* friends up complaining or worrying, then maybe the end was closer than I'd thought.

CHAPTER 16
VAL

Tuesday, I ran into Jason in the elevator again.

When he saw me, his face flushed as dark pink as his tie, and I leaned against the back wall beside him as the doors slid closed.

"I've been meaning to call you," he said.

"You don't have to lie to make me feel better." I searched out his face in the mirrored reflection across from us. "Barclay never has."

"You couldn't be more wrong about that."

"How do you figure?"

The doors opened, shattering his face into pieces. Three women stepped inside, so engrossed in their conversation they didn't even notice our presence. When the doors closed, I caught his stare in the reflection again.

"That man loves you beyond reason," he said quietly. I opened my mouth to protest, but Jason pursed his lips. "And he has for a very long time."

We reached the lobby and both of us followed the women outside and onto the sidewalk. They went left, chattering and gesturing madly. Jason turned toward me, looking down with a small smile on his face.

"Did you have lunch plans?" he asked.

"I was just going to get a sandwich at that place on the corner."

"Do you want company?"

I hadn't planned on eating there. I should have been used to eating meals alone, but I never got over the little bubble of embarrassment that settled around me every time I went to eat out by myself.

"Sure," I said.

It looked like Jason had a lot more to say, and I figured he and I both had a decent amount to talk about too. We'd gone on that date, I'd brought him to another man's house where we'd all fucked, and then he'd left and gone radio silent until ten minutes ago. I wasn't worried that I'd misread the situation with him on Saturday, and I didn't know what I had expected to happen after our hookup, but silence definitely hadn't been on the short list.

After ordering, we settled into a booth tucked into the corner of the cafe, and Jason dove right into the communal pickle jar and dropped a huge sour spear onto his plate. His eagerness was one of the most attractive things about him, and I was pleased that the nervous aloofness from our very first meeting seemed to be a thing of the past.

"Has he told you yet?" Jason asked, after chewing a slice of pickle and swallowing it with a very happy groan.

"Told me what?"

"That he loves you."

"Yes," I said softly.

Jason nodded like he'd expected it.

"You should have given up on him sooner," he said without a hint of malice.

The implication was one I'd thought of at least a thousand times in the days that had passed. But I was a believer in divine timing and I knew in my bones that an earlier decision would not have rendered the same outcome for me.

"Can we talk about us instead of him?"

Jason sliced another piece of the pickle off and popped it into his mouth, giving me a sweet grin after he swallowed. "What about us?"

"Are we friends?"

"Do you fuck all your friends?" he asked.

I snorted. "At one point or another. Generally."

"I wish I could do that," he said, working his jaw left to right. He set his fork and knife down beside his plate and looked up at me. "I'd like to be your friend."

"With fucking," I said.

"Obviously." We both laughed. "But also, I mean that sincerely. More than just sex."

More than sex was the plea I'd spent three years sending to the heavens, and now I wondered if it was something I was allowed. Because Jason looked at me like more than sex was still some kind of emotional commitment, and that felt off-limits.

"I have to talk to Barclay," I admitted. "I don't...we haven't talked about how things are going to go now."

"Are you not sleeping with other people now that you're together?"

"We are," I said.

"But you have to ask him if you can sleep with me?"

The question felt reductive.

"I'm not a threat to whatever the thing between you and him is," Jason said. He ran his hand through his hair, some of the strands falling loose over his left eyebrow when he finished. "I meant what I told you on our date. I don't want to fall in love. I won't. It's just...not programmed that way for me."

"I'm sure Barclay wishes that were the case for me," I muttered.

"That man would be unmoored without your love in his life." He inhaled a tired-sounding breath. "I want to be friends, Valentin. I mean that sincerely."

"Friends who fuck," I corrected.

He grinned. "Friends who fuck."

"I just want to make sure Barclay and I are on the same page," I said. "There's a lot that's changed between us and I think he and I need to talk a lot more about a lot of things before I can say one way or the other."

"That's fair."

Our food arrived, and it felt like a soft blanket settled over the conversation. There was no pressure to be anything more than we were or anything more than we could be. Just two friends having lunch who might get to fuck in the future. Again. It felt familiar and sacred, even though Barclay should have been the one bringing that sense of safety out in me. Not that Barclay had me feeling *unsafe*, but maybe unsteady. It wasn't something I would hold against him. I didn't imagine that I felt very sturdy either considering all the changes that had taken place over the weekend.

Maybe I'd asked for the wrong thing. I'd wondered it more than once since Sunday morning. Because before, Barclay had been predictable in his stoicism, reliable in the way I understood with a surgical precision how things were between us. I knew what I could expect from him and he knew what he could expect from me. And now…that all felt very uncertain.

Not bad.

But new was always scary, and new always meant there were different opportunities for failure. I did my best to stop my mind from wandering down that particular dark train of thought, instead trying to remember the feel of Barclay's shirt against my skin and the way he kissed me with so much nervousness and love.

The way he'd looked at me when he told me he loved me.

With that in the front of my mind, so many of my fears immediately lifted. He was still the same man he'd been before. If anything, he was *more* mine, and that should have offered me more certainty than before. He was invested in me as much as I was in him and that wasn't something that either of us could just walk away from.

I let those happier thoughts take me back to a brighter path, smiling at Jason as we ate. We were halfway through our sandwiches when he set his down and looked up at me, brow furrowed in confusion.

"What?" I asked around a mouthful of pastrami.

"Have you really slept with all your friends?"

I laughed, dropping my sandwich onto the plate and covering my face with my hands.

"Not all of them," I said from behind my palms. It wasn't a shameful thing, but calling it out was a level of exhibitionism I hadn't planned for over my lunch break.

He reached across the table and hooked his finger around one of mine, pulling my hand away from my face. "Don't act like it's something to be ashamed of."

"Most people are not like me," I shared the mantra I'd spent a lifetime telling myself. Sometimes I said it positively, sometimes not.

"I don't really know you at all." He ate the last bit of pickle on his plate. "But I feel like there's a lot of love inside of you."

I rubbed the tip of my tongue against the pointed tip of my canine tooth, the dull ache almost soothing against the truth of this man who was all but a stranger to me. A stranger I'd slept with. One of many, and he should have been a no one to me, but I felt seen by him in a way Barclay never had. In a way no one ever had.

Jason cocked his head to the side, seeing the thoughts across my face, I figured, and giving me a chance to respond. But I stayed quiet.

"Sex is just a way to share that," he said quietly, making sure no one at the neighboring tables heard.

"Is that it?" I countered.

He shrugged. "That's how it feels to me when you fuck."

It could have been a step away from the truth, but maybe not the whole of it. For me, sex had started as a self-esteem boost, but it had quickly grown into something that was much closer to necessity than reward. There were some nights when my body craved it, the need between my legs almost painful. And it wasn't a psychological thing. Not physical or neurological. I'd spent years in college in therapy and I'd had my testosterone checked and all of that. I just had a *healthy sexual appetite,* one of my doctors had said. After that, I'd stopped questioning the why of it.

"I haven't thought too hard about it," I told Jason.

"Just how it felt to me."

"I thought you weren't interested in that particular four letter word," I said.

"Just because I don't feel it doesn't mean I don't know it when I see it." He picked his sandwich back up and took a bite, saying to me through a mouthful, "I told Barclay as much on Saturday when I was leaving."

I huffed, closing my eyes. "I don't remember you going."

"You were well fucked," he said. "You're welcome by the way. But you were truly out of sorts. It was beautiful."

"You're going to make me blush." I shoveled a handful of fries into my mouth so I didn't have to say anything else in response to his praise.

"Just talk to your boyfriend and let me know if we can do it again sometime," he said.

"You and me or all of us?"

Jason smiled at me across the table, his eyes dark with want.

"Yes."

———

After lunch, I was half an hour into a ninety minute call about budget projections when my phone vibrated across my desk. The screen flashed Barclay's name pm the screen with the preview of a text message I didn't have time to read before a second one came in and then the screen went black.

I hadn't talked to him since breakfast, which wasn't unusual for how things had been between us before, even if it felt wrong for the new state of our relationship. But the change was a bigger thing for him than me, and the last thing I wanted to do was press him to see me more or talk to me more than normal. I didn't want to scare him off because he had a fatalistic enough impression of what dating was going to be like. The last thing I wanted to do was prove any of his fears or worries to be true.

Barclay: Come over tonight.
Barclay: Is everything okay? I haven't heard from you since Sunday.

I typed out a reply.

Me: I didn't want to run you off. I'm fine.
Barclay: Come over tonight.
Me: I heard you the first time.
Barclay: And?

There was no point in pretending the answer would be anything besides yes.

Me: What time?
Barclay: Six
Me: That's early for you.

Three dots appeared and vanished, appeared and vanished before his reply came through.

Barclay: Not early for dinner.

I bit my lips between my teeth, tracing my fingers over the words on the screen.

Me: Are you asking me on a date?
Barclay: I'm not really asking.
Barclay: I want to take you to dinner tonight, then I want to take you home.
Me: I'll see you at six.

CHAPTER 17
BARCLAY

Val knocked on the door at 5:58. I'd been ready since I called him, but beyond that, I was nervous too. Ever since the Sunday night ambush, my chest felt like the ocean in the middle of a tsunami. On Saturday, Val and I had talked about it and I told him I wasn't going to hide it from my friends, but finding out he'd told one of my best friends before I did had me feeling a little more slighted than I would have wanted to admit. I wasn't trying to keep the change in our relationship a secret, but I would have preferred to tell my friends on my own terms.

On top of all that, I hadn't been able to stop thinking about Val's date, Jason. He wasn't the first person we'd taken to bed together—and I hoped he wouldn't be the last—but there was some kind of imbalance there that had me feeling uncomfortable. I didn't know how to articulate it, so I hadn't bothered to try. I also wasn't sure if it was a conversation for Val and me to have, or for Jason and me. Time would tell, I imagined.

Val looked…

Handsome.

He always looked beautiful, but something about him showing up on my porch in plaid pants with white sneakers and a rolled-up button-up had that storm in my chest settling. Even if just for a moment of reprieve.

"You look great," I said.

He glanced down at his shirt, fiddling with the cuffed fabric below his elbow. "I came from work. Didn't have time to change."

"You…" I trailed off, clearing my throat. "Are you ready to go?"

He angled his head to the side, studying me. "After you finish the original sentence."

I stepped toward him, walking him back onto the doormat. I pulled the door closed behind me, listening as the lock audibly and automatically engaged. The move brought us toe to toe, and I snaked my hand into the back of his hair and yanked our mouths together. His head was already at the right angle for our lips to align, and he slid his arms around my neck, moaning softly into my mouth. He kicked at my toes with his feet and pressed my back against the door, shoving his leg between mine and lifting his knee up against my balls.

"Finish the sentence," he murmured again, the pressure there between my legs.

"You make it impossible to not want to fuck you every time I see you," I said.

He smiled and kissed the corner of my mouth.

"You do fuck me every time you see me," he said. "But that's not what you were about to say. I could see it in your face."

"What did you see?"

I reached between us and pushed his leg away. He leaned back and huffed an amused laugh at me, but his pupils were dilated and his cheeks were already pink from exertion.

"You were thinking."

"Aren't I always?"

"It was different." He took a step back, and my hand fell away from his hair. "Please don't make me fight you for it. I just…"

The air went out of him so fast I wondered if the waves in my chest had crashed right over him when they'd left me. His eyes were back to normal, his face almost white as the walls behind him.

"I was going to say you should keep clothes here," I said quickly, taking a step toward him and grabbing his hand. He kept moving backward and I kept going forward until it was him with his back against the wall instead of me. "I was going to say I *want* you to have clothes here."

"Why?" he rasped.

"So you're comfortable."

Val let out a low and miserable-sounding laugh that twisted my heart into a knot.

"I know I'm not good at this," I said, hoping he took it for the apology it was.

"What's this?"

"Dating." Our hands were still tangled and I brought them to my mouth, kissing the swoop between this thumb and first finger. "Knowing what to say. What to do."

"I know for a fact you have at least one ex-boyfriend," he said, expression guarded. "I don't believe that you don't know what to do."

"That's not what I said. I told you I'm not good at it."

"Out of practice then," he murmured.

I pressed the front of our bodies together and another quiet moan fell out of his mouth. It was a far nicer sound than the horrible half-laugh he'd just breathed out.

"I'm just asking you be patient with me for a little while longer," I whispered.

"I've already given you three years."

"I won't need three more. I swear it." I kissed his hand again. I kissed his chin. His mouth. The tip of his nose. "I'm not asking for anything revolutionary here."

Val thumped his head against the wall and stared at me down the long line of his nose. He wasn't taller than me, but the angle gave him an advantage, and I kissed his cupid's bow.

"You've asked me for everything."

He blinked slowly. "Did you want to go eat or just go inside and call it a night?"

"I want to take you to dinner," I said.

"Do you?"

"Maybe. After I take you inside and fuck this attitude out of you."

Val let loose a low laugh, shaking his head and bringing himself back down to our normal level.

"Am I being difficult?" he asked.

"A little bit, yeah."

"I'm honestly not that hungry," he admitted.

I curled my fingers around his wrist and pulled him back to the other side of the hallway. Turning around to shove my key into the lock, I didn't let go of him until we were both inside and the door was once again closed behind us. Val toed off his sneakers and eyed me with a tight frown while I undid the laces on my shoes and kicked them into place beside his.

"What do you want to do?" I asked.

"I want to have a glass of wine and sit down," he said.

"Do you want to put on something more comfortable?"

He looked down at his shirt, his belt, the slacks that stretched across his thighs. "I don't think your pants will fit me."

"They probably won't." I jerked my head toward the bedroom and he shuffled toward me. "All the more reason for you to bring something over."

Val made an agreeable sound and followed me into the bedroom. He sat on the edge of the bed, fiddling with his belt while I got him a pair of black sweats and another one of my white t-shirts.

"Off with it then," I said, gesturing at his state of dress.

He stood and undid his belt, his pants. He opened his shirt one button at a time, then unrolled the sleeves and shrugged out of it altogether. Val draped his shirt across the foot of the bed and I snatched it up, sliding it onto a hanger and hooking it in the closet next to mine. His stare flickered in that direction, and he stepped out of his pants. I clipped them onto a hanger and situated it next to his shirt. He watched every move I made like I was some sort of predator and he was prey that I just hadn't caught sight of yet.

When I turned back to him, he was dressed again in my clothes which fit him better than I'd expected. They were still a little bit baggy, but they looked comfortable and the pants stayed up without having the drawstring readjusted.

"Or you can just wear my clothes," I murmured, beckoning him closer.

Val stepped toward me and tipped his head back, leaning in and pressing a kiss against the base of my throat. Without thought, my arms went around his waist and he kissed his way over the curve of my shoulder.

"You should change too." He plucked at the buttons on my shirt until I was half undressed. He went to my belt and my pants next, going onto his knees as my pants went to my ankles.

"Val."

He nuzzled his cheek against the front of my underwear, breathing in the scent of me with a low and guttural groan.

This, I thought to myself, *this is what we're good at.*

"Let me suck your cock." His mouth was right there, words and breath burning hot against my quickly thickening erection.

"I thought you wanted to have a glass of wine and sit down."

"I do," he said. "But I want this first."

He blinked up at me and I nodded, then my underwear was around my knees and my cock was in the back of his throat. Val sucked and licked my length like it was his favorite flavor of popsicle, moaning and jerking his hips every time I bottomed out in the back of his mouth.

I cursed under my breath, bracing myself against the top of his head. He hollowed his cheeks and sucked any protest right out of me, along with all the cum in my balls. The orgasm was quick and hard, and I still shook from it when Val stood back to his full height and kissed me on the mouth.

"I feel better already," he said softly. "Now I can sit down and have some wine."

"You're going to kill me one day." My knees trembled, but I managed to get myself dressed in an outfit that almost mirrored the one I'd given him.

"I hope not. I'm rather fond of you."

"Fond?"

"That's a word for it." He left me in the bedroom long enough for the post-orgasm haze to filter out of my head.

I went after him and found him in the kitchen, two glasses and a bottle of wine in front of him, that stupid fucking wedding invitation in his hand.

"Ignore that." I leaned over the counter and taking the bottle of wine out of his hand. My reflex had been to go for the invitation, but I didn't want him to think I was hiding something from him. He knew about the wedding. There wasn't much else to discuss about the rest of it.

"You ignore it," he said. Val pulled the invitation out of the envelope and read the names and date and time with a frown.

"I'd love to."

I poured us both glasses of wine, then went to the couch. He slid the invitation back into the envelope and left it next to the bottle.

"You didn't tell me it was so soon," he said, sitting down beside me on the couch. In the months since the invitation had arrived, he'd never looked inside. He'd never asked. Val had diligently remained by my side, taking what I gave him and never asking for anything more. At least, not about that.

I passed him one of the glasses and he nestled in against me with a quiet sound of contentment. He was like a fucking cat, and I petted my hand over the top of his hair like he was one.

"The time's gone by quickly."

"It's next month."

"I can't wait for it to be over," I said, taking a swallow of Pinot Noir.

"And you're sure you have to go?" he asked.

"Long enough to be seen."

"Do you—"

"No." I patted the top of his head, ending my stroking of his hair and I kissed his temple, the taste of his sweat and the wine a heady combination on my tongue. "I do not want you to come."

He sucked in a breath like he wanted to argue about it, and I braced myself for the conversation, but instead he took the smallest sip of his wine. Val reached over me and picked the remote up from the side table and turned on the TV. The screen flashed to life on the History Channel, which was the last thing I'd been watching before going to bed the night before.

"You never struck me as the type," he said quietly.

"To what?"

He gestured toward the TV with the remote. "Aliens."

"I love the aliens."

He chuckled and burrowed in closer beneath my arm, his knees folded up and tucked on top of my lap.

"What else do you watch?"

"I like the old war documentaries. Oh, and I really love nature shows."

"What kind of nature shows?" He took a bigger drink of his wine.

"Like the universe and the ocean ones. The kind of shit Morgan Freeman narrates," I said.

"Hmn."

"What?"

"That's just surprising." I could hear the smile in his face.

"What did you think I watched when you weren't here?" I clinked the rim of my glass against his and we both took a sip.

"Honestly? Like something insanely boring like the stock ticker."

"I think I should be wounded by that."

I reached over and poked him in the ribs. He laughed and jerked away, stretching his arm out straight so wine didn't slosh onto the couch. Val landed on his back and I crawled on top of him, my wine still in hand. Our noses hovered inches apart and he smiled up at me with flushed cheeks.

He was gorgeous like this too.

In and out of his clothes, it was when he was happy that I wanted him the most. His excitement was breathtaking and contagious, and I wondered how I'd ever been able to say no to him for as long as I had. I hoped he didn't ask me about the wedding again because I knew beyond a shadow of a doubt I would tell him yes.

Yes, come to the wedding with me.

Yes, you can have a key.

Yes, you can take over my closet.

Yes, you can take over *my life*.

"This is all I wanted, Percy," he said softly, blinking up at me through the thick fan of his eyelashes.

"What do you mean?"

"I don't care about dating."

"I remember a very different conversation," I said, wondering what he was on about because, if anything, Val had been extremely adamant about dating. It had very much been an all or nothing kind of conversation for us when it had happened.

He wiggled underneath me until I eased my weight off of him. I leaned back and he pushed up alongside me, bringing our faces back within a breath of each other, just back in a seat.

"I mean I didn't care about dinner and going out. All of that was secondary," he said.

"What did you want, Val?"

"This," he said again, dropping his forehead against mine. "I just wanted you to let me in."

BARCLAY DIDN'T SAY MUCH FOR THE REST OF THE NIGHT, BUT WHEN the second episode of the alien show was over, he turned off the TV and stared at the blank screen. I was still tucked against his side, warm and content with his arm around my shoulders and my head on his chest.

"I do love you," he said, seemingly out of nowhere.

I righted myself, knees now nudging into the outside of his thigh. "I believe you," I promised.

"I really meant to take you to dinner tonight."

"It's barely eight," I said. "You still can if it means so much to you."

"What does it mean to you?" He kept his stare trained on the dark screen ahead of us.

"I told you." I pressed my palm against his cheek and turned his face toward mine. "I just want you to let me in, whether that's here or over a meal."

"Doing it here doesn't feel like dating," he muttered.

He was going to give me whiplash. "If you want to take me out, we can go out."

Barclay angled his mouth to the side and kissed the edge of my hand.

"I want to make you happy," he said softly. "What if…"

He cleared his throat, and I stroked my thumb over the sharp angle of his cheekbone. The stubble on his chin poked against my palm, but I didn't mind. His face flashed a myriad of emotions, some of them more decipherable than others, but the one it settled on made his fears clearer to me than they ever had been before.

He doubted himself.

"What if you let me in and I don't want to be there anymore?" I asked.

He rolled his head, pulling his face away from my hand. I let it fall into my lap when he stood up, all coiled nervous energy ready to pounce or explode. I didn't know which way it was going to go and I didn't think he did either. "It's a fair question."

"It's a risk. I may not know you as well as I want, but I think I know you enough to say that I don't plan on wanting to be anywhere besides with you."

He swallowed.

"Let's go get something to eat," I said, standing up and taking him by the hand.

This was a new version of the man I'd long been in love with. Barclay was always a walled-off kind of man, but the changes over the past week had done more than take a brick or two out. The shift in our relationship had taken a wrecking ball to his defenses and no matter how hard he tried, all the parts he'd worked so long and hard to keep hidden were coming to the surface. It was his biggest fears manifesting all at once, but seeing the soft and scared parts of him didn't make me want to leave.

It made me love him more.

In the bedroom, I changed out of his pajamas and back into my work clothes. Barclay donned a pair of jeans and a tight black t-shirt. Our discarded clothes lay flung across the bed, and the casualness of it sent a sharp twinge through the middle of my chest. Rubbing at my sternum, I waited for Barclay to finish tying his sneakers.

"Did you have someplace in mind?" I asked.

"Honestly?" He shook his head.

"Let's just drive then."

He held my hand the whole ride down to the parking garage, only letting go when he closed the passenger door of his car behind me. As soon as he was in the driver's seat, he reached over the console and settled his hand on my thigh. I rested my head against the headrest and cracked the window as he headed out onto the road.

We drove through the maze of the city for twenty minutes before Barclay pulled into a small parking lot and cut the ignition.

"Where are we?" I asked.

"No idea. But I'm too hungry to keep driving and this looks like a restaurant."

I laughed and unclasped my seatbelt.

We were definitely at a restaurant. The building looked like it had seen better days, and the interior decor hinted that it might be one of those greasy mom and pop kind of diners that had survived the influx of chains that popped up throughout the edges of the city.

"Does this look good?" he asked, taking a step around the car toward the fluorescent lit front door.

"Not sure," I admitted. "But I think we'll survive it."

A frazzled-looking woman with graying hair shouted out for us to take any seat we wanted, which wasn't going to prove difficult as they were all open. I wasn't sure why she looked spread so thin, but as soon as we settled into a booth against the window that faced the street, she was there with water and two sticky plastic menus.

"Can I get you anything to drink besides water?" she asked.

"Sprite," Barclay said. "Thank you."

I arched a brow at his answer. "I'm good with water," I said.

After she walked back to the kitchen, he leveled an amused look at me.

"What's that for?" he asked, pressing his finger against my eyebrow to pull it back down toward my eye.

"I just didn't peg you as a Sprite guy."

"I can't live on whiskey alone."

"No," I murmured, tearing off the straw wrapper. "I don't imagine you could."

Barclay flipped open his menu, eyes scanning down both pages before flickering back up to me.

"It's…" He sighed and leaned back. "It's easy when you're here."

"What is?"

"This."

"Eating?" I asked, opening my menu and giving it a quick scan before turning my attention back to him.

"I doubt it less when you're here."

Something like agreement pulled at the corner of my mouth. "I know what that feels like."

"Why do you think that is?"

"I don't know." I shrugged. "I've never really done this before either."

"Dated?"

"Dated someone like you," I said.

It made me somehow feel less alone that he also struggled with the change when I wasn't around, and it brought me an over-whelming sense of comfort that my presence softened the edges for him.

"Can I ask you something?"

"Anything," I rasped.

"I told you I was going to tell my friends about us." He picked at the corner of the menu with this thumbnail. "Why did you tell Archie before I could?"

"Are you mad about it?"

"No. I just…I wanted you to know that I would've made good on my word. You didn't give me a chance."

"I didn't mean to tell him." I stretched my arm toward the center of the table and Barclay slid his hand into mine. "I was having some issues with my sisters on Sunday and I'd already talked to him about things with Jason, and I just…wanted his advice."

Barclay's jaw tensed and his shoulders squared back. "Was it helpful?"

"Enough." I squeezed his hand. "What about that didn't you like?"

"It doesn't matter." He looked up at me just as the waitress came back to take our orders. I'd had pastrami for lunch, so I ordered a chicken sandwich and Barclay ordered a patty melt with onion rings. After she left, he tilted his head to the side in question. "Was that as shocking as the Sprite?"

"Not as much," I said. I didn't know how to explain it, but the fact that he was a patty melt and onion ring man made absolute perfect sense to me.

"What did you need advice about?" he asked under his breath.

The tender tone of his question instantly brought my own hypocrisy into focus. There I was, asking to be let in and I wasn't offering the same access in return. In another world, another time, that kind of question that I'd posed to Archie would have gone to Barclay. It should have gone to him, but asking anyone besides him was almost muscle memory after so long. It was going to be a learning curve for us both, and I clearly still had work to do too.

"I don't even know where to start." I untangled our fingers and leaned against the back of the cracked vinyl booth. "My sister figured out I was dating someone and she just… My family can be a lot."

"I can imagine."

"I didn't mean to tell Archie, but the conversation just went that way," I said. "I'm sorry."

Barclay shook his head, swirling his straw around his drink. "I'm not mad. You don't have to apologize for talking to a friend."

"Archie isn't my friend."

"No?" He sucked up some of the Sprite, scrunching his nose.

"He said no."

"At least I'm not the only liar in that group chat," he said with a soft laugh. "They ambushed me on Sunday night. I fell right into it."

I covered my face with my hands, silently vowing never to confess anything to Archie ever again. "I'm so sorry."

"It's fine." He kicked at my ankles until I let my hands fall.

"That wasn't what I meant to happen."

"It's fine," he said again. "I promise. I just...it *was* a lot and when you're not here, I go back into my head. I told them I didn't love you."

The confession hurt a lot more than I would have expected, and I rubbed my chest, but my fingers didn't come anywhere close to easing the pain of his words. Barclay had spent three years denying me; I didn't know why one more denial should come as a shock. Being in a relationship after so long *not* wasn't a light switch. The change was rocky and gradual, and I would have to get used to that...from both sides.

"Why?" I croaked.

"I don't know. I was feeling defensive. I...I took it back almost immediately."

That softened the blow slightly, but I made an effort to not hold it against him. Of all the pieces of his defense that had cracked and shattered in the past five days, there were still some in place, and I was sure his refusal was part of that.

"I just didn't want one of them to tell you that I didn't love you," he went on. "Because I do."

"I know you do," I agreed.

Our food arrived, and the smile that flashed across Barclay's face when he caught a whiff of his sandwich was enough to erase anything he'd ever done to wrong me. It was a glimpse of a man who was a stranger to me, even if I knew the truth of him in my bones. That was Barclay without the warnings and the caged protection. It was the man I knew to be inside, the man I wanted to know.

Suddenly, I knew that everything was going to be okay between us. It would take time and patience, and it was probably going to hurt, a lot...but it would be worth it for more of that smile. More of that man.

"I had lunch with Jason today," I said.

Barclay picked up an onion ring and bit into it. "How was that?"

"Good. I like him," I said. "As a friend."

I twisted open the lid on the ketchup and dropped a huge glob of it onto the corner of my plate, then I offered the bottle to Barclay, who declined.

"Are you serious?" I slid the bottle back toward the window. "You go in dry?"

He winked and bit another piece off his onion ring. "Back to Jason."

"Friends," I said again.

"Does he want to fuck you again?"

"He wants to fuck *us* again," I corrected.

Barclay licked his lips, a red flush coloring up the column of his throat. He chewed and swallowed, then switched to his patty melt. After the first bite, he let out an appreciative groan that sounded a lot like a sex noise, and I shifted in my seat while he enjoyed the food.

"I told him I needed to talk to you about it," I said.

"You never talked to me about it before."

"Things are different now," I reminded him.

My chicken sandwich was moist and juicy on the inside, crunchy on the outside. A silence fell between us while we both dug into our meals. I hadn't realized how hungry I was, nor had I noticed how heavy the two glasses of wine had been sitting in my stomach until I dumped mouthfuls of greasy diner food on top of it.

"Do you want things to be the way they were before?" Barclay finally asked after he finished the first half of his burger and two more onion rings. "Just...more?"

"I honestly don't know," I said. "Maybe?"

"We can try it and see...if you wanted."

"Would you not get jealous?" My upper lip twitched with the ask, unsure of whether I wanted him to get jealous about me sleeping with other people or not.

"I didn't before."

"But, like you said, things are different now."

He plucked the plastic-topped toothpick out of the other half of his sandwich, looking up at me with an unimpressed look on his face.

"You've loved me all along, Val. My friends say I've loved you the whole time too." He took another bite, chewed and swallowed. "What's really changing between us beyond a little more conversation and the sleeping situation?"

Well.

When he put it like that.

I'D NEVER BEEN NERVOUS TO GO TO RAPTURE, BUT I'D NEVER GONE TO Rapture with a partner before. Next to me, Val vibrated with excitement and I did my best to lean into that feeling instead of the nerves that threatened to take me out at the knees.

"You look miserable." He pulled me upstairs to the loft.

"That's not quite the word."

Val had met me at home a couple hours earlier. He'd brought a garment bag with two work outfits and some pajamas, clean underwear, and fresh toiletries. I sat on the edge of my bed while he busied himself hanging things up and putting them into drawers. I'd made room for him, which I think he noticed, because when he opened the bottom drawer of my dresser and found space there, he paused. He didn't say anything, though, and neither did I.

After he unpacked, I pushed him against the wall and shoved my hand down his pants. He came all over my fingers with my name on his tongue, and I felt tall enough to conquer the world.

The world was one thing, though. My friends were another.

"Let me get you a drink," he suggested, pressing a kiss against the top of my hand and shaking free of my vise-grip hold. I tried to protest, but he was back down the stairs before I could stop him.

Reluctantly, I took a seat, catching my breath and steadying my heart just in time for Flynn and his gorgeous little femme boyfriend, Rose, to appear at the top of the stairs. Archie and Rob were next, with Grayson and Owen following and engrossed in conversation. As the six of them settled in around me, Archie was the first to speak, clapping his hands together like a pleased school teacher.

"Where's your boyfriend?" he asked.

"Getting me a drink."

"Cute," Grayson teased.

"I liked you better when you were pouting and fawning over Rob," I said.

"So did he." Grayson kicked Rob in the ankle, and Rob just rolled his eyes.

"Where are Dalton and Royce?" I asked.

"Trailing behind," Flynn said, hauling Rose onto his lap. "They'll be here."

When Val made it back upstairs with our drinks, he was met with a raucous round of cheering and applause that had his face turning crimson, even in the dark of the loft. A soft rainbow glow danced across the back wall, reflected from the massive stained glass panels and the disco balls and dance lights, and I couldn't help but think he looked a little bit like an angel.

"You guys are too much." He moved through the crowd of my friends—our friends?—and taking a seat beside me on one of the many leather couches that decorated the space. He passed me a tumbler of whiskey and clinked the edge of his glass against mine.

"What's on the agenda tonight?" Flynn dropped a kiss on Rose's bare shoulder, his stare trained on me and full of trouble.

"Drake just got here." Rose had his phone in his hand and he leaned against Flynn with a wiggle.

"Who's Drake?" I asked, fairly certain I was able to keep track of the men my best friends had partnered up with, but not recognizing the name.

"My best friend," Rose said, throwing a look over his shoulder just as Dalton and Royce reached the top of the stairs. Rose cursed under his breath.

"It's fine," Flynn said. "We're all adults and most of us have slept together."

"Am I missing something?" Val asked.

"My best friend and Dalton used to…you know."

There was only one seat left in the clustered corner where we'd all sat down, and Dalton settled into it without even an offer to his husband, but when I watched the fluid and natural way the massive blond man went to his knees, I understood why.

"It doesn't matter." Dalton waved Rose's worries away. "It was before I was married."

"Was it really?" Flynn asked with a laugh. "I don't even think Drake was alive when we were in college."

Dalton flipped him off, then said something to Royce, who blushed and nodded.

I leaned my mouth closer to Val's ear so I could talk to him without everyone else getting involved in the conversation. Archie watched me, and I made a show of raising my hand to block my lips from his view.

"Do you feel like being shared tonight?" I asked.

Val swallowed, mouth parting, but no words coming out. It wasn't his normal reaction to the ask. He always wanted to be shared, and I only asked because things were different than before. The whole night was meant to be a test run and I didn't want to do anything he wasn't one hundred percent consenting to and excited for.

"I don't want them to think less of me for it."

"You know they won't."

He turned toward me, my hand still raised to hide our mouths. I gave him a gentle kiss, stretching my fingers to graze his cheek.

"Don't worry about them," I said, tapping him until he looked right at me. "Worry about me."

"I always worry about you," he murmured, lashes fluttering.

"You know what I meant."

He nodded, a low hum vibrating against my hand. "Yes."

"I promise I'll make sure it's good for you."

"I know."

I let my hand fall away because it was so easy to get lost in him, not that I allowed myself to. And we couldn't have been any further from alone.

Turning my attention back to my friends, I met Flynn's stare, finding that same level of mischief in his eyes.

"This is Rose's best friend, Drake," he said, jerking his thumb toward a pink-haired twink who had flopped down on the floor next to Flynn's chair.

"Yes," Val said under his breath.

"Nice to meet you," I said to Drake. "This is my boyfriend, Val."

"His boyfriend!" Grayson clutched his hands together and batted his lashes, pretending to swoon.

"Ignore him."

"I don't think I could if I tried," Drake said with a small smile. "It's nice to meet you."

"Same."

Drake took a look around the group, his stare landing on the empty St. Andrew's cross in the corner, which sent his entire face into a flush that looked like it would be hot to the touch.

"Are you all right?" Rose asked, swirling his hand in a small circle over the top of Drake's back.

"I'm fine."

"You want to play?" I asked.

Drake and Rose both snapped their attention toward me and, even closer, Val's body burned hot against mine.

"I'm not sure I'm one for dropping my pants in public."

"Just bathrooms and alleys?" Rose laughed, and Drake punched him in the arm.

"They're all really fucking intimidating." Drake gestured at all of us, and I knew better than to argue the point.

"You get used to it," Val chimed in, "when you realize they're all idiots."

"I am not," I protested.

"Says the man who almost lost that one." Rob pointed at Val, and I groaned at the truth of the statement.

"Back to the case of your pants, though."

"I don't think I'm up for a show tonight," Drake said, licking his lips.

"Party of three maybe?"

Drake looked at Val like he was a four-course meal, then looked at me like I was the man about to serve him his dinner.

"Three I can manage."

Drake unfolded himself from the floor, and I had Val up off the couch before either of them could change their minds. Another roar of hoots and hollers echoed around the loft, and Val pushed Drake and me into the first open playroom we stumbled by on our way to the stairs.

"You don't have to if you don't want to."

It was the first thing out of Val's mouth, but Drake already had his shirt halfway over his head.

"I want to," he said, throwing it onto the floor and fumbling with his pants like an overeager teenager, which he looked like he could have been.

"You're legal, right?" I asked, sitting down on the couch against the far wall of the private room.

"Very."

"And safe?"

"Also consensual." Drake pulled a condom out of his wallet and then dropped his pants.

"And eager," Val mused, beckoning the slender man closer.

Drake moved toward Val like he was magnetized, and then his arms were around Val's shoulders, his mouth on a direct path for Val's.

"Slow down, sweetheart." Val got his hand between them right before their lips touched. Drake kissed the tips of Val's fingers, eyes already heavy with arousal. "You're so much like me."

"He is," I agreed. "Always ready and willing."

"That's what makes life fun."

"No kissing on the lips." Val let his hand fall away and Drake pressed his mouth against the base of Val's throat.

"Is here okay?"

"Better than."

Drake walked them backward until Val's shoulders hit the door. There was something oddly arousing about watching Val get pushed around by a wisp of a man who didn't even look old enough to drink.

"If you want to play, Drake, you're going to need to take instruction," I warned.

Val peered at me from across the room, Drake's mouth tracing its way along Val's shoulder, his hands roaming over his sides.

"I listen well," Drake murmured. "But I don't wait for instruction."

"Bring it over here," I said, and Drake had Val in front of me before I could even bother with my belt. "You were looking at the cross out there. Do you want more than sex?"

"Can you give me more than that?"

Val chuckled. "He can give you anything you want."

How true it was, but how long I'd fought giving him the one thing he wanted above all else. Looking at him here and now, with another man ready to fuck him and suck him, and watching the way Val's body responded, I couldn't imagine any other way. There wasn't anything I loved more than seeing Val get off, whether I was the one who got him there or not.

I pushed up from my seat and finally got my belt out of the loops.

"Val, take out your cock and sit down," I said.

Drake whimpered when Val moved away, but once he was sitting down, I pushed Drake down to his knees. He settled his hands on Val's thighs, and Val fisted his shaft, teasing the tip of it against Drake's lips.

"Put his cock in your mouth," I instructed.

Drake approached orgasms with the same level of eagerness he had undressing, and Val had his hands in Drake's hair to steady himself in less than three pulls of the other man's mouth.

Val groaned, hips rising off the couch. "Oh, shit. Slow down, sweetheart," he said again. "We have all night. We have all night, okay?"

"I just love to fuck," Drake whimpered, letting Val's cock slide out of his mouth. He started leaving kisses up and down Val's swollen length, down around his balls and his thighs, and Val finally settled in with a shaking breath.

"I'm going to spank you with my belt, Drake," I warned.

He nodded vigorously, spitting on the leaking tip of Val's dick before taking it back into his mouth.

"Then I'm going to fuck you."

He still had the condom in his hand and he tossed it backward at me without another word. I looked up at Val, the air catching in my throat at the sight of him. He looked so happy, flushed and tended to. He looked so in love.

With me.

I forced myself to look away, only long enough to get the lube out of the cabinet against the other wall, and then I was back behind Drake with two slippery fingers in the crack of his ass until he got too excited around Val's shaft again.

I tested the snap of my belt, then laid the first strike down against his slender and pale ass. He cried out, dropping his forehead against Val's thigh. I struck him twice more and he fucked the air like it was going to get him off.

"If you stop making my boyfriend feel good, I stop making you feel good," I said.

And then Val was back in his mouth and the leather was back against his skin.

Val held out longer than I expected, and I waited until he was on the verge of his own release to roll the condom down my own length. I pushed my way into Drake's body, going slow enough that he wouldn't take his mouth off of Val again. Val steadied Drake with gentle fingers against the top of his back and I seated myself fully.

"Put his whole dick into your mouth, Drake," I grunted.

"Need help," he muttered the words with his lips around Val's flared tip.

"I'll help you," Val promised, slowly moving Drake's head down until he gagged. There were still a few inches of cock to be covered, and Val lifted off the couch, seeing how much more would fit.

Drake sputtered and spit all over Val, and I pulled out and fucked back into him with a rough and shallow thrust. Drake cried out, taking the rest of Val's dick into what I imagined to be the back of his throat.

All of Drake's muscles spasmed, gripping my cock like he wanted to cut it off and save it for later.

"I'm close," Val whined, and I started to fuck Drake in earnest then, using the force of my hips to make sure his whole mouth was around Val's cock when he came.

It didn't take long for Val to get there. With his eyes focused on me, I noticed when he lost his breath on the cusp of his release. I slid my hand up Drake's back, chasing after Val's hand. When our fingers connected, Val gasped, his mouth parting in a silent O as he spurted into Drake's mouth.

Drake cried out, even if the sound was messy and wet, the channel of his ass strangling me off at the base again. It was only three more thrusts before I buried myself fully and spilled into the condom. Val groaned, sliding off the couch and onto the floor. Drake was nearly crumpled in on himself, and it took one taste of Val's mouth around his cock before he was the last to come. It was loud and frenetic, and Val swallowed him down with as much fervor as the situation deserved.

After the three of us came down from the intensity of our joint orgasms, I made sure the two of them were cleaned up and that they had water. Val and Drake sat as they'd started, Drake fully naked and Val still mostly dressed. I was still dressed, save for my belt, but it didn't feel imbalanced.

I knew it would be possible to have sex with one person for the rest of my life and not get bored of it. There were so many positions, so many toys, so many role playing games, but all of it felt boring in comparison to the life I had with Val. There was something so exhilarating about finding new partners and learning their bodies, how to make each other come. Even if we didn't have repeats all the time, half the fun was the adventure.

I realized, watching him laugh with Drake, who still looked like he was halfway to another planet, that part of the reason I loved Val so much was because of that unique facet of our relationship. He trusted in us enough to share me, even if I'd been blind to that for far too long. And I loved to share him because I wanted people to know how lucky I was.

I wanted them to be jealous that it was my mouth he kissed, my cum that was allowed to go into his body. And if that hadn't been love all along, I didn't know what else it could have been.

DRAKE REMINDED ME OF THE TWENTY YEAR-OLD VERSION OF MYSELF, bursting at the seams with energy and interest, eager to explore everything the adult world had to offer. The force of my orgasm had knocked the wind out of my sails, and Barclay and I were content to send him off with a thank you and a good night.

But not before we got his phone number in case he was interested in a more drawn-out repeat.

Barclay saw him to the door, then came back to me where I'd planted myself against the corner of the couch, one leg bent up at the knee, the other splayed out with my heel on the ground.

"What's the verdict?" he asked.

I huffed a laugh, crooking my finger and beckoning him closer. He came to me easily, like we'd been doing it forever. One knee on the couch, then another, and he was spread out on top of me, nose drawing aimless spirals on my cheek.

"I think I liked it better," I admitted.

Sharing Barclay with others and being shared myself had always been exhilarating, but with the newfound commitment between us, there was a novel sense of…something between us that made everything feel more heightened, more alive.

"What about you?" I asked, angling my face to the side in search of a kiss.

He pressed his lips against the corner of my mouth, lingering long after the kiss should have ended. Shifting his hips, the hot length of his still hard cock dug into my thigh.

"I liked it," he murmured. "Do you think you have another one in you?"

"Another threesome?"

Barclay shook his head and chuckled. "Just me. For now."

"I always have one for you."

I hooked my hand around the back of his neck, crashing our mouths back together in a kiss that was far more urgent and eager than the peck he'd started with. Barclay moaned into my mouth, leaning back and breaking the kiss only long enough for us to both scramble out of our pants. The lube was still close and he slicked his length in what felt like record time. Then he was back, mouth against mine, one hand braced beside my face and the other around his cock. He teased the tip in and out of me, stretching me out until I was gasping and lifting off the couch in search of more than that throbbing first inch of cock.

"What do you need?" he whispered, lips curling into a smile against mine.

"Only you."

He finally slid home.

"Always you."

Barclay grunted, seating himself fully inside of me. His eyes rolled back a little as he grabbed me around the waist and yanked my body against his, ensuring that I had as much of him inside of me as would fit. When a look of satisfaction washed over his face, he went still, eyes glassy as he stared down at me.

"What?" I asked, starting to feel nervous from the attention.

He traced his fingertips along the curve of my cheekbones, entire body wracked with a shudder. My muscles clenched and contracted, and I closed my eyes.

"Always you," he repeated my answer back to me, barely louder than his next, jagged breath.

I swallowed, forcing my eyes open. Blinking him into focus,

gooseflesh rippled up my body when I registered the look in his eyes. With his fingers still feather light against my cheeks, he ghosted his way down to my jaw, then my neck. I still had on my shirt, and he worked his hand beneath the collar, fingers stretching around my throat. He didn't hold, he didn't squeeze.

He just held me there.

"I know."

He was realizing in that moment the things that I had known all along. That we were perfect for each other. In every way that mattered and all of the ones that didn't.

I'd had enough patience and strength to wait him out until he was ready to tear down his own walls, and that was what he needed more than anything else.

"You're not going to leave me," he said, alternating between blinking and squinting like he had a splinter in the corner of his eyes.

"I'm not going to leave you."

"Why not?"

He was still long and hard inside of me, muscles jumping with every word that left his mouth. His fingers flexed around my throat, and I grabbed his wrist with one hand, his waist with the other so he didn't get a single idea about going anywhere besides where he was. "Because I love you."

"That doesn't feel like enough," he muttered.

"It's everything, you stupid man."

He growled at me, a low rumble in his chest, then eased his way out of me before pushing back in with a long and slow slide of skin against skin. I arched my neck, pressing my throat against his palm. Barclay started to move then, with measured thrusts that had the tip of his cock dragging over my prostate with every pump of his hips. Beneath him, I shivered, and he let go of my throat to brace himself once again beside my head.

"It's everything," I said again, hooking my feet around the back of his thighs.

Instead of answering to that, he slanted our mouths back

together, kissing me to say what I knew his words never could. I deepened the kiss as much as I could from beneath him, my fingers scrabbling at the back of his neck, his shoulders, trying to pull him closer, deeper. I kept our mouths pressed together, tongues tangled, until his pace quickened and faltered, and then the familiar stutter and stillness of his orgasm.

Closing my eyes, I gasped, feeling the heat of his cum fill me while his thick length pulsed and stretched my rim. Before his cock had even stopped spurting, he took my dick into his hand and jerked me off in the way he knew always got me off, and it wasn't long until I followed after him. He barely managed to shove my shirt up and out of the way before my cock leaked all over my stomach and his fingers.

Even after I finished, he didn't let go, only sliding down my body to replace his hand with his mouth.

"Fuck," I cried out, grabbing his hair and flying off the couch when he licked a long stripe from my balls to my tip.

He hummed a pleased little noise and lapped up my cum and my sweat until I was clean enough to get his bill of approval, then he tucked me back into my pants and got me re-dressed as best he could considering the second orgasm had taken my bones and muscle tone with it.

Barclay collapsed half on top of me, his cock still out and his fingers still shiny with spit and cum. I worked my fingers through his damp hair, pushing it back from his face so I could study him while he rested. With his eyes closed and his brain half-deep in that post-orgasm kind of haze, he looked absolutely mindless and unbothered. Like he didn't have a care in the world, no weight or stress upon his shoulders. My first thought was to say he looked like an ideal version of himself, but that wasn't the case.

Barclay as he *was*, was ideal.

I loved him and all his faults, his flaws, his perfections.

"I'm not going to leave you," I said the promise from earlier, in case he had forgotten it in the heat of the moment.

His lashes fluttered, eyes blinking open. He stared up at the ceiling, still blissed out, but some of the worry I was used to creeping in around the corners of his eyes and the tight line of his mouth.

"Everyone else has."

I swallowed past the knot in my throat. "Dalton hasn't. Flynn, Archie, the rest of them."

He rolled his eyes. "They're friends. It's different."

"We were friends," I reminded him.

He rolled over onto his front and caught my stare, his own gaze intense and serious enough that the knot in my throat somehow felt amplified and now impossible to breathe around.

He literally took my breath away.

"You're different," he said.

He *implored*.

"Am I?" I whispered.

"I see it now."

"Do you?"

He nodded and moved into a seated position, taking me with him so I was half in his lap, almost like the cuddle we'd had on the couch earlier in the week.

"I see you," he said, kissing the top of my head. "I get it now."

I wasn't convinced he did, but I was certain he was close to it, if not. I wasn't going to argue the point considering how good the rest of me felt. It didn't feel like avoidance, just…delay.

I wanted to enjoy the peace of him a little while longer.

I got ten minutes before his phone started vibrating against his thigh and my knee like it was a child's toy that had been left on and unattended. He sighed, reaching beneath my legs to fish it out of his pocket. The screen flashed with text messages from the group chat he had with his friends.

The Trophy Doms Social Club, they'd named it.

"I told you they'll never leave," I said, untangling myself from him.

I was a disheveled mess and my knees felt like those of a baby deer, not quite able to hold my weight or bend at the right angle.

But I finished putting myself back together, trying to ignore the smear of cum against my shirt that Barclay's ever attentive mouth had missed.

"What do they want?" I asked.

"Wanted to make sure Drake didn't fuck us to death," he muttered, joining me on his feet.

"As if he could ever keep up."

Barclay laughed and grabbed me again, delivering another toe-curling kiss. Kissing wasn't new to us, but this frequency of it, this intensity, it was very new. I didn't hate it, but it was taking some getting used to.

He kissed me there until I got used to it.

Until his phone started buzzing again.

"We can go out," I said with much reluctance.

"Just see what's going on and then we can go."

"Why would we go?"

Barclay's brow furrowed. "To go home?"

"It's early." Confusion knit tight around my mouth. "Oh my god, do you think that because we're in a relationship that I want to just stay home and not go out anymore?"

"I know you very much want to go out," he said, giving me a spin and a push toward the door. "That's what got us in this situation."

"You know what I mean." I let him give me another friendly shove toward the door. "I'm not trying to turn into a boring home-body just because I have a boyfriend."

He looped his arms around my waist and yanked me back, breath leaving my lungs in a rush as my back landed against his chest.

"Boyfriend," he repeated, tone sounding somewhere between prayer and promise.

Burying his face in the crook of my neck, Barclay licked and sucked at the visible skin until my laughter and protests turned to moans and sighs. And then my chest was against the wall, his hand was down the front of my pants, and he had me seeing stars until he worked another orgasm out of my very sore and well-tended cock.

"Open the door," he said against my skin, my sticky cock still in his fist.

I managed to get the lock loose and knob twisted, then we stumbled together into the hallway. He caught our balance and walked us back to the corner of the loft where all of his friends still sat. Flynn and Rose had taken our place on the couch, but they scooted over to make enough room for one.

I'd never been embarrassed about being naked around them, and having Barclay as my boyfriend wasn't going to change that. I couldn't erase the history between all of us, and I didn't want to. Everything had worked together, lined up in place to get me to that very moment. On the lap of the man I loved with his hand around my cock. He teased me with his fingertips while verbally sparring with Archie about how long he'd taken in the other room.

"Close your eyes." Barclay nipped my earlobe, and I dropped my head against his shoulder and did as I was told.

Someone went to their knees between our legs. I didn't know who it was, and I wasn't going to ask. Because a hot mouth joined Barclay's fingers and nothing else mattered.

My life was fucking perfect, and I was going to enjoy it.

Val was off again at dinner with his family, and I was in front of my closet, mindlessly tracing my fingers over the crisp pleats in the slacks he'd hung up on Friday night. Stepping back, I crossed my arms in front of me, raising my thumb and scratching at my dry bottom lip.

I waited for any hint of discomfort or unease, but the only thing I found was a calm and quiet kind of pleasure at seeing his things mixed in with mine. His underwear was in my drawers, his toothpaste in my vanity. He was in my home, my life…and I didn't hate it.

I wasn't sure I trusted it, but I *wanted* to trust it. After sharing Val with Drake on Friday night at Rapture, something inside of me had shifted in an irrevocable way. It wasn't anything I could put a word to, because I'd loved him long before that encounter, but it was something monumental just the same. That night we'd played with Drake, I'd had Val for myself, and then I'd put him on display and shared him with at least three more people who'd been grateful for a taste of him.

Val had come until he wept against my shoulder, tears leaving dark splotches against the front of my shirt while cum stains dried against his pants. The night had been a blur for him, I knew, because when I brought him home and tucked him back in bed, he was so deep in subspace he was absolutely mindless. I loved him like that, loved being able to give him those ecstatic and easy moments of peace and pleasure. When I'd climbed into bed behind him and wrapped my arms around his chest, the ache between my own legs drew into sharp focus, but I knew for certain Val was done for the night.

Instead of fucking him again, I'd jerked off against his ass, spurting my own release against his tender and swollen asshole. He'd moaned and pressed back against me, still so far out of my reach I knew he'd sleep well until the sunrise. He had and then some, sleeping well past nine and not even complaining when I brought him coffee in bed.

All of my friends were dominant men by the letter of the word, but it wasn't a label I'd ever claimed for myself. I was dominant, sure, but I didn't want the same things they chased after. I was happy to control and take and give when necessary, but I didn't want a submissive, and I loved that Val walked the line as masterfully as he did. He knew when to yield and when to fight, and I think that was what had always kept me on guard around him.

If I wasn't careful, he'd see right through me, and that was terrifying.

That was when the hurt would start.

But that ever-lingering fear felt softer around the edges than it had before, and even when I tore myself away from his clothes in my closet and went to the wedding invitation in my kitchen, the tension wasn't as loud as it had once been. I still had to go to the wedding, and I still hadn't decided if I wanted him to come with me. I knew it was expected. That was, after all, what two people in an equal partnership did, but…

Dennis and I had never had an equal partnership and I'd had a whole lifetime to reflect on the imbalance and the betrayal. While I was a controlled man in most things, Dennis had always found a way to unnerve me and throw me off step, and I didn't want Val to witness that if it happened again. It was bad enough when the invitation had arrived. My reaction was far from reasonable—I saw that now in hindsight—but it wasn't anything I could take back. If anything, it only proved to me how much the defenses I'd put in place had been a necessary failsafe.

But…

Things were different.

Normally, Sunday nights were my quiet time, which I loved, but tonight it felt like I was just waiting for Val to come home and…

Wait.

Waiting for Val to…

Come home?

This wasn't his home—it was mine.

His things were here, but it was my apartment, my space.

With the invitation in hand, I turned to survey my surroundings, appreciating the glow of the city lights as they reflected up through the plate glass windows on the far wall. Most of my friends had bought houses, but I'd never wanted that kind of domesticity. I liked the distance, the view. Like a king in his tower, though I'd never admit the comparison to anyone else.

This was my home, but I could feel him in every corner. My mind worked through three years of memories, and I found there wasn't a surface in my home that Val hadn't touched and claimed for himself, even if that hadn't been his plan.

A sharp buzz from my phone across the room brought me out of my thoughts, and I tried—and failed—to tamp down the burst of anticipation over my hope that it was a message from Val.

Unknown: Barclay?

I set the invitation down and picked up my phone.

Me: Who's this?
Unknown: It's Jason. Valentin gave me your phone number.

It was unreasonable, but I hated that Jason called him by his whole name. It reeked of some kind of exclusivity that should have been far out of his reach. Jason was a stranger to both of us, he had no right, but it wasn't my place to dictate what Val did or what he allowed other people to call him. I thought about the way he'd called Drake *sweetheart*, how he'd murmured such reassuring words in his ear while things got underway.

I thought about how I'd only ever called him Val.

Unknown: I hope that's okay.
Me: It's fine.
Me: I don't really like texting, Jason. What did you want?

I didn't mean to be abrupt, but the group text with my closest friends really took most of the energy I had when it came to texting and if Val and Jason wanted to be friends, that was on them, not me.

Unknown: Checking if you wanted to get a drink.
Me: Val is busy.
Unknown: I know. You and me.

Two weeks before, I would have said no.

Me: Sure.
Unknown: Any preference?
Me: Cunningham's.
Unknown: LOL are you paying?

I huffed out a laugh, rolling my eyes which opened back up to stare at the wedding invitation on the table, half out of the envelope with the flourished and elegant script almost visible beneath the flap.

Me: Yes. An hour?
Unknown: See you then.

I saved Jason's number into my phone and went back into my bedroom to change into something a little more presentable than the jeans and old USC shirt I'd put on after the gym. Opting for a pair of gray slacks with a white button-up and white sneakers, I brushed my teeth and then headed down to Cunningham's.

Jason was on the sidewalk in front when I arrived and we fought our way through the awkward hug or handshake phase, settling on something that landed somewhere in the middle.

The hostess recognized me and walked us back to the normal cluster of tables and chairs I shared with my friends on Thursday nights. Jason looked around, and I could tell by the nervous flicker in his eyes that he was out of his element. I hadn't meant for that, but I *needed* to be somewhere familiar, considering how much everything else in my life had changed.

The soft leather of the chairs was almost like home, and when the waiter came over, Jason ordered a 7&7, and I got a whiskey. I chose to not make a comment about his selection, instead waiting for him to feel ready enough to talk.

I was halfway through my whiskey before that happened.

"This is weird," he blurted.

I chuckled, shaking the glass so the two large cubes shifted and settled. "What part?"

"I don't normally venture out so far above my paygrade," he said.

"You're not paying."

"I know."

"How does it make you feel?" I asked, genuinely curious.

"A bit like a whore," he admitted with flushed cheeks and a quiet laugh.

"I don't take issue with whores," I said softly.

The flush crept higher up his face, expanding up and down until his throat was also very nearly crimson.

Jason cleared his throat, taking a hearty swallow of his shitty drink.

"I wanted to clear the air between us," he said.

I thought about his fingers against my cock, pinched tight in the hot channel of Val's ass.

"I didn't know anything was murky."

"Has anyone ever told you you're insanely intimidating?" he asked.

Leaning back into the overstuffed seat, I crossed one leg over the other, eyeing him above the rim of my glass. "Daily."

He huffed an exhale and shook his head, looking down at his lap before finding his fortitude and locking his gaze onto mine. "I'm not interested in Valentin romantically."

"I know."

Jason swallowed. "I'm not interested in *anyone* romantically."

"A bit like a whore then after all," I teased, one brow raised in interest.

"Liking sex isn't something to be ashamed of."

"Neither is being a whore." I finished off my drink and raised the empty in the air, catching the attention of our waiter. "Finish your drink."

Obediently, he swallowed down the last of his cocktail just as our second round was delivered. He gave the straw a little swirl around the glass, and I waited once again for him to speak. He was the one who had asked Val for my number, who'd texted me and asked me to come out.

"What I mean is, I'm not a threat to you," he said.

"I know," I repeated.

I hated to admit it, but I'd spent a good portion of the last three years *hurting* Val, and I would have to spend far more than the next three atoning for that, but that horrible and unspoken history between us only served to solidify my confidence in my reply. If Val would stand by me through my doubt, my neglect...there wasn't a single man on the planet who was a threat to me.

"He loves you."

"I know," I said again, softer this time. "I love him."

"Good." Jason bit the tip of his straw. "He deserves that."

"Are you an expert now?"

"He's a good man and you know it."

I didn't have to confirm it because we both knew it was the truth.

"Better than I deserve," I admitted.

His mouth quirked up into a grin. "I know."

I laughed, a hearty sensation that exploded in the center of my chest.

"What do you want, Jason?" I asked when the emotion inside of me died down.

He chuckled, shaking his head and giving me a lopsided shrug. "I just wanted to get to know you," he answered.

"Not many people do."

His subtle head shake shifted to a nod. "I know. But Val thinks you're a good man too. And I think I trust his judgement."

Licking my lips, I rubbed them together until they were half dry and a spike of friction shot through my nerve endings.

"I've known most of my friends since college," I said. "Half my life."

"Are you saying you're not in the market for more?"

I frowned down at my drink. I didn't know for sure what I was saying, but what did know was Val knew me better than anyone. Dalton was maybe a close second, but I'd deliberately kept them all at some kind of arm's length. Sitting across from Jason in seats I normally shared with my four best friends, I realized none of them really knew me at all. And suddenly Val's things in my home meant so much more than they had before. They'd been just as patient, more patient even, than he'd been. They'd tolerated my distance for going on two decades and…

"Shit," I cursed under my breath.

Pinching my nose between my thumb and first finger a couple of times, I dragged my hand down the bottom half of my face, grimacing as the stubble on my jaw abraded my palm.

"I just want to be friends, Barclay," Jason said, head cocked to the side. "With both of you."

How had Val delivered me an ultimatum that had not only

turned my relationship with him upside down, but also every relationship in my life? I'd have never admitted that I'd held my actual friends off before, because the proximity I'd allowed then was far beyond my normal range of acceptance. Those five men—Val, Dalton, Archie, Flynn, and Rob…they knew me better than anyone in my life ever had and they barely knew me at all. Val had chipped away at my sharp edges and now everything I'd built was crumbling while I watched.

Val's voice in the back of my head promised me it was for the better, but the knot in my chest vehemently disagreed.

"You'll have to forgive me." I took a swallow of my drink. "I'm not feeling very much myself right now."

"Yeah," he agreed. "I'm told love will do that to a man."

CHAPTER 22
VAL

MONDAY AFTER WORK, BARCLAY WAS WAITING FOR ME ON MY welcome mat when I got home. He looked a little scattered, but not the worst I'd seen him.

"Is everything okay?" I asked.

He pressed his chest against my back, doing a decent job of distracting me from trying to get my key in the lock. I finally managed and got us both into the apartment. He closed the door behind him and leaned against it while I bent over to take off my shoes.

"Everything is fine now," he said.

I turned to regard him, cocking my head to the side in a quiet appraisal. "I'm not sure I believe you."

Loosening my tie, I headed into the living room where I settled down on the couch. Barclay followed after me, taking a seat beside me, so close our thighs touched. The proximity wasn't unwelcome, but it was out of character for him, though I supposed the relationship side of him wasn't one I was familiar with and neither of us knew what was the norm here anymore.

"I had drinks with Jason last night," he blurted.

Something like curiosity or arousal exploded low in my belly and I did my best to not show him any part of that reaction. He tapped his fingers against the side of my kneecap, a nervous habit, and I grabbed his hand and kissed his knuckles before returning it to my leg.

"How was that?" I finally asked.

"He seems like a good man."

"He is."

"He said the same about you."

I cleared my throat, the compliment catching somewhere that didn't allow me to ingest it fully. "What else did he say?"

Barclay's fingers went still on my knee.

"We talked about what the future of our relationship was going to look like," he murmured, glancing up at me like he was some damsel in distress. I waited for him to elaborate, but it was clear he wasn't going to do it without prompting.

"And?"

Barclay chewed the inside of his cheek so hard it hollowed out, then he shook his head and raised his hand from my leg to my chest. His fingers worked nimbly at the buttons on my shirt, and I was happy to lean back and let him divest me of my clothes. He kissed his way around my throat and my neck, then stopped himself with a groan, his forehead pressed against my collarbone.

"What's wrong?" I brought my hands around him and stroked my fingers up and down the knobs of his spine.

He was half on top of me, chest heaving as he breathed, and I wished more than anything I could have made this whole thing easier for him. That I could get what I wanted without sending his entire world into a tailspin like I had.

Barclay hummed and kissed the side of my neck, then pushed himself off of me.

"Let's get dinner," he said softly.

I groaned, palming my already half-hard cock and pointing the bulge at him. "Are you serious right now?"

"Dating and all that." He mumbled something under his breath and stood, holding his hand out for me.

Reluctantly, I slid my palm against his and let him pull me to my feet. He was quick to do up the buttons on my shirt, and then his hands were down my pants, adjusting my cock behind the waistband of my underwear.

"I hate you for this," I told him.

He chuckled and shrugged, almost looking like a younger version of himself. "I'm trying to do right by you."

"I'd rather you do me right," I said, gesturing toward the bedroom. "Right now and right there."

"Believe me, I want to. But...after."

He stared at me with such an earnest expression on his face, there was no way I could tell him no.

"Alright," I begrudgingly agreed. "Let's go."

I put my shoes back on and let him drive us to a restaurant in mid-city with a one word name that I'd never even heard of. He didn't have a reservation, and apparently we didn't need one because it took less than two minutes for us to be seated in comfortable upholstered chairs on opposite sides of a small square table with a white candle and pink flowers in the middle.

"Are you trying to impress me?" I asked, sliding the candle and the flowers toward the edge.

"Is it working?"

I huffed a laugh and shook my head. "I was impressed by you three years ago. You don't have to keep trying."

"Yes, I do." His tone was beyond serious, and I swallowed, looking up at him. His stare bore into me until I managed to nod in agreement with him. "You deserve it."

"What the hell did Jason say to you last night?"

"Nothing I didn't already know."

"Well." Licking my lips, I tore my stare away from him and turned my attention to the menu. I wasn't sure if I owed Jason a thank you or not, but every day with Barclay seemed to bring a new level of intensity and variance to our relationship. I wouldn't go so far as to call it unpredictable, because I knew he was reliable, but it definitely kept me guessing.

"How was your family dinner?" he asked.

Yeah.

For what had to be the hundredth time, I reminded myself that Barclay as a boyfriend was definitely going to take some getting used to.

"It was uneventful compared to the week before," I answered. "My older sister is like a mother hen."

"Which one is she?"

It seemed absurd that I'd been with this man in some form or another for going on three years, and he didn't know which of my sisters was which. But I didn't know anything about him really at all, either.

"Angie," I told him. "She's a year older than me and Teresa is a year younger."

"And they know…know you like men?"

"They know I'm gay." I laughed softly. "At this point, they don't really care who I bring home as long as I bring someone home. They're both married."

"Do they expect you to get married?"

There was an edge to his question that felt a lot like fear, and it was impossible to not remember the way he screamed and cried the night he'd gotten the wedding invitation from Dennis. Just as Barclay didn't know anything about my history, the only thing I knew about Dennis was that he'd broken Barclay's heart—apparently beyond repair—by cheating on him with one of their professors in college. He'd never shared details beyond that, let alone what the relationship had been like before the affair came to light.

"I don't think they would be mad if I did."

"Do you want to get married?" The edge sharpened, and I leaned away from him so I didn't get cut. "It doesn't make a difference to me one way or the other."

"Your face says that's a lie."

"Are you an expert on me now?" I asked, brow raised. "You know all my secrets and hopes? You didn't even know which of my sisters was the older one."

I could taste the anger as I answered him, only stopping because a waitress came up to the table and asked if we were ready to order drinks. Barclay ordered wine for us both then sent her away, his jaw tense as the silence settled back over the table.

"I don't know if I want to get married," I said softly.

Marriage had always been more of an idea than a real thing to me. Like a dream that I'd sometimes fantasized about when I was younger, but not so much as I got older. I may have been a romantic at heart, but I didn't see the point of it. Even after sitting through Angie and Teresa both tying the knot, it hadn't ever felt like something for me. Of course I wanted that lifetime commitment, but I didn't need a piece of paper to give me that. It was something between two people, no third parties. Though, I supposed in a way, my relationship with Barclay was built around third parties.

"I always assumed you would want that," he said.

"Maybe in a perfect world, but this isn't one of those."

"You deserve that kind of commitment."

"I deserve a lot of things."

The waitress brought us wine, and I wished we'd stayed home and fucked because it would have felt a lot better than this conversation.

"It's just paper," I said with a shrug. "That invitation you have sitting on your counter is made of the same stuff."

Barclay cleared his throat, leveling a wounded look at me before reaching for his wine.

"Is that where you think this is going?" I asked, mirroring the action and taking a drink of my own. "You think dating me and then marrying me?"

"I don't know what I think. That's why I'm asking."

"I've always just wanted you," I told him simply. "But not in pieces. The whole of you."

"I'm not..." He licked his lips and taking another sip of his wine. "I'm not whole."

"You may not see it."

"I'm not," he snapped.

I arched a brow. "I'm sure all the pieces are there," I said.

"And what?" He scoffed, lip twitching up into a disgusted smirk. "You want to put them all together?"

"I'll take them in pieces," I answered him quickly. "Take you in pieces."

"Why?"

"Because you deserve that kind of love."

He sucked in a shaking breath and scrubbed a hand down his face, looking everywhere in the restaurant besides my face. I sighed, twisting the stem of my wine glass between my finger and thumb while he took the time he needed to get himself back together. It felt like he needed privacy, so I counted the petals on the pink daisies at the edge of the table.

"You can't just have these conversations talking about what I deserve," I reminded him. "You deserve those things too."

"Then why haven't I ever had them?"

I finally looked back up at him, ignoring the glassy sheen that had taken over his eyes.

"Why haven't I ever had them?" I countered instead. "I can answer it for you if you want me to."

"Sure."

"Because you're the only person who gets it," I said. "The only one who understands me, and if you don't think I understand how terrifying that can be, then I don't think you've been paying attention."

He took another sip of his wine, hand trembling as he raised the glass to his mouth.

"Are you scared of me?" I asked.

The way his lips turned down at the corners said yes.

"It's not that simple." He set his glass on the table, then wiped his hands on his thighs.

"This is…this has gone off the rails a little." I braced myself on the arms of the chair and gave it a shove back so I could stand. Barclay's eyes went wide with panic and I gave him a soft smile. "I'm just going to go get some air, and we can let some of this tension dissipate."

"Are you coming back?" he asked.

I saw the fear in his face when he asked the question. I saw what it cost him, in the tight stretch of his shoulders and the proud puff of his chest. Everything about his body said he was ready to fight and prepared to lose, ready to pretend that loss wouldn't cost him everything.

"I'm coming back," I assured him.

Dropping my napkin on the chair, I navigated my way back through the restaurant and right through the front door. I didn't realize I'd been holding my breath until I sucked in a lungful of fresh air so fast I almost choked on it. With my hand against my chest while I coughed and sputtered, I walked down the block until I found a stretch of wall that begged me to rest against it.

I love him, I reminded myself.

I wanted him.

I wasn't going to let his prickly edges scare me off and be the thing that proved *him* right. I was more than the men he'd been with before, and I was surely far more than Dennis ever could have been for him. I knew it. In my bones, I knew that the love I had for Barclay was unlike the love I'd have for anyone else ever in my life, and I knew it was the same in the opposite direction too.

I just needed to find a little bit more patience.

"I'm sorry." Barclay was there in front of me, his arms around my shoulders as he pulled my face into the crook of his neck. My next breath sounded watery, and I tried to swallow it back when he tightened his hold on me. I gently slid my hands around his waist, barely holding on. He didn't waver, grunting happily when I finally held him with purpose.

"You don't have to apologize for anything," I assured him.

"I want to be better," he said, kissing the side of my head. "I want to be a better...boyfriend...for you. Better friend for Dalton, for the rest of them."

"You're a good friend."

He laughed, breath ghosting over the shell of my ear. "I could be better," he murmured. "And I want to be. I'm going to be."

I nodded, wiggling my shoulders so I could lean back and get a good look at him. The panic from earlier had faded from his eyes, instead replaced with that ever-lingering exhaustion I was so used to seeing on his face.

"I love you," I reminded him. "I'm not giving up on you."

"I want to deserve that kind of dedication. From you."

"You're perfect *for me*," I said. "In pieces or otherwise."

"I love you."

Every word dripped with truth and need. And, between us, my stomach growled. Barclay cracked a smile, pressing a kiss against my forehead with a quiet laugh. I was hungry and I was tired, but I wasn't going to walk away from him. Not now and not in the foreseeable future. Unless the foreseeable future didn't involve a basket of warm bread and a plate of olive oil. Then, I might.

"Let's get back inside?" he suggested.

I held my hand out for him and he twined our fingers together.

"Yes," I agreed. "Let's."

CHAPTER 23
BARCLAY

Dalton was home getting Royce settled after his move, and Flynn was running late because he was too busy fucking Rose before work to be on time, so I found myself at Cunningham's with just Rob and Archie. We'd ordered our first round, and I could *feel* their attention on me.

"What?" I asked, closing my eyes and taking a sip of my whiskey.

"I want to know when you're going to invite Val to the wedding," Rob said.

"I'm not."

"Why bother putting in all this work if you're just going to blow it in three weeks?" Archie asked.

"I'm not going to blow it." I forced my eyes open just so I could narrow them at him. "Taking him to the wedding would blow it."

"Why?" Rob pressed. "Are you still in love with Dennis?"

"I haven't loved Dennis for years."

"Then what are you scared of?"

Archie sucked his tongue across the front of his teeth, leaning away from Rob after the question left his mouth. I sucked in a breath that didn't come anywhere close enough to filling up my lungs.

"I'm not scared," I said. "Dennis is the past and Val is not, and I don't see the need to mix the two."

"Then why are you going?" Archie asked.

"You grew up in a split-level floor plan home in Maine, Archie. I don't expect you to understand the obligations of another tax bracket."

"I've signed deals this week worth more than you make in five years." He raised his glass, arrogant smirk dancing across his smug fucking mouth.

"How much money of that do you see?" I countered.

"You're missing the point." He clanked his ice around. "I'm not as removed from your realm of understanding as you think I am."

"Calm down," Rob said quietly, rolling his eyes. "I get enough of this at home."

"Grayson giving you a run for it?" Archie directed the question at Rob, and I used the reprieve to try again to take a breath…and a drink.

Rob ignored Archie entirely. "I think you should take Val to the wedding. It would let him know you're all in."

"He knows."

Even if he hadn't known before, there was no way he *couldn't* have known after our borderline disastrous dinner date earlier in the week. It had taken all of my willpower to watch him walk away from me in the middle of the restaurant, and the door had barely closed before I was up and chasing after him. I'd yet to figure out what it was about *that* Val that had my head all screwed up, but maybe Jason was right.

Maybe it was love.

"Are either of you taking into account that Val might not even want to go?" I asked.

"Of course Val wants to go," both of them answered me at the same time.

I groaned and rolled my eyes, crossing one leg over the other and looking toward the door. No sooner had I looked up than Flynn walked in, red-faced with his shirt unbuttoned at the base of his throat. His sleeves were rolled up to his forearms and he smelled like lilacs when he flung himself into the empty seat beside me.

"Sorry I'm late," he said, raising a hand and flagging down our waiter for a drink.

"Did you get your man sorted before work?"

"I made sure he ate."

"Jesus," Archie muttered, pouring a healthy swallow of whiskey down his throat.

"You looked annoyed," Flynn said to me. "What were we talking about?"

"Val," Rob answered.

"Val does the opposite of annoy him."

"They were on about the wedding again," I said.

"Are you really still digging in about not taking him?" Flynn asked.

"Please don't tell me you're on their side."

"I'm on the side of reason," he offered with a shrug. "You're together. You're in love. It's just what people do."

"If you don't, he'll think you're hiding something," Archie said.

That couldn't have been further from the truth.

"Val knows me better than I know myself."

"All the more reason," Rob said.

The waiter brought Flynn his drink and was gone in a flash, leaving the three of them staring at me, which was so much worse than when it had just been the two of them.

"Val and I are still trying to figure things out," I explained.

"Looked like you both had a good handle on it last weekend at Rapture," Flynn murmured.

"The sex has always been easy. And don't pretend that you don't know what I'm talking about."

Flynn sipped his drink and gave me an unimpressed look. "I take it that the two of you are still…" He gestured vaguely.

"Open," I said. "Physically."

"Not romantically?"

Archie snorted a laugh. "He barely wants to be with Val romantically, let alone anyone else."

"I'll be happy for our weekly get-together to break up if they're going to turn into the three of you bullying me into having my relationship on your terms," I warned, pointing a finger at them, one after the other.

"We just love you." Flynn punched me in the shoulder. "You stubborn son of a bitch."

I was suddenly so very tired, so desperate to be back with Val, tucked in the privacy of my condo where none of my asshole friends or his meddling sisters could find us.

"My relationship isn't going to look like yours."

"No, I don't imagine it will," Rob mused.

"If I promise to think about the wedding, can we stop talking about it?" I asked.

"Yes," all three of them agreed.

"Deal." I lifted my glass toward them and they all leaned in, clinking the rims together.

After my concession, the conversation turned to easier topics, and I spent the next two rounds hyping myself up to go over to Val's at the end of the night and invite him to the wedding. Or, at least, see if he wanted me to invite him to the wedding. I didn't want him to feel obligated, but then I thought about the possibility of him not wanting to go, and I didn't know which answer had me feeling worse.

If he wanted to go, I'd have to bring the best part of my life back into the worst time of my life. If he didn't...well...why not? Val was the one who had wanted me to let him in. He'd wanted more from me, but was that a bridge too far? Would he not *want* those parts of me?

By the time I said goodnight to Rob, Archie, and Flynn, I didn't know which way was up. I knew I was a little too buzzed to drive, so I took a car to Val's apartment. Counting my steps from the sidewalk to his front door, I rehearsed what I wanted to say to him until the words didn't even sound like words anymore.

I hated this version of myself.

This man who was scared and nervous, and it was all Val's fault. I'd let him into the most palatable corners of my life and he still wanted more and where did that leave me? Naked and terrified apparently, at least if we were doing anything besides fucking. Though, spending time with him in general had started to feel the same way to me, and I didn't *hate* that change for us.

But still.

I knocked on the door, listened to the commotion on the other side. I hadn't bothered to let him know I was coming over, and I suddenly worried that had been an oversight on my part. What if he had company? What if he was with Jason or someone else and I'd interrupted them?

The door opened, and I squeezed my eyes closed, blinking out the shape of my shoes on his straw welcome mat.

"Do you want to come to the wedding with me?" I asked, not looking up.

"I don't think my husband would be too thrilled," a woman's voice answered, and I sputtered, eyes flying open as I took a step back.

The woman who opened the door was a near spitting image of Val, but with long and curly dark hair that tumbled past her shoulders. It was half pinned back and she had an explosion of flour on her shoulder.

"I..."

I didn't know what to say.

"I told you to wait, Teresa."

There was Val, coming up behind his doppelganger, hands covered in dough and matching splashes of flour on his shirt. It was in his hair, on his neck.

"I can come back," I said, holding up my hands in apology.

"Don't you dare." The woman, Teresa...his sister, grabbed me before I could retreat and, with a surprising amount of strength, hauled me into the apartment. Val closed the door behind us with a worried sigh.

"Is this him?" Teresa asked. "The man you're dating?"

"Yes," Val answered. "Barclay."

"Barclay, do you like gnocchi?"

"I…" I blinked quickly, unsure of if there was a correct answer or not. "I don't know."

"Haven't you had it before?"

I shook my head.

"Valentin hasn't cooked it for you before?" she asked, incredulous. She moved to smack him with the back of her hand against his forehead, but he anticipated her move, blocking her and smacking her against the back of her head instead.

"We just started dating," I said, as if that was some kind of explanation.

"Teresa, can you give us a minute." Val swatted at her again and ushering her back into the kitchen.

Her eyes twinkled with a mischief I'd often seen light across Val's face, and she backed away from where we stood in the entryway. Val had an apron on, I realized, when he pulled the edge of it up to wipe his hands off, but it was futile. There was flour everywhere.

"I didn't mean to interrupt. I'm sorry."

"You're not interrupting." He glanced over his shoulder toward the kitchen, then stepped closer to me and lifted onto his toes, pressing a kiss against the corner of my mouth. He tasted like chocolate and wine. "Is everything okay? What did you say when Teresa opened the door?"

Shit.

I'd lost the momentum. Now I had to ask him and mean it.

Swallowing, I managed to ask, "Did you want to come to the wedding with me?"

Val pursed his lips, almost puckering his mouth into a kiss, but he didn't say anything. He untied his apron and crumbled it up.

"Hold on." He headed into the kitchen. I listened to him and his sister talk in hushed tones, and then he was back in the entryway, his arm around my waist. "Let's go talk."

Val ushered me into his bedroom and closed the door behind him, eyes wary. I sat down on the edge of his bed, hands resting on the tops of my thighs. He'd gotten flour on my slacks somehow, and I tried to rub it off but it only rubbed in.

"You're making it worse," he said from the door.

I folded my hands in my lap.

"Ask me again."

He was going to be the death of me.

"Do you want to come to the wedding with me?" I asked.

"Do you want me to come with you?"

"That wasn't what I asked."

He folded his arms in front of him. "That's what I'm asking."

"I don't even want to go," I reminded him. "Of course I don't want to subject you to the spectacle."

Val let out a quiet breath and pushed off the door. He was barefoot, I noticed, wearing a worn pair of gray sweats and a tattered-looking college t-shirt. He looked comfortable, and he sat down next to me on the bed. His clothes were a stark contrast to mine, but all of that disappeared when his pinky finger stretched out and dragged against mine.

"And you have to go?" he asked softly.

"Keep up appearances."

"Would it be easier for you if I was there?"

I turned toward him, our knees brushing together. Sucking in a deep breath, I caught his stare and truly took time to look at him. Like, really look at him. I studied the finest lines that spread out from the corners of his eyes, and the single gray hair that stuck out a little wildly above his ear. I made note of the deep swell of his cupid's bow and the way his mouth was always slightly upturned, ready to smile. That was Val at his core, a man who was always ready to please, ready to be happy.

"I love you," I said.

That wasn't what I'd meant to say, but they were the only words in my brain. When I looked at Val, it was the only thing I knew, the one thing I truly understood. That gorgeous mouth of his quirked up into a full smile, and I grabbed his face in my hands, leaning in and pulling him toward me at the same time. He gasped, lips parting, and I slanted mine against his to kiss him. Val whimpered, curling his fingers around my wrists to hold on. He leaned into me, opening his mouth wider to make room for my tongue to slide past his lips.

"I love you so much." I kissed the words against the corner of his mouth.

I pulled away because the moan that tumbled out of his throat went straight to my cock and I was achingly aware of his sister less than fifty feet away from the haven of his bedroom. Stroking my thumbs across his cheeks, I couldn't do anything besides shake my head in disbelief. I'd known before I loved him, I'd known it far longer than I'd been willing to admit, but this was one of the first times when I truly felt it. One of the first times I became aware of what it would be like to lose him.

"Is that a yes?" he whispered, cheeks flushed.

"Everything is easier when you're with me."

He hummed, giving my wrists a squeeze before letting his hands fall into his lap.

"Then yes," he said. "I'll go to the wedding with you."

SOMETHING HAD CHANGED WITH BARCLAY. I KNEW IT WASN'T THE first time I'd had the thought, but it felt different this time. Over the years, I'd come to expect a lot of things from him, but an invitation to his ex's wedding wasn't anywhere close to even the bottom of that list.

"I'm...I'm worried that..." he trailed off, lips twisting into a frown.

"I'm not going to think differently of you," I assured him, "if that's what you're worried about."

He let out a self-deprecating laugh. "I'm honestly worried about a lot of things, but I think...it'll be okay if you're there."

"Percy." I softly brushed my fingers over the scruff on his cheeks. "I think that's the sweetest thing you've ever said to me."

"I love when you use my first name," he said softly.

"That might be the second."

He laughed, cheeks darkening beneath my fingertips.

"I don't know what you've done to me."

I leaned in and brushed my mouth against his. I didn't have an answer, but I was ready to pinch myself because sometimes I didn't believe it either. How we'd been in a holding pattern for so long and then a stranger had sent us shooting headfirst into coupledom and now...love.

Now, this…

"Valentin Russo!" Teresa shouted from the kitchen. I closed my eyes and dropped my forehead against Barclay's. "This gnocchi isn't going to cook itself!"

"I forgot she was here," he murmured, using his head to give me a bump.

"I've been trying that my whole life and you've managed it in ten minutes?" I scratched the side of my neck and unfolded myself from the bed, pulling Barclay to his feet beside me. "You don't have to stay if you don't want to."

"Is this a repeat of me asking if you wanted to come to the wedding?"

I exhaled, shoulders slumping. "My sister can be a lot. And she's the easy one."

"I can handle her," he promised me, "if you want me to stay."

"Are you hungry?" I asked. "I didn't expect to see you tonight since it's Thursday and you're normally with the boys all night."

"They bullied me into asking you about the wedding."

He'd said the comment offhandedly, but something about it poked at me the wrong way. There was an implication there I couldn't quite get my head around, so I asked him, "Did you *not* want to ask me yourself?"

"It's not so much that. They just helped me see the error of my ways, I think."

"I'll take it," I said, inclining my head toward the door. "Of course I want you to stay. You're always welcome. You may just not always want to be here."

He laughed, taking a step toward the door. "I can handle your sister."

"Famous last words."

Barclay's palm slipped against mine, clammy and cool with sweat. Bless, he was nervous after all. Beneath that relatively unflappable demeanor, my sister had gotten under his skin. But, maybe, so had I.

"Are you ready?" I asked.

He nodded, and I opened the door.

My sister was bustling around in the kitchen, rolling and sizing more gnocchi than an entire army would need. I doubted there was any flour left in my kitchen and every surface was covered in a sheen of starch from the potatoes, but I appreciated her attempt at keeping herself busy instead of eavesdropping on us in the bedroom.

"I didn't know you had company coming over, Valentin," she said, brushing her hands off on her apron and turning to face us with a smile.

"I came by unannounced," Barclay said, giving her a professional smile.

"Are you hungry?" she asked.

"I should eat."

"Then you should cook," she said.

Teresa threw an apron at him—my crumpled and flour-covered apron. It landed against his chest, an explosion of starch and powder puffing over the otherwise clean lines of his black button-up. He pursed his lips, and it looked like he was fighting a smile. Barclay shook the apron out and tied it around his waist, a lopsided bow that hung down over the swell of his ass.

"We'll clean up later," he promised, brushing as much of the mess off himself as he could manage.

Teresa laughed, grabbing Barclay and hauling him toward the stove. "The water's boiling so come on."

"I've never…"

"You just drop them in until they float," she said, scooping a ladle of gnocchi into the pot of boiling water. "They work quick. Valentin, get some bowls."

Teresa had a pot on the back burner of sauce that she'd been fiddling with since she'd gotten to my house. It wasn't our mom's recipe and it wasn't Angie's, which would have sent them both into a tailspin. Hers was heavier on the garlic than mom's, but there was some tarragon which was very off-recipe for our family and she wanted to make sure it was perfect before she even entertained the idea of trying to sneak it in for Sunday dinner.

Barclay and my sister made quiet and casual conversation while she showed him how to scoop out and strain the little balls of dough. Heat swelled in my chest as I listened to them, and I pulled three bowls out of the cabinet and set them down beside her. She opened her mouth and I smacked the back of her arm.

"I'm getting the grated cheese not the shredded," I said, horrified at my little sister's preference for crappy store-bought granules of Parmesan cheese. "Don't even try to argue with me."

"Is he like this with you?" she asked Barclay.

"He knows how to get what he wants."

I puffed out my chest at the acknowledgement, scooping cheese into the bottom of each bowl. I pressed my way up to the counter, shoulder against Barclay's left arm so I could reach around him to the sauce at the back of the stove. I didn't give Teresa the chance to argue or protest about the taste before I dropped a full spoon of sauce on top of the cheese in each bowl.

"What if it's too strong?" she muttered.

Barclay strained another batch of gnocchi and dumped them into the serving bowl in my sister's hands.

"The sauce is fine."

"How do you know?" she asked. "You haven't tried it."

"He has a sense for things," Barclay said, adding another round of gnocchi into the salted, boiling water.

Teresa looked doubtful, but as the red sauce melted the cheese and my kitchen filled with the mixed scent of potato and tomato and cheese, there wasn't any going back for us. Just like there was no going back for Barclay and me. A small smile danced across Teresa's face as Barclay started to cook the gnocchi without her instruction, and she smirked in my direction, one eyebrow raised. I shook my head, warning her away from a comment that could undo all the work I'd put in over the past three years.

"That's good for now," she said, giving him a pat against the outside of his arm. "We can cook the rest after we eat. It's best when it's hot."

Without being prompted, Barclay spooned gnocchi from the serving bowl into the sauced bowls, humming happily as all of the pieces of our dinner came together in front of him.

"I'll take these to the table," Teresa said, gathering the three bowls in her hands with the practice of a youngest child and aunt of two. "You two get wine and forks."

She bustled out of the kitchen with the bowls, and Barclay rubbed the back of his neck nervously. "I don't know where your forks are."

"That drawer." I pointed to the narrow drawer beneath the microwave, and when he turned, I tugged the strings on his apron. It unraveled and fell loose, but I kept the tie in my finger and whipped it off of him with a flourish. He'd already knocked most of the flour off of it onto the floor, but he turned to me with three forks in his hand and the most unreadable smile on his face.

"What?" I asked quietly, tossing the apron onto the counter.

He shook his head. "This is nice," he said.

It *was* nice. It was domestic and homey. It was boyfriend-y. Though all of his friends had boyfriends now, I couldn't imagine any of them ever doing anything like this, and that somehow made it feel more special and more private. For as much of ourselves that we shared with others, this felt explicitly ours.

"It is," I rasped. Clearing my throat, I shoved the bottle of wine in his direction and he took it without question. "I'll get the glasses."

Barclay headed into my very small dining nook with the wine and the forks, and I braced myself against the counter to catch my breath. The last half-hour had been an absolute whirlwind of emotions, and between Teresa and Barclay, I hadn't had a moment alone.

"Glasses, Valentin!" Teresa hollered out like she was five hundred feet away, not fifteen.

"Yes, Ma!" I shouted back.

"Fuck you."

Barclay said something that I couldn't make out, but the rumble of his baritone was already engrained in my heart. Teresa laughed, and I was quick to get three wine glasses out of the cabinet and join them at the table.

"What's so funny?" I asked, walking in on their hushed laughter.

"Nothing," she said, trying and failing to school her features.

Barclay was a lawyer and had a better poker face, but he didn't even try to hide the amusement that tugged at the corners of his mouth.

"I hate both of you," I grumbled, sliding into my seat and snatching one of the forks.

"No, you don't."

Barclay patted my thigh and busied himself with opening the wine and pouring it out for the three of us. Teresa frowned down at the bowl, using her fork to roll the gnocchi around in the sauce that had my entire apartment smelling like a Michelin-starred restaurant.

She finally took a bite, frowning the whole time. "More tarragon," she mumbled.

Barclay mimicked her little gnocchi roll before taking a bite. As soon as he sealed his lips around the fork, his eyes went wide and he groaned appreciatively, shoving another bite into his mouth before he'd even finished chewing the first.

"This is delicious, Teresa," he said, adding another forkful of food into his mouth.

"It's not right."

"The sauce is better than Angie's," I told her after my first bite. "The gnocchi are good too."

"Thank you both for dinner," Barclay said quietly, attention very focused on his bowl.

"You cooked it," she said to him.

"You made these." He raised a fork with two gnocchi on the tines. "And the sauce. I just dropped them into the water."

"That's the most important part," she said.

He took his bite and chewed thoughtfully. "I would say the sauce is the most important part here."

"And it's delicious," I said to her before she could argue again.

Teresa sighed and dropped her fork, reaching instead for her wine.

"What does Drew think?" I asked.

"He's biased."

"Her husband," I explained to Barclay, who gave a knowing nod.

"Maybe if I'm buzzed, it'll taste better." She took a drink of her wine, and I rolled my eyes at her.

There was no pleasing my sister. Except when it came to Barclay, she seemed far beyond pleased. She seemed happy and willing to accept him right into the fold like there had always been a place for him there. I'd been cooking with my sister for my entire life and she'd never stopped telling me what to do, but after one roll through the process, she'd let Barclay fend for himself. I didn't think it had anything to do with him being more capable than me, because that was improbable, but she was going easy on him. That was for sure.

I didn't hate it. There was something about the comfort of having him and her in the same space, sharing a meal and a bottle of wine, that had me believing everything was really going to work out okay in the end. Even though I'd been invested in him for years, things had been more slow-going in return. Barclay was worth the wait, being loved by him was worth being patient, and I hadn't been lying when I told him I'd wait him out. But this unprompted Thursday night meal felt like the first time I was seeing the light at the end of the tunnel. Barclay had seemingly turned a corner with the wedding invitation, and he was doing so well with my sister. The life I'd never dared to think possible was suddenly within my reach.

Teresa grumbled her way through another drink and another bite, the tension in her neck softening enough that she didn't look like she wanted to burn every potato on the planet and never cook again.

"Better?" Barclay asked her, amusement coloring his voice.

"It's edible."

"You're too hard on yourself," I said.

"Enough about this disastrous meal." She fluttered her hands around like she could magic the entree into the garbage. "Barclay, my brother hasn't told me a single thing about you. Where should we start?"

After Teresa left on Thursday, I didn't even have the energy to fuck Val, but he didn't seem to mind. We'd kissed and snuggled and fallen asleep before midnight. Even though he'd brought clothes over to my house, I didn't have anything at his place. I hadn't even meant to spend the night, so Friday had me up earlier than normal so I could get home in time to shower and change. Friday at lunch, I found an either horrible or great idea percolating in my brain and by the time I was finished with work for the day, the deal was done.

Val and I were going on a double date.

He'd told me the act of dating wasn't what he really wanted with me. He wanted the closeness and the intention of the whole thing, but the dating part had the potential to be fun. He and I had barely had more than one successful date, but I wasn't ready to give up. So much of my nerves around having a relationship with Val had started to fade, the act of sitting in a restaurant with him for an hour didn't feel as scary as it had before.

When I'd called Val and asked if he was available, the smile in his answer was the loudest thing I'd ever heard. We set the plans, and I picked him up at seven. He looked handsome as always in a well-tailored pair of charcoal gray slacks, black loafers, and a dark red button-up. He reminded me of a Christmas present, ready to unwrap.

"Have I ever told you I love that you don't shave down to your skin?" he asked, leaning over the console and pressing a soft kiss against my mouth. His fingers danced over my cheek and I smiled against him.

"I'm sure you have."

"Where are we going?" he asked, leaning back and pulling the seatbelt across his chest.

"Some restaurant Dalton picked," I said.

I'd already keyed the address into my nav and Val reached over to hold my hand as I drove us through the city. He told me how Teresa had called him first thing in the morning to rave about how much she loved me and ask when he was going to bring me to Sunday dinner. He told me how he'd been talking to Jason and he wanted to get together with the both of us again soon.

As much as that one interested me, it reminded me that I'd committed to not just being a better partner for Val, but also a better friend and I hadn't been focusing on both of those in equal measure. Dinner with Dalton would be a good start, and then we could make plans with Jason later next week. With the wedding coming up closer every day, it would be nice to see him and let some steam off.

"Are you nervous?" I asked after handing my keys off to the valet in front of the restaurant.

"Most of your friends have seen me naked. Dinner is nothing." Val winked, and I grabbed his hand, pulling him close for a quick kiss before heading inside.

He'd been right. The proximity and the intimacy that came with this change in our relationship was something I enjoyed. I'd always liked being with him and touching him, and now I got to do it more often. There wasn't a loss here, as far as I was concerned. Save for my own personal protections, but Val was someone I could trust even if I had to remind myself of that more often than not. Every day it got easier, despite the wedding growing closer, and nothing about that felt safe.

Dalton and Royce were already at a square table in the middle of the restaurant, and the hostess walked us right to them. They both stood up when we arrived, offering hugs and handshakes, which Val accepted like he had been for his entire life and not just a handful of weeks. But that was wrong too. My friends had always loved him. They'd always known. Settling into our seats, I fanned my napkin across my lap and ordered us both drinks.

"How are you finding the city, Royce?" I asked.

Dalton's husband had just moved from New York and the two of them had done a decent job at keeping to themselves, which made sense as soon as I saw them together. They were almost always touching, like a planet and a moon orbiting each other. The connection between them felt tangible, and every minute I sat next to them I became painfully aware of how in love they were. It was enviable.

"It's slow," he answered with a laugh.

"I went to college in New York," Val said, giving him an agreeable nod.

"You what?" I asked.

Val's mouth quirked into a smile.

"Stern?" Royce asked, and Val nodded.

"I've been out here for years, though. I'm from California and I couldn't wait to get back home after graduating."

"If not for Dalton, I don't think I ever would have left," Royce said.

I tried to not fixate on the fact I was still learning things about Val. How had it escaped me for three years that he'd gone to school in New York? I'd never bothered to ask, so I wasn't sure how I expected myself to have known, but it only highlighted how dismissive I'd been for the beginning stages of our relationship. I'd really treated him poorly, and he'd taken it. Over and over again. Reaching over, I grabbed his leg. He glanced over at me, still in conversation with Royce about New York, and gave me a soft smile.

"Is Val coming to the wedding?" Dalton asked me quietly, not interrupting their conversation.

"Yes."

He chuckled. "Proud of you for that one."

"I'm trying."

"I know." Dalton nodded, stare flickering between the two of us before drifting over to Royce. "The trick is that you shouldn't have to try."

"What does that mean?"

"It comes naturally," he answered.

"It's unlearning muscle memory," I murmured, hand still on Val's thigh.

"I've always known that you loved him."

I huffed out a laugh. "I haven't."

I was still getting used to the fact my friends had seen through me for years, that Val had somehow known better too. He had to have known there was more beneath the surface or he would have told me to fuck off years before. The sex couldn't be *that* good.

"I think you have," Dalton said.

I swallowed, wondering about the truth of that.

Maybe, subconsciously I'd known there was something more to Val than other men. While I hadn't been faithful to him, because that hadn't been the bounds of our relationship, he'd always taken a sort of priority over everyone else. Even though there were other people I'd slept with more than once, he was the only one who knew my friends, who'd come around and been accepted into the fold. He was the one who'd been to my home, in my bed. He was the one I fucked bare.

"Shit."

Dalton laughed and leaned back in his seat. "I wish you could see your face right now."

"Are you being mean?" Royce asked.

The air swirled around us like a vacuum, and I became aware

of Val's attention on me, his hand on top of mine, mine still on his leg. I hadn't let go of him since we sat down.

"Just helping my dear friend see the truth," Dalton said.

Val threaded his fingers through mine in a soft of awkward reverse handhold, but it was everything.

"So." Dalton clapped his hands together. "Let's talk about the elephant in the room."

"Let's not," I muttered.

He went on, unperturbed, "The wedding."

Val squeezed my hand. "We don't have to talk about it," he said.

"We have to stick together," Dalton said. "None of us want to go."

"Then why are we?" Val asked with a sad little laugh.

"Do you want the short answer or the long one?" Royce asked.

"Long."

"Because the only thing that matters more than money in life is appearances, and weddings aren't about love, they're about being seen. How many hands you shake, deals you make," Royce explained.

I was grateful for him being there, finding a way to articulate the nature of my upbringing to Val in a way I never had before.

"They're front page social events," Dalton added. "The who's who kind of shit."

"That feels backwards and wrong," Val said.

"Very," Royce agreed. "But that's the way of it. You're lucky that you don't have to deal with family like this."

"I have my own family to deal with."

I laughed, thinking about how easy his sister had been, even though her aggressive friendliness was overwhelming at first. Walking in on dinner with Teresa had caught me off-guard, but it was nothing compared to what I knew the wedding would be. My parents would be there, and that would be bad enough. I avoided them whenever I could, as their scorn over breaking up with

Dennis after his affair had been one of the hardest pills I'd ever swallowed.

"It's different," I assured him. "Your family is like mice compared to the vultures the three of us grew up around."

Some of the color drained from Val's cheeks. I wasn't trying to scare him, but I wanted him to understand what he was walking into. What he'd asked for by asking for me.

"You'll be fine." I raised our hands to my mouth and kissed his knuckles. "I'll have to be cordial to Dennis like nothing ever happened between us. It'll be perfunctory and then it'll be over."

"And we'll be there," Dalton said.

I gave him an appreciative nod. I was trying to be a better friend.

Val's brow furrowed and his jaw worked from side to side like he was deep in thought. I much preferred his face when he was deep in his pleasure, but a side effect of being in a relationship meant that I got both now, so I didn't look away.

"And…" His voice hitched. He cleared his throat. "And what do you need from me?"

"Not a thing," I rasped. "I just need you. This."

Lifting mine and Val's joined hands above the table, Dalton made a soft noise of approval from his seat. He leaned over and slid his hand around the back of Royce's neck and pulled him in for a blistering kiss that had all of the color rushing back into Val's cheeks.

"Just don't judge me for it." I turned toward him. "This wedding is about survival. And keeping you safe."

"I'm fine. I'll be fine."

"I know that, in theory. But…I don't want you to think of me differently. If you meet my parents, if you meet him. If…no…when you understand the life I came from."

I turned my stare down toward my lap, toward Val's slender fingers twined between mine. This man was everything and I'd almost lost him. I didn't think taking him to the wedding was a way to keep him, but he didn't understand.

"My family isn't like yours," I explained. "This…"

"I can handle it," he said, and his face looked like he meant it. "I know I wasn't brought up like you three were, but I went to school with plenty of people like you. Like your family. I know how to play the game, Percy. I just haven't had to do it in a while."

"Hey!" Dalton interrupted, voice loud over the chatter of the restaurant. "Why does he get to call you Percy?"

"Because he lets me come inside of him."

"Jesus." Val yanked his hand out of mine and covered his face with a groan under his breath.

"What?" I laughed. "Was that the wrong thing to say?"

The tension over the table and the threat of the wedding evaporated. Val reached for his wine and took a drink, shaking his head at me, cheeks flushed like they normally were when we were together.

"No," he said, shaking his head. "It was exactly the right thing to say."

"I love you." I grabbed him and yanked him closer to me, slanting our lips together and kissing the words against his mouth. With my tongue, I begged him not to think less of me after he learned more, and the small moans that left his mouth promised me that he wouldn't.

"I love you," he whispered back, breaking the kiss, much to my regret.

"I love *this*," Dalton said, clapping his hands together. "Now, let's get some fucking food. I'm starving."

THE WEDDING WAS A WEEK AWAY AND I DIDN'T HAVE A TUX.

Barclay had a tux, because of course he did, and that was how I found myself at a boutique on Beverly that was so upscale it didn't even have a sign out front. It felt a little *Pretty Woman*, with Barclay lounging on a circular couch behind me and a thousand mirrors in front of me. I could watch him in the reflection, and I made note of the way he pretended to busy himself with his phone like I hadn't caught him at least four times stealing glances at me in the mirror.

"I could have rented one," I said when he looked up and didn't bother to look away.

"I know," he said simply, turning his stare back toward his phone and mumbling something under his breath.

"What was that?"

He raised a brow. "I said I wonder if this is how Flynn felt with Rose."

"I don't think our income gap is that dramatic," I assured him.

"I don't suppose it is, but you're still acting like Rose about this whole thing. You want to date me, Val? Then date me."

"Oh, how the tables have turned."

His mouth twitched into a smirk and he tapped out a message on his phone before sliding it into his pocket and giving me his full attention.

"My only regret," he said, "is that I didn't ask you sooner."

"To date you? You didn't ask me at all."

"To the wedding. I can only imagine how good you'd look in something custom tailored." Heat flared in his eyes, and my cheeks burned. Now it was my turn to look away.

"This feels pretty tailored to me," I said.

"This is off the rack with changes." Barclay waved a dismissive hand at the row of matching tuxedo slacks to his right. "Not *made* for you."

His voice got scratchy and rough at the end, and I pulled at the heavily starched collar of the white shirt I had on. I swallowed, thankful for the breath, and then the tailor was back, a tomato full of pins on his wrist and a tape measure around his neck.

"Sorry for the delay," he said, quickly busying himself with tugging at the tails of the coat and the hem around my ankles. "Thank you for your patience."

"Val is nothing if not patient," Barclay said, amused.

"Thank you, Mr. Barclay."

I chuckled, forgetting that Barclay was his last name not his first. It was easy to forget the Barclay name and the Barclay family, because even though I rarely called him as much, he was Percy to me.

Fact of the matter, though…I was nervous about the wedding. Barclay was an otherwise unflappable man. He was always collected and confident, but having witnessed his unraveling upon receipt of the invitation and the turmoil that followed, I appreciated the gravity of the situation—and the relationship—for him. Being invited to his ex-boyfriend's wedding was a bigger deal than his agreeing to date me had been. I wasn't worried that he still had feelings for Dennis, but the aftereffects of what Dennis had done to him when they were in college echoed through every choice he'd made in life since.

The tailor, Eduardo, busied himself pinching and pulling and pinning me, and the entire time I studied Barclay in the mirror. He had on a pair of dark wash jeans and a black t-shirt that hugged his chest and shoulders in the way I preferred to do myself. His hair was tousled, dark brown with wisps of sun-kissed gold…a side effect of living in Los Angeles. He was broad and tanned, his hands thick without looking out of place on his body. He cradled his phone in his hands, brow furrowed while he tapped out another message.

"Who's texting?" I asked, hoping the question wasn't out of bounds. We were still navigating the limits and rules of what dating meant for the two of us. So far we had overnights and shared meals, both in and out of the house, and I had some clothes and his house, but he still had nothing at mine. And, of course, the wedding. I was a plus one, which felt more monumental than anything else that should have come first.

"Jason," he said, resting the phone on this thigh.

"I didn't know you and he texted."

"You know I hate texting in general, but…trying to make plans."

My nostrils flared when he caught my gaze in the reflection. "What kind of plans?" I asked.

Barclay's stare flickered to Eduardo, on his knees tucking pins into the back of the slacks he'd picked out for me upon our arrival, then back to me.

"The kind you like."

I licked my lips and stared at my shoes, urgently begging myself to not get an erection. Eduardo worked his way up, bringing his face dangerously close to my cock, his fingers working quickly up my inseam while he checked measurements and added chalk marks and pins.

Barclay let out a low rumble of a laugh, and I wanted to smack him for it. He adjusted himself in his seat, making it clear to me he was far less concerned about the state of his cock than I was about mine. That just wouldn't do.

"Tell me what I need to know about the wedding," I said.

His mood immediately soured, which hadn't been my intent, but I needed us both to keep it under control until we were out of the store and it wouldn't be considered publicly indecent for us to have hard-ons.

"Just stick with me and we'll get through it."

"I didn't plan on ever leaving your side."

Regarding me in the mirror, he licked his lips slowly, tongue tracing back and forth over one of his canine teeth. The stare didn't do much for the blood flow I'd been trying to control, and with a sigh, I gave up trying. Eduardo was at my waist now and then he was on to the shirt and the coat, and before I knew it, we were finished.

Barclay ignored my protests and paid for the tux and the rush fee on the alterations. He also ignored me when I almost choked at what the rush fee turned out to be, but I knew arguing wasn't going to change the outcome. He wasn't going to let me pay and, frankly, I would have never paid that amount for anything, let alone a tuxedo I was going to wear exactly one time.

"Thank you," he said softly, taking my hand after concluding the transaction.

"What for?"

"For understanding that even though you're in it now, my life is different from yours."

"You're just a man," I muttered.

"But that." He pushed the door to the tailor shop open and waited for me to step out onto the sidewalk. "That was nothing for me. That's just life."

I exhaled, shaking my head before conceding, "You're welcome. And thank you."

"For what?"

"For doing it. For...I guess for letting me into those parts of your life."

He squeezed my hand in confirmation of something, though I wasn't sure what.

We walked down the street to his car. He opened the door for me and I sank down into the passenger seat while he walked around to the other side of the car. Barclay dropped his keys into the cup holder in the console, but didn't press the ignition button.

"Do you have plans for the rest of the day?" he asked.

"No plans until dinner with my family tomorrow," I said. "Which…you're invited to, if you wanted to come."

I'd been debating the ask since he'd stumbled into dinner with Teresa a couple days before. I knew it was a risk, not because I thought he couldn't handle it, but because I didn't want the matchmaking marital plans of my oldest sister and mother to scare him off. Things had just calmed down since we'd started dating and I wanted to enjoy the time with him before things went south. But he'd been so open and honest with me over the past week, I wanted to give him the same in return. There was no point in him letting me in if I didn't take risks and do the same for him.

He reached over the console and rested his hand on my thigh, his thumb stroking a soft arc from side to side.

"I appreciate the invitation, but let's wait until after the wedding," he said.

"Why after?"

"I want you to be sure about me before you get their hopes up." He offered me a small, almost embarrassed smile.

"They know your name," I reminded him. "Their hopes are already up."

"You know what I mean."

"What will it take for you to stop thinking that I'm going to leave you?" I asked, covering his hand with mine. His thumb kept swiping, and it almost felt like a nervous habit.

"A wedding ring, probably, and neither of us wants that," he mumbled.

My heart stopped and I clamped down around his hand. "What did you say?"

"I don't want to get married, Val," he said, wriggling his hands free and then drying his palm off on the top of his own thigh.

"You just said a wedding ring."

"I don't want to get married," he said again.

"So you'd rather spend the rest of our relationship worrying that I have one foot out the door?"

"Do you?"

"No," I answered quickly.

The small smile quirked up in the corner and he shrugged. "Then I believe you and that's enough."

"That doesn't feel like enough."

"It's enough." He cleared his throat and said something under his breath. I didn't bother asking for clarification; I just angled away from him and faced the windshield.

"Did you have something you wanted to do?" I asked him. "Is that why you wanted to know if I had any plans today?"

"I wanted to see if you were interested in getting dinner and maybe playing a bit."

He knew what he was doing. He knew how to distract me and it was by sending all the blood in my brain straight between my legs with the tease of a good time. I hated that it was in an attempt to deflect the conversation away from something we probably really needed to talk about, but like all things with Barclay, there would be a time and a place.

"We can get dinner," I said.

"And play?"

"Don't we always?"

"With Jason," he said.

I rolled my head to the left, the look on his face enough to wipe all of my unhappiness at his earlier avoidance right out of me. I was too soft for him because I was always too hard. There wasn't enough common sense left to think things through when I was so wholly focused on getting him into bed.

"Jason."

"Or not."

"Jason is fine," I assured him. "I think it's cute that the two of you are becoming friends."

"I'd hardly call us friends." He turned the car on. "I feel a little more like your secretary to be honest."

"Is that such a bad job?" I leaned over and pressed a soft kiss on his cheek, the scruff on his jaw abrading my chin. He slid his hand around the back of my neck and turned so our lips connected.

"It's my favorite job." He puckered and kissed the corner of my mouth. "It's the best job I've ever had. The only job I'll ever want."

"Now you're being dramatic."

He licked across the seam of my lips and I opened my mouth so he could dig in deeper.

"I think you underestimate the power you have over me," he murmured between licks and nips and kisses. "You have me doing all kinds of things I never thought I'd do."

"Like dating."

He smiled against my mouth.

"Talking about marriage."

The idea was out there in the open, getting water and air and life, and it was rooted already in both of our imaginations, whether we liked it or not. I'd thought about many futures with Perceval Barclay, but none of them had ever involved marriage. That one was straight from his mouth to my ears, and I couldn't un-hear it. I could maybe water it…or I could starve it. I hadn't made up my mind which one I wanted to do. At my comment, his smile faltered, but didn't fall.

I didn't press it more than that. And I wouldn't. Not until I knew what *I* wanted.

Sex was always where we connected the most, understood each other the best. Laughing and giving him a kiss of my own against the wet swell of his mouth, I said, "Making friends so you have an endless line of men on the ready to fill your boyfriend's throat with cum."

Barclay growled, fingers tightening around the back of my neck.

"Is that a yes, then?" he asked.

"It's always yes for you, Percy."

CHAPTER 27

BARCLAY

It pained me to admit, I didn't know how to make friends. I'd stumbled on Dalton during college, and he was friendly with Flynn and Archie, and Archie was friends with Rob, and the rest was history for us. But since then…nothing had stuck. Not that I'd been interested in making new friends or anything. I was happy with my four closest friends. We had shared interests—and proclivities—and being with them had always been easy. I'd never meant to be friends with Val, but he'd always had other plans for me, and now we were in love and sitting across the dinner table from a man who was very close to becoming my first new friend in over a decade.

Jason threw his head back and laughed at something Val said, and Val's hand was warm and still against mine. Val finished off the last of his wine, the only glass I'd allowed him, and then shoved the empty glass toward the center of the table. Jason's laugh quieted down, and I found myself smiling at my lap, wondering about the complexities of life and love in ways I'd never even cared about before.

"This was great," Jason said, taking the last swallow of his wine.

He also only had one glass, and I'd stayed with water for the night. I was an active drinker and had been for so long that one glass of whiskey didn't even faze me anymore, but whenever I knew things were going to go a very specific way with Val, I tried to stay as close to sober as the situation allowed. I gave Val the same instruction, and without being told, Jason seemingly had agreed to follow suit.

"It was nice," I agreed.

Shaking free of Val's hand, I pulled my wallet out of my pocket and dropped one of my credit cards on the edge of the table for the server to pick up on her way back by. The air between us immediately thickened, and Jason cleared his throat.

"Did the two of you have plans for the rest of the night?" he asked.

"You," I said. "If you find that agreeable."

"More than." He folded up his napkin and dropped it on top of his plate. "Check please!"

Val laughed.

"My treat," I told him.

"You don't need to do this."

"He does it anyway," Val explained, reaching toward me and rubbing his hand back and forth across my shoulders before letting it fall down my spine like a waterfall. "You just have to get used to it."

"I swear we've talked about this already."

"About getting used to you?" Jason arched a brow.

"Sure."

"If I may be so bold as to say you're a completely different man from the first time we met," Jason said to me, and Val's fingers flexed against the small of my back.

"How do you figure?"

"About a thousand percent less defensive," he said, "of yourself and of Val."

"Oh, shut up," Val muttered.

Jason shot me a knowing look, and I licked my lips, very content to count the sixteen digit number on the front of my credit card instead of admitting the truth of his observation. Admitting my feelings for Val had changed me, and every day was a new and unexpected shift in my life. From dinner with his sister, to the wedding plus one, to the clothes of his in my house...I was different than before. I wasn't sure if it was a better version of myself or not, but I did know—in my bones—that I loved Val and didn't want to lose him. So I would change and change a hundred more times if that was what he demanded of me.

"To your question, though, I don't have any plans for later," Jason said.

"Would you like to come over?" I asked.

His nostrils flared and he answered with a jerky nod.

The waitress walked by and discreetly snatched my credit card from the table.

"Perfect," I said.

Val leaned over and pressed a kiss against my cheek, and I didn't think I'd ever been happier. The negative thoughts were few and far between these days when it came to Val. Most of my defenses were muscle memory, but Val was repetitive and tender with his assault against me and he'd worn almost all of them down. I did still have legitimate fear about how things would go after the wedding, but I had to hope that after three years of dedicated patience, he wouldn't give up on me now.

The server returned with my card and the slip to sign, which I did as quickly as I could. Val was on his feet before I had my card back in my wallet.

"Eager much?" I teased.

"I don't blame him," Jason said, also rising to his feet.

"You'd think I don't fuck him at all," I said, standing and wrapping my arm around his waist. "Just last week I had half of Rapture sucking his cock and here he is about to whimper like he's been deprived of attention under my care."

Val pressed against me, burying his face against my armpit. "You know I'm just horny."

"I love it," I assured him, kissing the top of his head. "I love you."

"The two of you are goals," Jason said with a laugh. "For someone else, not for me."

"Do you still have my address?" I asked.

Jason checked his phone and nodded. "See you there shortly then?"

"Yes, please," Val said.

He was practically vibrating, fired up and ready to go at even the hint of playtime. We said our temporary goodbyes, and when Val and I were back in my car, I leaned over and unzipped his pants. His cock was hard and hot to the touch, and I rubbed him over the already damp cotton of his underwear.

"You're my best little slut, aren't you?" I whispered against his ear.

He gripped the seat, leather groaning beneath his hands.

"Hungry for as much cock as I'll let you have, aren't you?"

"Yes," he whimpered, hips lifting off the seat.

"Tonight I think I want his hand inside of you."

Val's cock jumped against my hand, and I chuckled, pulling away and turning on the car. He still had his fingers curled around the edge of the seat, cock throbbing in time with his pulse.

"Do you like that?" I asked, backing out of the parking spot.

I knew the answer or I wouldn't have suggested it, but I wanted to hear him say the words just the same. Beyond what Val would like, it was something *I* would also like. I'd never been a jealous man, at least not until recently, but I was pleased to find those feelings remained dormant when it came to Val sharing his body with other partners. It was his heart that I felt ownership over, which was what he'd wanted all along. But when it came to sex, watching Val get fucked to within an inch of comprehension was the best kind of porn for me. Maybe because after all was said and done, he was still there with me. Sweaty and limp and boneless for me to take care of, for me to nurse back to sanity.

"Yes."

"Is two cocks enough for you?"

Another whimper.

"It's okay to want more," I assured him. "It's okay to want it all."

"I do." He turned toward me, pupils shot and cheeks flushed. "I want everything."

Something bubbled over in the middle of my chest, and I chewed the inside of my cheek when I had to turn my attention away from him and back to the road. I was already in love with him. How many more new feelings could there possibly be to discover? How would they stack up against all of the shame and disgust I felt over my past with Dennis?

I shoved that idea to the back of my mind. It would keep until another day.

"It's yours," I said instead.

The drive to my condo took a lifetime, and Jason was leaning against the front door with his arms crossed over his chest when we came out of the elevator. He pushed off the wall and smoothed his hands down the front of his snacks. His stare tracked over me and then Val, lingering on Val's still undone fly.

"He was very eager," I said by way of explanation.

I opened the door and pushed it open for both of them to step inside. Locking it behind me, I toed off my shoes and dropped my keys in the bowl.

"No need for niceties," I told them both. "Go into the bedroom and get naked."

Jason smirked. "Demanding."

"Is it a problem?" I arched a brow, the question serious even if the tent between my legs called the validity of it into question.

"No," he said softly, unbuckling his belt and whipping it out of the loops. "It's not a problem at all."

"Jesus Christ," Val groaned, already half naked and halfway down the hall.

I gave Jason a gentle shove in that direction and followed behind the two of them, undoing my shirt one button at a time. Val was naked and crawling backward up the bed, eyes locked on Jason, who stood at the foot of the bed with his cock in hand.

"You don't have to ask to touch him," I said.

"What if I'd like to?"

I laughed at that, but it came out more like a growl than anything else. Shrugging out of my shirt, I set to work on my belt, studying Jason and trying to make sense of him.

"We can play those parts tonight if you both want that."

"What do you want?" Val asked.

"I want you." It was always that simple. "And I want you mindless from pleasure before you fall asleep in my bed."

"I want that," Jason murmured.

"Alright."

This wasn't the first role play we'd done and it wouldn't be the last. Even though Val and I weren't traditional with the Dom and sub things, it was fun to play into it sometimes. I'd given him a spanking on more than one occasion, tied him up and edged him until he'd forgotten his name. But they were just games for us, not a lifestyle like it was for some of my friends.

"Get up on the bed and eat his ass." I stripped out of everything except my underwear, watching Jason crawl between Val's legs like a predator. "Get him ready to fuck."

Val cupped his cock and balls in his hand, lifting them up and putting his pucker on display. Jason groaned and buried his face beneath Val's balls. I couldn't see what he was doing with his mouth, but I could hear the messy kissing and sucking, and then there were Val's gasps and moans. Jason curled his fingers around Val's legs and pushed them wide, making more room for him to feast. Val's eyes were barely open, but he focused on me at the foot of the bed and gave his cock a lazy stroke, letting his balls fall against Jason's temple.

Walking around the side of the bed, I pulled lube and some condoms out of the nightstand. I dropped one condom on the bed and tore the other open with my teeth, pulling my underwear down behind my balls and rolling the condom down my length. Jason grunted and sighed happily between Val's legs, adding his hand and what I imagined was at least two fingers, judging by the sound that left Val's mouth.

I cracked the lube and drizzled some down the cleft of Jason's ass. He tensed and shivered, then returned his attention to using his mouth to get Val ready to fuck.

"Is this okay?" I asked, pressing one hand against the small of his back. He arched and fucked his hips toward the bed. I teased the latex-covered tip of my dick against his hole, and he ripped himself away from Val's ass with a gasping breath.

"Yes," he panted, reaching behind himself and grabbing my wrist. He pushed my cock against his ass more insistently. "It's very okay."

"And you said Val was the eager one," I murmured.

He wanted my cock, but he was nowhere near ready for it. I shifted and pressed the tips of two fingers against his hole, swirling around the edge before easing inside of him. He groaned and Val cried out, then I pushed one past his tight ring of muscle. Jason's body was as receptive as Val, and it didn't take long for me to be confident that he was ready for more.

"You can suck his cock if you want," I said, lining myself up with his prepped and slick hole, "or his balls. He loves having his balls sucked."

Even after my fingers, Jason was still a tight fit. The flared crown of my cock popped inside of him and his movements stuttered. I waited for him to adjust and then gave him inch after inch until I was fully seated inside of him. He'd gone mostly still, fingers of his left hand curled into Val's thighs, the others lost between Val's legs. He wasn't touching himself. Just touching me and Val, and I closed my eyes, content to lounge in that feeling of perfection for a moment longer.

CHAPTER 28
VAL

JASON'S MOUTH WAS HOT AS A FURNACE, AND WATCHING BARCLAY'S face morph into that beautiful mask of relaxation as he slid into Jason's ass was almost enough to send me right over the edge. Barclay grabbed Jason's hips and bowed over his back, letting out a trembling breath.

"Fuck, you're tight."

Jason hummed happily, the vibration sending shockwaves right up my spine. His hand came around, taking my cock into his fist and I dropped my head back, trying to focus on the ceiling so I didn't blackout from how good it felt. I didn't think he was intentionally edging me, but I was walking the finest line right on the cusp of a very premature orgasm.

"I'm already close," I warned.

"Good." Barclay grunted. "You loosen up after the first one and I have plans for that hole of yours."

My lashes fluttered and my hips lifted off the bed. Jason sucked my balls into his mouth and I saw fireworks. The tight grip of his fist and the wet heat of his mouth…the way his tongue and teeth grazed over my most sensitive spots because of how hard Barclay fucked into him…

"Close," I murmured again.

"Come." Jason dropped my balls out of his mouth and swallowed my cock into his throat.

I cried out, jets of cum shooting against his tongue and the roof of his mouth. He groaned greedily as I drowned him with my spend, and as soon as the last burst had emptied, Barclay curled his hand around Jason's shoulder and yanked him up. It changed the angle of his penetration and a full body tremor wracked through him as he sank down onto Barclay's cock.

Still shaking, I curled up and crawled onto all fours, lifting his balls and flattening my tongue against where their bodies joined. Jason let loose needy little moans with every pump of Barclay's hips. Even through the latex, I could taste their sweat and fluids, my cock pulsing out another valiant leak against the sheets.

Barclay and I had never had a steady third for our bed. We did repeats, but part of the thrill was finding new partners who had new kinks. There was something to be said, though, for the consistency of someone who knew their way around your body and your bed. Even though it was only our second time with Jason, he fell right into the dynamic that had always existed for Barclay and me. I didn't want to say it was perfect, but it was damn good.

"No," Jason whined, shifting away from me when Barclay pulled out of him before either of them had finished.

"Patience."

Barclay softly smacked the side of his ass before falling onto his back and arranging himself beside me. He hauled me onto his lap, and I reached behind me to pull the condom off of him. I was still slick and ready from Jason's mouth and fingers, and Barclay found a home inside of me with little resistance.

"I haven't been able to stop thinking about your hands," he murmured.

As if it had been a demand itself, Jason situated himself behind me, fingers dancing softly around my stretched hole and Barclay's cock. He groaned and rested his forehead against my shoulder. He was sweaty and slick, and his free hand slid around my waist to support himself.

"Not my cock?" Jason asked with a laugh, tracing the shape of my hole with the tip of his finger. After my first orgasm and the consistent, hard thrusts of Barclay's cock, the sensation was electric. Gooseflesh broke out, racing down my arms and up my spine, and Jason splayed his hand across my stomach to steady me.

"That's more for him than me, I think."

"What about my hands, B?" Jason asked.

Barclay's mouth quirked into a smile at the shortening of his name, but the expression was gone as soon as the tip of Jason's finger entered me alongside Barclay's dick.

"Fuck, you're so tight when we're both in here," Barclay whispered.

I perched my hands against his chest, pressing back against Jason's front. His fingers moved swiftly at the place where our bodies came together and I sighed happily, vision going dark around the edges.

"More lube," Barclay said, but Jason was already moving like he'd read his mind.

I was half mindless with both of them paying attention to me, and I barely noticed when my crease became drowned with lube. It was cold and slippery, and then everything went white and burned. Fuck, it burned.

"Slower, slower," Barclay coaxed, two of Jason's fingers inside of me now, pressing flat against Barclay's dick. He still fucked me, just slower with longer thrusts of his hips up from the bed. Every withdrawal left me gaping around Jason's fingers, and then there was another finger, and another. And I was so impossibly full.

"That's enough," I murmured, grabbing Jason's hand which was back around my stomach, sliding toward my chest.

"Did you want to stop?" Barclay asked, going still.

"I mean it's enough prep. I can take his cock too."

I could do more than take it—I would devour it.

There wasn't much for me to think about besides getting the both of them inside of me, my brain quickly reminding me what it felt like to have Barclay spill into me and Jason chasing after into the condom. I thought about what it would be like to take both of their cum inside of me, having it mix and swirl together before sliding out of me. I shook so hard I almost forced Barclay's cock out of me, but he and Jason both held me down.

"You're not taking his cock," Barclay said.

I blinked my eyes open until I was able to bring his flushed face into focus. He looked like a god beneath me, with the pink blooming from his chest to his cheeks, the short dark hairs that sprouted from his sweaty and tanned skin. He was a man to be worshipped, and how I loved to kneel at his altar.

"I want it."

"I want something else," Barclay said, thrusting extra hard into me. The breath left my lungs in a rush and I collapsed against his chest.

Jason chuckled behind me, fingers still there.

"I know what you want," Jason murmured, "but this isn't a good angle."

"What do you want?" I asked, the words muffled against Barclay's sweaty chest. I'd give him anything. Everything.

"I want his hand inside of you, wrapped around my cock while I cum."

"I...I don't..."

"Of course you can." Barclay stroked his hands through my hair, over the back of my neck, down my spine. "You can do anything I want, can't you?"

I huffed a laugh. "I'm not sure that's how the saying goes."

"But it's true, isn't it? And think about how good it would feel. This cock that you love so much, this cock you dream about, tucked up so nice and tight inside of you with those fingers that got you stretched and ready for it. My cum against his fingers, against the deepest parts of you."

I shivered, mind floating back toward the blissful state of pleasure where nothing counted besides getting off. Barclay's hands were still on my back and Jason's were still dancing around the backs of my thighs and my hole.

"Do you think you'd feel it if he smeared my cum against your prostate?" he rasped, voice rough and low. "Do you think he could use my cum to milk some more out of you?"

I was fairly certain that yes, I would be able to feel that. But more importantly, I was certain that I wanted to find out.

"How do you want me?" I asked.

"I think…" Jason pulled away, and Barclay lifted me off of his cock with a slippery pop. Lube raced down my balls and my thighs, sticking to my hairs as I waited for them to decide how to make this happen.

"B, sit on the edge of the bed."

Barclay chuckled, and I tried to think of another time in the three years I'd known him that anyone had ever told him what to do before. Before I could find one, he sat on the edge of the bed, cock glistening and hard, pointing toward the ceiling. Jason climbed off the bed and stepped back, and I blinked slowly when my brain focused on the amount of lube on his hand.

"Valentin."

My name didn't even sound familiar through the lust-drunk haze.

"On his lap, but facing out."

I moved on reflex, and Barclay grabbed my waist to stop me. I looked at him, mouth softening at the sight of him. I loved him so much, and I'd almost lost him. How was any of this life possible?

"This is a lot," he said, taking my face into his hands and stroking his thumbs across my cheeks. I sighed and leaned into his touch, and he pressed a kiss against my forehead. "If it's too much, I'm happy to change course."

"It's not too much," I said. "Now that you've said it, it's all I can think about."

He hummed and lifted me onto his lap. "This work?"

"I think so." Jason grabbed the lube again and went to his knees at Barclay's feet. "Now put him on your cock."

I'd had a lot of sex in my life, and I'd had a lot of sex with Barclay. Even when things had been casual between us, I'd always felt cared for by him in a way that I knew he'd never admit to.

Even when he rough-fucked me until I had bruise-shaped finger-prints around my thighs or slammed so hard into the back of my throat I'd rescheduled a dentist appointment out of embarrass-ment, I couldn't remember a time when he'd ever relegated me to a fuck toy, which was exactly what Jason had done with his last instruction.

My balls ached to release a second time.

I fucking loved it.

I was getting ready to tell them both, when Barclay seated me back onto his dick and I sank down until he was as deep inside of me as he ever had been before. He was painfully hard, stretching and pressing against my pucker with every beat of his heart. I could feel his pulse batter against my ass, his heart against my back.

"That works," Jason said, taking Barclay's cock into his hand when it wasn't inside of me. "But I think…"

I couldn't see what he was doing down there, and Barclay couldn't either, I realized. It was an unexpected level of trust and closeness that had no place—or rather, every place—existing in a filthy threesome between a couple and a stranger.

"Do you need me to lift him?" Barclay asked, continuing to talk about me like I wasn't there and, honestly, I wasn't. I couldn't have made a decision to save my life because the only thing I wanted was for both of them to be inside of me and I wanted all of us to come again, and again, and again, until we weren't anything besides a mess.

"A bit," Jason said.

My legs didn't work, so Barclay hoisted my weight and Jason's hand replaced Barclay's cock, what felt like all four of his fingers, if not half his hand.

"Can you fuck him on my hand?" he asked. "It'll help loosen his hole."

I groaned and let my head fall back. There was only sensation and need left inside of me.

Barclay lifted me and eased me back down, and I cried out

when Jason's knuckles pushed past that ring of muscle. I'd taken both of their cocks before, and recently, but something about his hand felt thicker and more intrusive. Maybe it was the way they were talking about me like an object, like I was just a sleeve for them to fuck.

"I love it," I whimpered, because it was the only words I could string together and it felt important to let them know.

"I know you do." Barclay nipped at my earlobe.

I'd been sweating the whole time, but with Jason's hand fucking in and out of me, it was a cold sweat. I trembled in Barclay's hands, his fingers painfully tight around my arms as he worked me up and down on Jason's hand.

"Okay, slower now," Jason said softly, and there was another stretch. An impossible stretch as his hand made an O shape to accommodate the addition of Barclay's dick inside of me.

"Oh, God," I whined, fighting against the burn even though there was nowhere I wanted to be besides right there. "Help me take it. Help me. Help…"

"We've got you." Barclay's mouth was hot against my ear, whispering and kissing every bit of my face he could reach, and then my cock was in Jason's mouth and my entire life flashed before my eyes. The world around me went white and Jason's knuckles dragged over my prostate and then it was Barclay's cock. I shivered uncontrollably, every nerve in my body going absolutely haywire.

"Tighter," Barclay grunted, and then he groaned.

With short pumps of his hips, he fucked his way through Jason's fist, right into my ass.

"You're so fucking thick," Jason said, letting my cock slide out of his mouth. He kissed his way up and down my length, but it hurt. It was too sensitive. I wasn't even a fuck toy—I was just sensation and an orgasm that I knew was going to leave me unconscious.

The last thing I remembered seeing was Jason leaning back and jerking himself off. Cum sprayed out of his cock, landing against his chest and my calves.

"Fuck." Barclay growled in my ear, pace stuttering. "I love you. You're fucking perfect. You're fucking mine."

He bit down hard on the soft skin behind my ear and I cried out so loud my voice cracked. Jason cursed under his breath, and Barclay lifted me off his lap. His cock slid out of me, leaving Jason's hand inside. He searched out my prostate and with insistent circles, he massaged Barclay's cum into my gland until the floor fell out from beneath my feet.

I heard Barclay.

"Let him breathe."

And I was on my back, on my side. Barclay brushed my sweat-soaked hair away from my face and petted his hands down my sides. I moaned when he reached my ass, giving me a gentle spread before letting my cheeks fall back together. I groaned, and he kissed my temple, then Jason kissed right below him. And then I fell into a quiet and soft darkness, wondering what I'd done to deserve this perfect life and this wonderful man.

CHAPTER 29

BARCLAY

I FIDDLED WITH THE ENDS OF MY BOWTIE, BEYOND FRUSTRATED THAT I couldn't bring them anywhere close to even. They should have been good enough, but my nerves had gotten the better of me and my hands were shaking. Giving up with an annoyed grunt, I braced my hands against the mirror and let my head hang low.

Fuck Dennis and his stupid wedding.

Behind me, I heard the distinct click-clack of shoes, and then Val's gentle voice from the doorway.

"How do I look?" he asked.

I brought my head up enough to search him out in the reflection of the mirror, immediately needing to turn away as soon as I saw him. He was beyond breathtaking. The tux I'd paid to have tailored for him was well worth the money, and even with a quick glance I could see how the wool hugged the slim angles of his muscles.

"That good?" He let out a low laugh and walked closer, footsteps growing louder until his arms were wrapped around my stomach and his cheek pressed flat against my shoulder. I brought one hand down to cover his, straightening up with the intent to turn around in his arms. He was always so warm, always smelled so good, always felt like home, which was a new thing for me to make peace with.

It wasn't so much that I'd set myself apart from my friends or from people who'd felt the overarching need to pair up and settle into relationships, but after Dennis, I didn't think that was in the cards for me. Or more accurately, I hadn't wanted it to be in the cards. I'd fought against it so long and so hard, I'd almost lost the best thing to ever happen to me. And even though it was by no means smooth sailing yet, I was holding on to Val for dear life in the meantime.

"You look amazing."

"You didn't even look."

"I saw you." Using my hip to dislodge him, I turned until we were facing each other and then took his face in my hands. I'd seen him alright, and he'd looked so good I couldn't bear to watch him a moment longer. I dipped down and pressed a kiss against his mouth. It wasn't wet and I didn't use tongue. I wasn't trying to taste him, even though I'd know him anywhere. The kiss was a confirmation and a promise of all the things he'd taught me, even if I didn't know how to tell him as much.

"Do you still hate me being here?" he asked softly.

"You're just better than all of this," I said. I hated him being here because I didn't want him to see the ugliness I'd tried so hard to separate myself from.

At my answer, his mouth quirked into a smile and he puckered a kiss toward my thumb. "I know I am, but so are you."

"This is what I'm from," I reminded him. "Formality and hierarchy and financial transfers. Not from loud and rambunctious dinners around a too small table where everyone cares about each other."

"I know you're not like any of that," Val assured me, but it did little to calm my unease about the whole thing. I was right on the precipice of buying into this future he'd built for us in his head, and I wasn't sure how I would react if he pulled it away from me now.

"Is it that? Or are you worried about me meeting your parents? Meeting Dennis?"

The question was like a bucket of cold water. I licked my lips and took a step away from him, bringing me flush with the mirror. The meeting my parents part was something I hadn't even taken into account until earlier in the week. Dalton had brought it up casually on Thursday, laughing at how I'd held Val off for three years only to immediately bring him around my parents and my ex-boyfriend. Trial by fire, he'd called it, but the idea had grown like a disease in my stomach, only compounded by the guilt I already felt over bringing Val into a part of my life he was far better than.

"I'm not worried about any of it," I lied.

Val's bowtie was perfect. I picked at mine again, undoing the knot, ready to start from scratch.

"Are you sure?"

He smacked my hands out of the way and made effortless work of the thing, finishing and fluffing it before I even felt the fabric tug against the back of my neck.

"My parents don't care about my love life," I said, and it was true. "Dennis won't either."

It was true that my parents had gotten me into school, gotten me my first internship, but the things I'd earned for myself since then were fully mine. My condo was bought and paid for with money I'd earned. I wasn't daft enough to deny the leg up their money and name had gotten me, but I didn't rely on them the way I had before. Pissing them off would offer no substantial change to the state of my life, but it would have ramifications around my inheritance, which I did want to get my hands on one day.

I'd always taken it on the chin and entertained the things they'd demanded of me. Shown my face at the events they felt mattered, pursued the degree that they said would be the most beneficial to my future—and the family name—but beyond that, we lived very separate lives. I was thankful for it.

After the shock from the wedding invitation had worn off, I'd spent plenty of time debating if this was one of the events I could avoid, but it was too complicated. Between the parental expectation and Dennis's familial ties to the partners at the firm where I worked, it was easier to swallow my pride and go to the stupid wedding. I had no idea at the time that the wedding was going to become such a big deal and send everything into a state of upheaval, but…

"It's just a lot," he said, smoothing his hands down the front of my shirt. His fingertips danced along the top edge of my belt and I closed my eyes, trying to hone in on the way he touched me and not feel anything else besides him.

"It is a lot," I agreed. "Do you want to not go?"

"That's not what I meant. It's just from nothing to so much so fast. It would be fine if you were worried about it."

I laughed, rolling my eyes at him, but finally able to admit the truth between us. "It hasn't been nothing between us for a very long time."

"You know what I mean."

"It's just a fancy function," I told him, wanting desperately to believe it myself. "We'll make the appearance and then come back home."

"And then tomorrow…" He trailed off.

"I'll meet your family. If that's still what you want."

Val smacked my chest and turned away from me, waving his hand in the air. His footsteps grew fainter as he went from the bedroom to the living room. A cork popped out of a bottle and then wine glugged as Val poured himself a glass. I took a look in the mirror at the bowtie knot he'd made.

"Perfect," I muttered under my breath.

When I joined him in the kitchen, he had a glass already poured for me, one for himself, and two more ready to go.

"I do want you to meet them," he said. "But don't slip up around Angie and talk about marrying me, or we'll be hitched before sundown."

I clinked the edge of my glass against his, hoping my face didn't betray the flurry of emotions that churned at the idea of marrying him. I knew it was a lot, to go from being so against it to so on board, but that was his magic, wasn't it? He made every-thing feel so perfect, so attainable.

"Thank you," I blurted, and Val furrowed his brow, taking a sip of his wine and eyeing me over the rim of his glass.

"For the wine?"

"No. For…" I trailed off, sucking my tongue across the front of my teeth. Looking around, I found his sneakers by the front door, his keys in the bowl on the table. I knew he had dirty underwear in my hamper, and my Netflix watched list had started to include a surprising number of foreign language films.

"For?" he prompted.

"For waiting me out, I think."

Val huffed a laugh, cheeks turning pink. "It wasn't a hardship," he murmured.

"Wasn't it?"

Any chance at an answer was interrupted by a loud and demanding knock on my front door. Val startled, and I cursed Dalton under my breath for knowing how to ruin a moment.

"I'll let them in," Val offered.

I nodded, because of course he would. Because my house was much his now, so of course he'd let Dalton and Royce in. I listened to them exchange pleasantries at the front door, and then the three of them were in the kitchen and Val was offering them the wine he'd already poured and laughing like they were old friends. It was a sight to see, and my chest ached at the comfort of it.

"You all right?" Dalton asked.

Royce patted Val on the shoulder and the two of them turned away, engaged in a conversation that Dalton and I were clearly not meant to be a part of.

"I'm fine," I told him. "Just thinking."

"Penny for your thoughts?"

"I don't make deals with loose change, Fox."

Dalton laughed and came around to join me on the other side of the kitchen island. We turned our backs toward Val and Royce, resting against the edge of the counter and admiring the view of the city through the far window.

"You look distracted."

"Wouldn't you be?"

Behind us, Royce laughed.

"There's not a single thing in the world that could take me away from living and breathing for that man back there," he said, bumping his elbow into mine.

"Sounds miserable," I teased, even though my heart wasn't in it.

"He's the best thing to ever happen to me."

"Val is…Val is too," I said.

"I know. I'm glad you didn't ruin it."

Scoffing, I took a drink of my wine. "I don't think Val would have let me ruin it."

"You were both pretty close to the edge there at the end," he said under his breath.

"I know that too," I agreed. "Thank you for always being here to talk sense into me."

"Are you sure you're all right?" he asked, left eye squinting at me. "The Barclay I know hasn't ever been the thankful type."

"He's the quiet type, asshole. That doesn't mean I'm not thankful for you and your friendship."

"Are you dying?" he asked, cheeks flushed as he held back a laugh. "Is that why you gave into Val? Trying to give him what he wants before you kick the bucket?"

"I'm not dying."

"Then why are you being so fucking nice?"

"I'm not being nice." I finished the last of my wine and set the glass down on the counter with a soft clink. "This whole…relationship…has just put a lot into perspective for me. Meeting Jason…"

Dalton cut me off, raising a hand. "Who is Jason?"

"This man that we sometimes…you know."

He laughed. "Don't get coy now."

I thought about how very *not* coy I'd been earlier in the week with Jason's hand around my cock and both of us so far inside of Val that I'd wanted to make a new home there.

"It doesn't matter who he is. He's a friend who has also helped me see that I could have spent a lot of time being a better man to him," I gestured over my shoulder, thumbing toward Val, "and a better friend to you and the rest of them."

"You're my best friend, Barclay. As you are, and as you always have been."

My eyes started to burn at the inner corners, and I blinked long and slow to try and get the feeling under control.

"I feel the same." I cleared my throat.

Dalton swallowed down the rest of his wine and clapped me on the back. "Now that that's out of the way, let's go get this fucking wedding over with."

WE SKIPPED THE WEDDING ITSELF, WHICH HAD ALWAYS BEEN Barclay's plan and I didn't have any protests about it. The four of us finished the bottle of wine I'd opened at his condo, then arrived at the reception right on time. The venue was a little ostentatious for my taste, with lots of white roses and glass, but it was the first time the depth of the wealth I'd surrounded myself with really hit home for me.

I'd always known Barclay made more money than me, that he came from more money than me. In an abstract sort of way, I'd understood the trappings that came with having last names that carried weight and bank accounts that followed close behind, but seeing it in real life was something else entirely.

"This is a lot," I murmured, giving Barclay's hand a tight squeeze. It was nearly impossible to hold his hand tighter than he was holding mine, but I wanted to support him. I wanted to him to know that while I might not understand all of it, none of it scared me, and he was worth whatever came up.

"I know."

"This is tacky as fuck." Dalton flanked me on the left, adjusting his bowtie with one hand and clutching his husband's hand with the other.

To my other side, Barclay snorted.

The four of us were near the door, taking in the cocktail space, when a man to Barclay's other side stepped up and cleared his throat. Barclay's posture straightened, but his shoulders sagged under the movement. He didn't let go of my hand.

"We didn't see you at the ceremony, Perceval."

"We were running behind, Mr. Barclay," Dalton offered, reaching past me for a handshake.

"Dalton. Good to see you again. How are your parents?"

Even before Dalton had interjected and addressed the tall, older man, I knew it was Barclay's dad. Their faces were the same shape, but the elder Barclay wore the name like it was a shield, when the younger had always carried it like a burden.

"They're well enough," Dalton said. "Have you met my husband?"

"Your father told me about him."

Royce made a sound in the back of his throat and offered a handshake. "Carter Royce," he said.

"I know who you are," Barclay's father said, his stare dancing between the three of them before landing on me. "I don't know who this is."

Barclay hadn't let go of my hand, and at the comment, he still didn't.

"Valentin Russo," I said, fighting my way out of Barclay's death grip so I could shake his father's hand. "It's nice to meet you."

"Isn't it." It wasn't a question. "This is my wife, Monica. Perceval's mother."

"A pleasure to meet you," I said, giving her a softer shake than I'd offered her husband.

"Perceval hasn't told me a thing about you," he said, and I could tell it wasn't meant to be a barb, but these people didn't matter to Barclay and they surely didn't matter to me. I thought about how Angie would have read him for filth after a dig like that, and a small smile flickered across my mouth.

"We've been together for three years," Barclay said, stunning all five of us.

"And you haven't thought to tell us about him?" Monica asked. She didn't look offended, just…like she was making some kind of conversation about the weather or endangered animals in Africa.

"You've never asked," Barclay said simply, taking my hand back in his. "If you'll excuse us, we have to find our table."

"And offer Dennis your best wishes," Barclay's father said. "It's still a shame about the two of you."

Another barb that I shrugged off as best I could. Dalton rolled his eyes and jerked his head toward the other end of the room.

"Barclay, my mom is dying to see Val again," Dalton said, a lie. "Let's go find her."

Barclay gave a nod to his parents, and then we followed after Dalton and Royce. We were halfway across the room before he breathed again, and I smoothed my hand up and down his spine until the sounds of his inhales and exhales went quiet.

"One down," I reminded him.

"Thank you," Barclay said to me, then he turned to Dalton. "And thank *you*."

"That's what friends are for, Perceval," Dalton said with a smirk.

"I fucking hate that name."

"Maybe some drinks are in order," Royce suggested, which felt like the best idea anyone had come up with all day.

The bar was, of course, open, and we were on the back half of our second round, engaged in a conversation that had even Barclay laughing at the absurdity of it, when a man I'd never seen before came up to our group and softly cleared his throat.

"Barclay," he said gently, and judging by how rigid Barclay went at the sound of his name, I knew who'd joined us.

Dennis.

I wanted to touch Barclay, even something as simple as resting my hand against the small of his back, but the whole event was precarious and I didn't want to make him uncomfortable. I didn't want to overstep and make things harder for him or worse. For once, I didn't know what he wanted from me. I was standing half behind him when he turned, and Dalton and Royce both crowded in, flanking Barclay like they were his own personal defense.

"I didn't think you'd make it," Dennis said, tilting his head to the side.

He was an attractive man, or he at least could have been at some point. The lines around the corners of his eyes were deep and while he had sharp cheekbones, his mouth pulled down into a near constant frown. It looked like it took real work for him to smile, so he'd just given up.

Admittedly, he was exactly the kind of man I'd pictured Barclay with, at least up until I'd gotten peeks of the *real* Barclay underneath the hard shell of his public facade. Because my Barclay, my Percy...he was fun and lighthearted, even if he didn't always want to be. He wasn't dour or unhappy, and both of those feelings rolled off Dennis in waves, even though we were at his wedding.

"The invitation made that nearly impossible, and you know it," Barclay said. His tone was clipped, abrupt.

"Right." Dennis offered a half-smile at that. "Well."

It was almost conniving, and I settled by hand against the small of Barclay's back because he deserved to know I was there for him, just like his friends. It was important that he understood that even though there'd been a time when he was jealous of me being with another man, I didn't harbor the same feelings.

His past was the past and his future was mine.

Dennis's stare caught my proximity, and his mouth was back in a frown when he said, "I don't believe we've met."

"Theme of the night," Dalton muttered from behind me.

Barclay scoffed, a low noise in the back of his throat, and I offered Dennis my hand as graciously as I could manage, considering the circumstances.

"Valentin Russo," I said. I didn't say it was nice to meet him because it wasn't, and I wasn't in the habit of being a liar.

"How do you know our dear friend here?" Dennis asked.

"He's my boyfriend," Barclay answered for me.

I took my hand from Dennis's grasp and slid it back around

Barclay's waist, and he matched the move with his around mine. He was so warm, so solid. I leaned into him, hoping he understood that even in the face of this uncertainty, he was still all the support that I needed.

"Your parents didn't say you had a boyfriend," Dennis said.

"It's not their business."

"So it's a new thing?" he asked.

"It's not."

If we were going to lie to everyone about the duration of our relationship, I wasn't going to argue about it. Admitting that we'd been *just friends* for three years before things changed wasn't my proudest moment, but I also knew the shift in the timeline didn't come from a place of shame or embarrassment. Barclay really had considered himself in a relationship with me for the past three years, even if he'd done everything in his power to avoid admitting it to himself or even calling it that. Because the things between us that had changed over the past few weeks were perfunctory, at best. My feelings for him were the same as they'd always been, and his for me were also unchanged.

"I don't want to keep you from your guests," Barclay said, which felt like a dismissal. Dennis received it like one, reeling back at his words. "But before you get caught up with the celebrations, I did want to…thank you."

The words almost sounded choked out, but I did my best to not react.

"What for?" Dennis asked.

Barclay leaned in and dropped his voice. "For fucking Professor Danielson."

There was that weird twitch of Dennis's permanently frowning mouth. He shuffled half a step back, trying to smile like the two of them were in a cordial conversation and not whatever they'd just dipped their toes into.

"How do you mean?"

"I'm sure I would have caught you eventually," Barclay said, "if not with him, someone else. But I spent a long time thinking the way you treated me was what I deserved."

Dennis rolled his eyes, dragging his tongue back and forth across his teeth, and it was the first time I caught a glimpse of the man underneath his exterior. Much like the way Barclay kept himself tucked away from the public, Dennis apparently did the same. But whereas Barclay was a good man beneath the bravado, a kind and loving man, Dennis looked rotten to the core. "Isn't it, though?"

"The way I love Val…" Barclay trailed off, shaking his head. "No. The way I allow him to love me…you paved the way for that."

"What do you mean?"

"You made sure that I would never settle for someone like you ever again. The way you treated me, treated our relationship…it all but ensured I would only take the absolute most. And that's what Val has always given me. So, thank you."

I sniffed, splaying my fingers against Barclay's waist and digging in hard.

"That's stupidly romantic," Dalton said under his breath, and I let out a nervous laugh at his comment.

"I love you too," I said to Barclay, resting my head against his shoulder. "Thanks, Dennis."

"Thank you, Dennis," Dalton said.

"Thanks, Dennis," Barclay said again

"Thank you," Royce chimed in, and more of that attitude rushed off of Dennis before he managed to get his head out of his ass and leave.

"Come dance with me," Royce said, taking Dalton's hand and tugging him onto the dance floor.

When it was just the two of us, Barclay let out a shaking breath and set both our glasses on a nearby cocktail table. He took my face into his hands, eyes searching my face like he was desperate to find something there, even though he didn't know what he was looking for.

"Did you mean that?" I asked, covering his hands with my own.

"I can't believe I almost lost you."

Tears pricked at the corners of my eyes, but I wasn't going to let go of his hands to swipe at them as they overflowed and raced down my cheeks and over his fingers. The truth was a horrible thing to admit, but it was important to me that he knew.

"I never would have left you," I whispered. "I know I said, I know I..."

He cut me off, crashing our mouths together in a fiery kiss. His tongue speared past my lips, and Barclay kissed me so hard my body bent backward toward the floor. He supported me so I didn't fall, then yanked me back onto my feet. His cheeks were pink, his pupils shot, and his breath came in unsteady gasps. Nothing like the way he'd breathed when Dennis had been around.

"I never would have let you," he said softly. "I would have done anything—"

"You did," I reminded him, "You did everything."

"Will you dance with me?" he asked, leading me onto the dance floor beside Dalton and Royce because he already knew my answer.

"Always, Percy," I whispered. He pulled me against his chest, sliding one arm around me and raising my right hand in his. "Always."

Dennis's wedding changed my life.

I hadn't realized how badly I needed to see him, how much I needed to face the truth of my relationship with him to understand what a special gift Val had given me. We danced and drank together, we laughed, we touched. Everything felt new in an unexplainable way, and even though I'd been as *in* with Val as my heart allowed, I was really and truly *in* with him now.

"You're not yourself," he whispered in my ear, head resting on my shoulder in the back of the car.

The four of us had stayed more than an hour at the reception, but we'd still left well before midnight. Dalton and Royce invited us over for a nightcap, but I promised them another time. I wanted to get Val home and I wanted to get him in bed.

"I haven't been myself since I met you."

"That admission is also achingly out of character."

I traced the shape of his hand, fingers splayed against the top of my thigh.

"Do you still want me if this is how I am now?" I asked. "If I'm comfortable this way?"

The driver pulled alongside the curb in front of my building, and Val busied himself getting out of the car instead of answering me. On the curb, he took my hand and followed me into the building, resting his head against my shoulder again in the elevator for the ride up to my place. His silence finally started to wear on me, and I stopped him in the hallway before I put my key into the door lock.

"You didn't answer," I said.

"I'm tired, Barclay," he replied, lips stretched into a tight line. "It's been a long night."

"But hasn't it been a good night?"

"Can we go inside?"

I think I liked it better when he wasn't talking, I decided. But I unlocked the door and stepped aside so he could go in. I followed after him, tossing my keys into the bowl by the door. In my head, this was as far as we'd gotten before I pressed him up against the wall and kissed him until he begged for more. The reality was different, with Val bending over and loosening the laces on his shiny black shoes. He kicked them off and shuffled away from me, into the bedroom without another word.

I didn't bother with my shoes, chasing after him with the urgency my nerves demanded. I found him sitting on the edge of my bed, bowtie knot already loose. He toyed with the buttons of his shirt, but they were small and the material was starched, and I went to him immediately, going down to my knees between his spread legs so I could reach him. He sighed heavily when I plucked the first button, and his shoulders sagged when I got to the second.

"I thought you had a nice time," I said softly, finishing with the buttons and moving on to his belt.

"I did."

"What's wrong, then?"

"What's wrong with you?" he countered.

I undid his fly and tugged. Val lifted up enough that I could wiggle him out of his pants. He shrugged out of his jacket and then popped the cufflinks around his wrists to get out of his shirt.

"I feel great," I said. "Or I did until we got into the car and you asked me why I was acting funny."

He snorted and shook his head, chin to his chest. I braced myself against his thighs and angled my head so I could get a look at his face. This was a new fear, the realization that Val maybe didn't really love *me* or want to be with me. That he was interested in the version of me that I'd been for so long it felt real, but wasn't. Because after seeing Dennis and having Val by my side, I felt more myself than I had in years. It was like the pieces of a puzzle had clicked into place and I saw everything clearly for the first time.

"It's hard to not think that if you'd done this sooner, there would have been someone better for you than me," he said.

I laughed, because the idea sounded so preposterous to me that it had to be a joke. But Val didn't laugh. His jaw tightened and his lips pulled into a thinner line than before. I swallowed back the rest of my amusement, the noise choking off in the back of my throat.

"Are you being serious?"

"Deathly," he whispered.

"Even if I'd faced the truth of him before, there wouldn't have ever been anyone like you."

"You don't know that."

"Of course I do." I lifted onto my knees, bringing our faces closer together so he could see the sincerity of my words. "I've never met anyone like you."

"You deliberately didn't meet people before me."

"I met plenty of people before you," I said.

He rolled his eyes and the tension in his mouth softened slightly. It was still there, but it was a step in the right direction.

"You're the one who changed me," I said. "No small task."

He scoffed.

"Look at me," I went on, waiting until he angled his face enough that I could see his eyes. "Look at *me*. On my fucking knees for you."

Val sucked in a breath, and on a deep inhale I caught a whiff of his arousal. I was shit with emotions, and I would be for the rest of my life, but this...this I could work with. Val and I had spent three years communicating with our bodies, and just because we were boyfriends in love didn't mean that should stop.

There was such a thing as multiple fluencies.

"On my knees for you because you deserve to be worshiped," I murmured.

His cock was inches from my face, half hard, but the tip was slick with precum already. My own erection pressed insistently against the fly of my slacks, but I would ignore it for as long as I had to.

"The man who changed my life." I tilted my head closer to his lap. "The man I love."

"Percy."

"Tell me what's wrong."

I kissed the flared ridge of his cock and his hand immediately went to the back of my head, fingers threading into my hair. I kissed his cock again, then I licked him. I kissed his balls and his shaft, drug my tongue across his leaking slit. He still didn't protest, so I took him into my mouth entirely. Val was still half soft and his cock sat heavy against my tongue. His fingers tightened in my hair and I hummed around the size of him. Almost immediately, he started to thicken and grow, but I fought against the gag so I could keep him in my mouth. He stretched against the roof of my mouth now, inching toward my throat.

"I'm scared," he rasped, bringing his other hand around to cradle the side of my face. I leaned into him, letting the base of his swelling cock slide out of my mouth so he could touch me the way he wanted. "Scared of what I want. Scared of what you're offering."

I let loose a knowing hum that made his dick pulse against my tongue. I related to everything he'd just said, even if he didn't know the depths of it. I'd spent three years damn near being scared of the way I wanted him. Except finally admitting it had been the most liberating thing I'd ever done.

There was no way I could keep breathing with his now fully-hard cock pressing into the back of my throat, so with hollow cheeks I eased back slowly and slid back down. His fingers dug into the back of my scalp and he let his head fall back. His thumb aimlessly dragged back and forth and back and forth across my cheek as I slowly worked my way up and down his shaft.

"When we were at the wedding, when we were dancing…"

I grabbed the base of his dick with my hand and held him pointing toward the ceiling. Out of my mouth and in the dark of my room, the city lights reflected through the window and off the spit on his shaft. I gave him a hot and slow lick from my fingers to the tip and waited for him to go on.

"When we were at the wedding," I prompted before giving the underside of his cock a wet kiss.

"I let myself pretend."

With my lips still spread around him, I nodded, encouraging him to keep going. If Val thought his confession was going to scare me, he had another thing coming entirely.

"That maybe one day you and me…"

"I'd marry you," I told him.

Val made a pained noise and shoved me so hard I fell away from him and onto my ass, barely catching myself before my head banged into the floor. He was a sight there on my bed, naked save for his dress socks with his hair still perfectly styled and his cock hard enough to cut glass. I looked down at myself, still completely dressed, but I knew he'd made a mess of my hair. Balancing myself on one arm, I scrubbed a hand down my face, wondering if the truth had been the wrong thing to give him.

"Why?" he asked.

"Because I love you."

"Why?"

I moved to crawl back toward him, but he was off the bed in a flash, pinning me to the floor. His cock smeared precum over the black wool of my slacks and he pinned my biceps to the floor with trembling hands.

"Why do I love you?" I asked.

He nodded.

"Because you've given me my life back," I told him. "Because you saw the truth of me when no one else did. When I didn't even see it."

"And what is the truth of you, Percy?" he croaked.

"That all I want is to be known."

He licked his lips and angled his eyes toward the window to avoid my stare. I didn't have it in me to worry that the truth was too much for him anymore. I couldn't find it in my heart to be afraid of losing him. Running on faith and fumes, I trusted that my assumptions about Val had been right all along. Even though I'd kept myself locked away and hidden from everyone, even my closest friends, he'd seen the crack in my facade. Maybe not from day one, but for a very long time he'd seen that gap and he'd happily picked away at it until he found room for himself inside my heart.

Inside my life.

And it was the only thing I'd ever wanted. For someone to care enough to put in the work, because my parents had given up on me long ago, and Dennis... My life had been one long line of people taking what they wanted from me and offering nothing in return, convincing me that was all I was worth. Val was the first person who had seen more in me. Whether he'd been the first person I'd *allowed* to see more or not didn't feel important to me. He was the only one who'd even bothered to try.

For three years he'd chipped away and waited for me to see him standing there in front of me. I'd come so treacherously close to losing him...thinking about it still sent a shiver up my spine.

"And do I?" he asked.

I shoved off the floor, bringing my hands around his back to stop him from falling after the move. He let out a startled gasp at the proximity, and I relished the heat of him, the feel of him.

"You know me better than I know myself," I told him. "Does it scare you?"

He shifted his weight, bearing down on my throbbing erection.

I grunted, hips bucking off the floor of their own accord and pressing against him.

"I know it's what I've wanted, but this feels too fast sometimes."

"You've waited three years."

He huffed out a noise that almost sounded like a laugh, if not for how miserably sad it came out.

"*I've* waited three years," I said next, pressing his chest against mine. He was on my lap, a little taller than me for once, and I tilted my head back to gaze up at him. "I've waited longer than that for you. I didn't even know."

Val rolled his eyes, but a tear fell from the corner. He blinked quickly, lashes clumping from the ones he'd managed to hold back.

"I understand why you are the way you are." He took my face into his hands, thumbs stroking across my cheekbones. "After meeting your parents, meeting Dennis."

"I am the way I am because of you," I said. "The way I was before had to do with them, sure. But now? Out here in love with you, talking about marrying you?"

My voice cracked, and Val leaned in and pressed his lips against mine. It wasn't even a kiss. It was just shared breath, a moment to regroup.

"You've shown me the importance of all the things I didn't think I needed, but I do need them. I need them as much as I need you," I murmured against his lips. "I don't think you understand how much you mean."

"Understand what?" Val leaned back just enough for me to speak unhindered.

"I'm a jealous man, Val. I'm possessive and I'm greedy, and I feel all those things when I think about you."

"You share me."

"I share you because I know that you're mine." I crashed our mouths together and swallowed down the moan that bubbled up in his throat. With my lips parted, I speared my tongue against his, kissing him until I couldn't breathe. Gasping, I told him again, "I know that you're mine. I don't have to be greedy because I know when everyone else is gone, you'll still be here."

"And the possessiveness?" he murmured.

"Of course I want everyone to see what's mine."

"They do more than see."

Finally.

Finally the pursed line of his lips softened into a smile.

"They do more than see because *you* want them to do more. You want them to touch," I said.

"You like when they touch."

"I like when you feel good. I like seeing you smile and I love seeing you come." My cock pulsed against him at the thought of it. "I like when they know their time is limited with you and mine isn't."

"Jealous." He dropped a kiss against my mouth.

"I'm not a good man, Val. But I'm yours."

"You're the best man."

Another kiss, longer and softer.

My head was spinning a mile a minute, from Val's earlier hesitation to the way I'd talked him around. It was what I wanted, but it wasn't. I didn't want to convince him to be with me. It was important he want that on his own, like he always had. He'd waited while I realized it was what I wanted, what I needed, and it mattered that we stand together in those feelings.

"Are we okay?" I asked. "Is this okay?"

"It'll be okay once you're inside of me, I think."

I tightened my arms around him and pushed us both up enough so I could get him onto the bed. Tearing open my belt, I shoved my pants down and used my body to shove him further back on the bed so I could nestle between his legs. His fingers scrabbled at my bowtie and my buttons, then my cufflinks. My shirt was half off when I found the lube, and I still had one leg in my pants when I got my cock wet for him.

I lined up and shoved inside with a grunt. Val gasped, arms

coming around my shoulders and fingers digging into my bones. I should have prepped him, should have gone slower, but *this* was what he did to me.

He made me frantic for him.

"God," he whimpered. "You feel so good."

"Is this okay?" I asked again, pulling out an inch and pushing back inside. "Are you okay now, Val?"

Everything about Val had me on fire. The way he looked at me, the way he touched me, the way his muscles clamped down around me when I was buried inside of him. He was a drug, and I'd been a goner since the first taste.

"We're okay," he whispered. "I'm okay. I'm okay."

I started to move in earnest, chasing after an orgasm that had been within reach since we left the wedding. Reaching between our bodies, I grabbed his cock and gave a long stroke to the tip. I needed him to come. Needed to see the orgasm wash over his face and the cum stick to my fingers.

Val had turned me into a desperate man, and when he hooked his ankles around the backs of my thighs and cried out into the crook of my neck, I was done for. Jets of his release splashed against my fingers and his channel grabbed my dick so hard I thought it would snap off.

"Don't be scared of this."

"Come inside of me, Percy," he pleaded, voice shaking.

I let my head fall against the sheets, right beside his ear. With his legs and his arms, he pulled me deeper, and when it was time for my orgasm, I didn't have a thing to say. I took a mouthful of the bedding between my teeth, no sound falling past my lips as my cock swelled and spilled inside of him. Everything went white and then black, and then there were fireworks against the backs of my eyelids when I came back to myself.

"You're okay," he said softly. "I love you and we're okay. I'm sorry, I just..."

"I love you so fucking much." I said it to him once and then over and over again because I needed to be sure he believed me. I'd spent so long…I needed him to believe me.

"I know." Val kissed my temple. "I'm okay, Percy. But if you really meant what you said, I'll be even better once you put a ring on my finger."

I woke up Sunday morning with a delicious ache between my legs and a heavy weight on my chest. Barclay snorted softly, his breath puffing over my nipple on every exhale, and I didn't bother to open my eyes. I shifted enough to get one arm around him and the other one up so I could tangle my fingers into his hair. He still had product in it from the night before, but there were pockets of softness to be found. With a quiet hum, I worked my way through his hair, tightening my arm around him when his snoring turned into stilted breathing.

"Did you mean what you said last night?" he asked quietly.

"Good morning." I kissed the top of his head. "I said a lot of things."

"You know which one."

Licking my lips, I rolled my head back and forth, deepening the pillow indent I'd made while I slept. Barclay was still half on top of me, his body a comfort instead of a hindrance. His question was a fair one because we'd said a lot of things to each other over the three years we'd been together, but I'd never once lied to him and he knew that.

"Yes."

"You're sure this is what you want for the rest of your life?" he asked. "Even after meeting my parents, seeing that debacle last night?"

"All I saw last night was the man I love dressed to the nines, whirling me around a dance floor in front of people who don't mean anything to us."

It was as much the truth as the rest of it and I needed him to understand it. Just as I understood that being in a relationship with him for the long term wasn't going to be an easy road. Barclay was a jaded man with a laundry list of insecurities brought about by the circumstances of his upbringing and the people he used to know. It would probably take the rest of his life to break him of some of those old habits, but they'd kept him together this far and I wasn't keen to knock him down any more than being with me already had. And besides, it wouldn't be a hardship to show him often—and ardently—that I was in love with him.

He rolled the rest of the way onto me, straddling me and sitting up. It was a change in one of our more familiar positions, and I tucked my hands behind my head, perfectly content to stare up at the messy morning version of him. I loved the broadness of him, the dark hair and the tanned skin, the soft but visible muscles in his stomach and shoulders. Everything about him was perfect, as far as I was concerned.

"Are you sure?" I asked, dragging my palms up his thighs and back down. "For someone who didn't want to even date me, you've made a quick turn."

"I never want to be without you."

"Is marrying me…dating me…is that just a compromise so you don't lose me?" I asked.

"Isn't that the point of a relationship?" He cocked his head to the side, the question sincere across his face. "You want to be with a person, so you do what you have to do to be with them?"

He was right.

I was pushing and poking at meaningless semantics. At the end of the day, he'd decided I was worth fighting for and he'd fought.

Even though I had to push him all the way to the edge and very nearly over, the outcome had been the same. I'd gotten the man I wanted…and so had he.

"You're right," I conceded.

"I need you to trust that I want you."

"I do," I whispered.

"That I'm committed to this."

"I do."

The corner of his mouth quirked up. "Say that again."

"I do." The words were barely louder than a whisper, but they were practice.

On the nightstand, my phone screen blinked on and the device vibrated with two sharp buzzes. He glanced at them and I reluctantly took one of my hands away from his leg to check the message.

"Anyone interesting?" he asked.

"Jason texted last night to see how it went," I said, scrolling through a couple other that had come in overnight to find the new one, which was from my sister. "And Teresa is asking if she has to set an extra place at the table tonight."

"And every Sunday after," he answered.

"Say that after you survive the first one."

"If you can make it through the wedding, I can make it through a family dinner at the Russo household."

I laughed, dropping my phone onto the nightstand before wiping sleep from my eyes. "So you say."

He bent down and pressed a kiss against the corner of my mouth, and I gripped the back of his head to deepen the kiss into something more suitable for the two of us. Barclay smiled against my lips, but broke the kiss before my cock had gotten all the way hard.

"Breakfast," he murmured.

I reached for his cock, and he grabbed my wrist before my fingers could make contact.

"You're mean," I whined.

"You're the one who said you wanted to marry me."

"I was drunk."

He let go of my wrist and rolled off of me with a chuckle. I turned onto my side so I could watch him stand and stretch, admiring the gorgeous view of him. He must have sensed my eyes on him because he threw a coy look over his shoulder at me before padding into the bathroom. The door didn't close, but the shower turned on, and he shouted out, "Are you coming?"

"I wanted to," I grumbled, kicking down the tangle of sheets so I could join him in the shower.

For months, Barclay had treated the wedding invitation like a curse, but as I stood and stretched my fingertips toward his ceiling, I knew it was a blessing, a catalyst. Even after he'd agreed to date me, things had felt rough between us, sharp. At first, I had worried it was a concession, but after the conversation we'd just had, I knew that wasn't how *he* saw things between us. This was the progression that made sense to him. It maybe wasn't conventional, but then again, neither were we. The way things went for us was what worked best, and that was all that mattered.

For the first time since I'd told him about Jason, it felt like the air around us had settled. There were times when I'd worried I was forcing Barclay into something he didn't want, but after the past few days, the wedding…I knew that wasn't the case. He was as dedicated to things with me as I was to things with him, and that was the strongest foundation we could ask for. Even though part of me didn't believe he would follow through with marrying me, I didn't mind. We were as together as Dalton and Royce were, legally bound or not.

"Get in here, Val," he called out again from the bathroom.

I snorted, rolling my eyes.

"Yes, Sir," I yelled back with a laugh, heading toward him.

———

All things considered, we had a nice and calm breakfast. Barclay fielded texts from Archie and Flynn about the wedding and the state of our relationship. It was fine, he said. It was better than fine, he said. He didn't let go of my hand, always seeking out some kind of physical contact with me, even while we ate. I had to swat him off so I could cut my waffle without elbowing him in the ribs, but I didn't think he would have minded if I did.

It was a new piece of him, another block out of the wall around his heart. Maybe the biggest yet, revealing the most tender and vulnerable parts of him. Over the course of the day, I understood the care I had to give him as we stepped into the next chapter of our relationship. Barclay was taking a massive risk on me, and I needed it to pay off. It was important he believe he'd made the right choice in me.

After we ate, I convinced him to come back to my house so I could get some laundry done. We spent most of our time at his condo, which was fine with me. It was bigger, brighter, and nicer. But he made himself at home on my couch like it was his, content to scroll through my Netflix while I sorted weeks-old laundry in the other room. It had been so long since I'd spent a meaningful amount of time at home…

"Hey," I said from behind the couch, laundry basket propped on my hip.

He turned around, remote still in hand.

I pulled a pair of plaid slacks out of the hamper and gave them a little shake. "It's been weeks since I wore these," I said.

"You should wear them again. I like how they make your ass look."

Heat flooded my cheeks. "Thank you, but that wasn't the point."

"Was the point that you need to do laundry more?" he asked.

"The point is that I haven't been here to need to do laundry."

My washer and dryer were in a small closet in the hallway, and I carried the hamper that direction, dropping it on the floor in front of the machines.

"Because you're always at my house," he said, missing the point entirely. He watched me throw clothes into the wash.

"Exactly."

I dropped a detergent pod in and started the cycle.

Barclay was still watching me, and I saw the moment when realization dawned on him.

"The answer is yes." He let go of the remote and reached his arm over the back of the couch for me. I went to him without protest, letting him drag me over the couch and halfway into his lap. One leg sprawled over the back and the other kicked into the arm, but just like breakfast, he never let go of my hand.

"What was the question?" I whispered.

He flashed a smile that turned his entire expression soft and tender.

"Yes." He brushed hair back from my forehead. "I want you to move in."

"You're zero to one hundred, aren't you?"

He jokingly covered my mouth with his hand, and I licked him.

"When is your lease up?" he asked.

I nipped at his palm and he pulled his hand back so I could answer. "Two months."

He hummed, frowning.

"Too quick?" I asked.

Barclay pulled me upright, taking my face into his hands. "Too slow."

"Zero to one hundred indeed," I repeated, the words disappearing into his mouth as he quieted me with a kiss. It was a better kiss than the last one, giving my cock enough time to get hard. I circled my hips against him, reaching down between us to grab the hem of his shirt and get it off of him. He let me, but with a low rumble of a laugh that vibrated my whole body.

"What?" I ripped my own shirt off before he could stop me.

At the sight of my bare chest right in front of him, his nostrils flared and he flattened his hands against my back, fingers splayed wide like he was trying to cover as much surface area of my body as he could manage. I suppose it should have made sense that he would turn out to be as tactile as he was because, even in the before times, he'd always been there for me physically. Even if it had been different parts of his body most of the time.

"I want to get you off."

"Good," I said quickly, going for my fly next. "You should."

"But I need you to get me ready for dinner."

"Great. I'll get you off too." I slid out of his arms and went to my knees on the floor. He grabbed my fingers before I could get his belt undone, and I blinked up at him with a frustrated pause.

"I meant I wanted a crash course about your family."

In any other circumstance, his interest would have caused my heart to expand five times too large, but all the blood in my body was well on its way between my legs and there wasn't much else for me to think about besides getting off. Sometimes, I hated how much I thought about sex, how much I wanted it, but…it wasn't my fault he was so fucking sexy. I couldn't be blamed for giving into the need he brought out in me every time he looked at me the right way.

"Can we not talk about my family when your cock is in my mouth?" I had his pants open enough that I was able to wrestle his dick out from behind the waistband of his underwear.

"My cock isn't—"

His words ceased abruptly as I swallowed him into the back of my throat. With a happy groan, he lifted off the couch to push the rest of the way into my mouth, his fingers tangling into my hair. With his cock in my mouth and my cock in hand, it didn't take long for either of us to come. Barclay coated my tongue with it and I spilled all over my hand and the front of my pants. He watched with hooded eyes while I licked us both clean, and when the timer on the washing machine went off, I flopped back onto the floor with a groan. I was still throbbing and Barclay was still hard, shaft pulsing like a heat-seeking missile.

"Angie is a teacher and Teresa is a veterinarian," I said, still struggling to catch my breath from my orgasm.

"Can we not talk about your family while my cock is inside of you?" he asked.

"Your cock isn't ins—"

But he launched off the couch and landed on top of me before I could finish the sentence, proving to me once again that everything besides me and him could—and would—wait.

CHAPTER 33

BARCLAY

My nerves about meeting Val's family didn't show up until the front door to his childhood home was already halfway open and the sounds of a loud argument tumbled out onto the porch.

"Should we wait?" I asked.

"Why?"

I gestured toward the door with the bottle of wine I'd insisted on bringing. "It sounds like they're arguing."

"They're not," he said simply, stepping inside. "But they will be if we leave the door open for much longer."

I followed him inside, taking stock of the house that didn't look like it had been updated since the late nineties. The front door opened right into a living room with beige and brown carpet that had definitely seen better days. The entertainment center was made from oak and the couch was brown leather and well worn. Family photos in mismatched gold and black frames were speckled across the walls, and two young kids sat in front of the TV watching a show I'd never seen before.

There were two men Val's age on the couch, both of them drinking beer. They looked up when we walked in and one of them smirked before shouting over the noise, "Val's boyfriend is here!"

"Fuck you, Drew."

"Do I need to take my shoes off? I asked Val, who snorted a laugh and rolled his eyes at me.

"It'll be harder to escape the inquisition if you do."

I wasn't going anywhere, but I knew it would take time to prove that to him. I kept my shoes on and closed the door behind me.

"This is Teresa's husband, Drew," he said, pointing at the man who'd announced my arrival. "And this is Marcos, Angie's husband. This is Barclay."

"That's a name," Marcos said with a grin.

"Better than my first name," I assured him with a nod. Some good-mannered teasing wasn't anything I couldn't handle. I got more than this from Archie on any given Thursday night. "But nice to meet you just the same."

"Please be nice," Val begged his brothers-in-law.

Drew made an X over his heart and Marcos shrugged.

"Ange is mad Teresa has met him already," he said.

"It wasn't planned," I said.

Marcos smiled as the noise from the back of the house started to move closer. "She won't care. Good luck."

Val's expression flickered, but I grabbed his hand and dragged a kiss across his knuckles.

"I'm fine," I promised before he could ask. "Let's go."

Teresa pushed her way ahead of two women who looked very much like her, coming at me with an apron around her waist, a glass of wine in her hand, and her arms outstretched.

"Barclay." She hugged me like we were old friends. "It's about time."

She bumped Val out of the way and hustled me through the living room and into a kitchen that looked about as old and loved as the front of the house. Ignoring the protests of another woman, who I assumed had to be Val's other sister, Teresa walked me right to the older woman in the kitchen, who gave me the longest appraisal anyone ever had.

"Mrs. Russo," I said, extending the bottle of wine in her direction. "It's nice to meet you. My name's Percy Barclay."

"Percy."

I recognized Marcos's voice already, much closer behind me than I had expected it to be. He was right there with Drew beside him, Val shouldering them both out of the way to make it back to me.

"Told you," I said to him, before turning back to Val's mom. "My friends call me Barclay."

"What does my son call you?" she asked.

"Barclay most of the time," I answered. "Percy when it's important."

Val pressed against my back, his hands bracketed over my hips and his chin poking over my shoulder.

"Barclay, Mama," he said.

"He's good, Mom," Teresa said.

Val's mom traced the front of her teeth with her tongue, then clicked it against the roof of her mouth and nodded. Behind me, Val exhaled loudly.

"If he's so good, what took so long?" she asked.

I coughed, choking on my spit. "Things have only been serious for a short amount of time."

"Really?"

I shrugged, still holding out the wine for her. "I've loved him longer than he knows, but yes."

"Stop," Val pleaded in my ear. "You'll make me cry."

"It's true."

"Where's Dad?" Val asked, pushing his way next to me and shoving Teresa into the wall.

"Out back," Angie said. "I'm Angela, by the way. The sister you haven't had dinner with yet."

"A glaring oversight," I said by way of apology. "Maybe next time I'll stumble into you on accident at Val's house."

"Well," he mumbled behind me, hand sliding off my waist and searching out my hand.

"One thing at a time," I said.

"We're going to find Dad."

Val gave my arm a rough tug and pulled me through the kitchen, past his sisters and his mother, past a dining room table with twice as many chairs as it looked like should fit there, and toward a sliding door that led to a small concrete back patio. Outside, it was easier to breathe, and Val's dad looked up when we stepped out onto the concrete pad.

"Finally," he said, sliding an unopened bottle of beer toward the empty seat beside him and dipping his chin toward his chest. "Valentin, go help your mother."

"She's fine," he said. "Angie and Teresa are in there like always."

"Go help your mother," he said again.

I hadn't dated much, hadn't dated ever really, but I'd seen enough movies to know what this was. Turning, I pressed a kiss against the side of Val's head and let go of his hand.

"I'll be in soon," I told him. "I'm fine."

"If he's not back in five minutes, send your mom out," Val's dad said.

Val groaned and shook his head, then trudged back into the house and pulled the slider closed behind him. After he was gone, I sat down in the chair next to Val's dad and waited for him to speak. He didn't for a long moment, so I opened the beer and took a drink to calm the nerves that threatened to collapse my spine for how tight of a hold they had on me.

"I heard you say your name is Percy?"

"Perceval," I corrected. "It's a family name."

"So is Valentin." He tapped his hand against his chest. "It's mine too."

"I didn't know Val was a junior."

"He's not." The elder Valentin shook his head. "Different middle names, after his mother's brother."

"That's nice," I said, realizing I had already moved him in and decided I wanted to marry him, but I didn't know Val's middle name. It wasn't like his name had any bearing on my dedication to him, but it only served to highlight how backward and misguided our relationship had been.

"You look like the kind of man who knows what to say in situations like this."

I barked out a laugh because that couldn't have been any further from the truth.

"Admittedly, I'm out of my depth. Val is the first person I've dated since college."

"Why's that?" his father asked.

There were a thousand ways to answer that question, but the truth of it came down to one simple fact. "No one was him."

We both took drinks of our beers.

"What do you do for work?"

"I'm a lawyer," I said.

"Partner?"

"Yes."

"Good." He nodded, bottom lip pushed out in thought.

"I love you son," I blurted before he could get another question out. "He's changed my life, and I love him for it. I hope it's not a problem that I'm a man."

"I don't care that you're a man." He waved me off dismissively. "Would your family care that my son is a man?"

"My relationship with my family is complicated and it doesn't matter to me what they think," I said.

"But would it?"

"No."

That was also the truth. My parents had regulated many things in my life, but they'd never cared whether I was involved with men or women. I was thankful for that as, in some small way, it had given me more grace than some of my friends had grown up with.

"Here comes Margie," he said, stare flickering toward the sliding door behind me.

I was glad he'd spoken because in the mess of our arrival, I hadn't caught her name. I didn't know if that was intentional, but I filed it away just the same, standing when the door slid open.

"This is nice wine, Barclay," she said, closing the door behind her and walking around to the seat opposite me.

"Thank you."

I sat back down and took another drink of my beer. Her arrival had to have indicated I'd made it past the first five minute mark, which felt like a win. When it came to my life, I didn't care what my parents thought about Val. I'd be happy for them to never see him again after Dennis's wedding, but this was a different situation altogether. Val had a big family, a loud family, a loving family. If they didn't like me, there was a very real possibility there was no future here for me.

I couldn't stand the idea of that. After all I'd done and fought through to get to the point where Val and I now were…the thought of losing all of it because of a botched dinner introduction had my blood ready to boil. Adrenaline coursed through my veins, the fight or flight instinct ready to kick in at any moment. I took a deep breath, swallowing it down and counting to five. Using court tricks I hadn't needed in years, I brought myself back under control.

"When my son told us about you, he said you'd known each other awhile but it had just gotten serious," Margie said, and I answered her with a slow nod. "Why the delay?"

I huffed, the nod turning to a helpless head shake. "Because I was a fool."

"Rightly so," she murmured.

"I'm making it right."

"How?"

"I'm getting a new drink." Val's dad flattened his hands on the edge of the patio table and shoved his chair back. It grated against the concrete, but Margie didn't flinch. She regarded me quietly until her husband was back inside, the door was closed, and we were alone.

It was that shift where I realized, even though I should have always known, this family was a matriarchy and the meeting with Val's father wasn't a test. It was a warmup.

"How are you making it right?" she asked again. "He's my only boy. He deserves the world."

"I'm giving it to him," I said.

She arched a brow, and I shoved my hand into my pocket, searching out the smooth gold band I'd bought earlier in the week. I sat it on the table between us, knowing that even if Val peered out the window, my body would block his view.

"Are you now?" she asked.

"If you'll allow me."

Margie hummed a thoughtful sound and raised her glass, taking a healthy drink of the wine I'd brought with the intent to impress her. She didn't say anything, and I covered the ring with my hand and slid it back across the table so I could return it to my pocket for safekeeping.

"Are you going to wait three more years?"

Chuckling, I shook my head. "I wouldn't dare."

"Do you make him happy?"

"I like to think so," I said.

"Teresa said she thinks you do. She said to be nice." Margie's mouth quirked into a wry smile that let me know she knew exactly what she was doing with this hard and intimidating act.

Inside the house, one of Val's sisters shrieked and then everyone's voices rose far beyond a conversational level. Margie's stare went over my shoulder and her smirk turned into a soft smile. I glanced back, finding Teresa with a spice jar in her hand and Angie trying to bodily remove her from the kitchen. Val leaned against the wall, glass of wine in hand and a happy look on his face while he watched his sisters battle it out for the seasoning.

"The tarragon is a nice touch," I said, turning back to face Margie.

"I know," she agreed. "But don't tell her that at my table."

I pressed my hand over my sternum. "I would never."

She cleared her throat and stood, taking another drink as she righted herself. I could tell this was the end of my interview, so I pushed my chair back as well. Checking my pocket for the ring, I finished my beer and waited because even though I was sure I had passed, I got the impression there was still something on her mind.

"Are you going to elope?" she asked me softly.

Another cry from inside the house and then Teresa was at the stove with a spoon in her hand, dumping seasoning into a bubbling sauce pot.

"I'll give him whatever he wants."

"My son is a romantic at heart."

"I know." I looked inside in time to catch Val's eye, and he gave me a small wave. His mother saw it, and she tutted her tongue against the roof of her mouth before walking around to my side of the table and patting me on the back.

"Invite us to the reception at least," she said. "Whether he wants that or not."

"Of course," I promised, breath leaving me in a rush.

"And don't forget about the sauce." Margie's hand was on the slider, and her eyes were narrowed in warning.

She pulled the door open, letting all the smells and the sounds roll out onto the patio. They crashed into me with the force of a storm, and I was assaulted with the understanding this wasn't anything new for her. This was a normal Sunday night, a normal *every* night if she'd wanted it. In that moment, I'd never been more certain of the richness and vibrancy Val brought to my world and how desperate I was to never be without it again.

"Tarragon is a sin," I confirmed.

She nodded her approval.

Her blessing.

"Welcome to the family, Percy."

CHAPTER 34
VAL

THE NEXT MORNING, MY ALARM WAS THE MOST UNWELCOME SOUND I'D ever heard in the entirety of my life. Barclay stretched across me and turned it off, burying his face into the dip of my throat and licking his way up to my chin.

"Call out of work today," he murmured against my mouth.

"Why?" I arched back, giving him more access to my body.

"So I can marry you."

"You don't even have a ring."

He reached beneath the sheets and took my half-hard cock into his hand. "It's on the bathroom counter next to your toothbrush," he said, giving a slow pull up my length.

I pressed my body against his with a low and scratchy moan.

"My mom will kill us," I said.

"She knows."

I sucked in a gasping breath and shoved him off of me, sitting bolt upright in bed. The sheets pooled around my waist, doing nothing to hide the erection he'd already coaxed out of me. "What do you mean?"

He rolled onto his back, dropping his head onto my lap and blinking up at me innocently. "I asked her permission to marry you last night," he said.

"You just *met* her last night."

"I can multi-task, Val."

"What did she say?" I asked.

"Do you really think I would be proposing you take off work and marry me if she had an issue with either the act itself or the attendance level?" Barclay's mouth twisted into something that almost resembled confusion before it settled on a look I hadn't seen in weeks.

Doubt.

"We don't need to get married. I know we talked about it, but..."

"I want to marry you." Barclay crawled over me and went down onto one knee on the floor. "I need to marry you."

"You know it's a yes," I whispered. "I just..."

"All I've ever wanted is for you to be happy. I love seeing you happy, making you happy, making other people make you happy."

He had both of my hands in his and I chuckled at the last part, but it came out sounding a little watery.

"On the bathroom counter, you said?"

He nodded and then jumped up, running off buck naked into the bathroom. He came back and went onto his knee a second time, a thick gold band held up between his finger and thumb.

"I never want to be without you," he said softly.

"Even though I'm needy?"

"Especially because you're needy."

"Are you going to get tired of sharing me?" I asked. "When we're living together and married, are you still going to be okay with those parts of me?"

"Sharing you is the sexiest thing I've ever done." He scooted closer, knuckles brushing against my cock and the ring still clutched between the tips of his fingers. "As long as it's what you want, it's what I want."

Barclay's words were almost too good to be true. It was impossible to sit in his bed with a ring right in front of me and not reflect on how much had changed between us over the past handful of weeks. It hadn't been so long ago that I'd stood in front of his bedroom window and worried about losing him for good. When I'd bartered pieces of myself for a sliver of him because I was terrified of letting go. Maybe it was desperate, but my heart had always been true in its course.

I held my left hand out and he slid the ring onto my finger.

"How does it fit so well?" I rasped.

"Because I know you."

"Yeah." I bent down and took his face into my hands. "You do."

The ring weighed a ton on my hand and his lips dusted across my mouth like they were feathers. I pushed myself off the bed, deepening the kiss and lowering down onto Barclay's lap. He snaked his hands around me and angled his head to the side, licking into my mouth with a new and somehow calm kind of insistence. Like he had all the time in the world to sit on his floor and kiss me.

"I have to be honest about one thing, though," he said, hands roaming over my body as torturously slow as his mouth.

"Tell me."

"I don't know your middle name."

I chuckled, fingers digging into his shoulders. "Anthony."

"Valentin Anthony Barclay," he whispered, and I moaned, loving the sound of it almost as much as I loved the idea of it.

I was lost in a years-old fantasy that had somehow become my reality, and I barely noticed when he opened the lube and slicked his fingers, but I definitely felt the cool and wet press of them inside of me. Out of instinct, I sank down onto his hand, throwing my head back with a groan. He kissed along the underside of my jaw and up to my ear, nipping at the lobe while he prepped me to take him.

"Is it wrong that I want you to be full of my cum when you marry me?" Barclay grunted in my ear, fingers sliding out of my body. He quickly notched the slippery head of his cock against my still gaping hole and arched his hips up to get inside.

"No." The answer punched out of me with a sharp breath as I settled down fully around his thick length.

He crashed our mouths back together, coming to me urgently, but kissing me with the same kind of lazy possession he'd started with. Tangling my fingers into his hair, I tried to pick up the slow and steady pace he'd set with his hips, but a firm hold around my waist kept me anchored to him. Barclay pumped into me with short and sharp thrusts, his mouth still as close to mine as he could manage.

Between our stomachs, I took my cock into my hand, letting the force of his thrusts fuck my shaft through my fist. It was a steady repetition that started the goosebumps against the back of my neck and sent them down my spine. The familiar heat in my balls as his cock dragged over my prostate with every slide of his body into mine.

"I'm close," he murmured, breaking the kiss and gasping for breath as his entire body went tense and still beneath me.

With our foreheads together, his cock swelled against my rim, pumping me full of his cum, just as he'd promised. Listening to the way his breathing turned labored and shaking with his release, I fell over the edge with a short cry. Cum spurted out of my cock, smearing against my fingers and stomach until it hurt to touch myself. Barclay's cock was still hard and firm inside of me, and I shivered, falling against his chest with a tremulous laugh.

"Guess we should get going," I choked out, lashes fluttering as I gave myself a breath to enjoy the sharp scratch of his coarse chest hair against my cheek. "Before you have to put another load inside of me at the courthouse."

He groaned, adjusting his arms around me and lifting enough to get my ass and his knees onto the edge of the bed.

"Please don't threaten me with a good time." He kissed the corner of my mouth and then very slowly pulled his cock out of me. His hand was down there as soon as my hole gaped after him, scooping up any cum that had slicked out and pushing it back inside with his fingers.

"Marrying me today isn't good enough on its own?" I teased, but the jest had his expression quickly turning somber.

"It's everything," he said, so seriously.

I pushed up onto my elbows and gave him a soft smile.

"I know," I said. "Let me email my boss and then we can go?"

Barclay's mouth twitched into a smile, and he looked like a boy, a younger version of himself who had never found cause to build a fortress around his heart. He looked happy and ready to face the future...

With me.

———

Three hours later, we were married and sitting at a small table outside a coffee shop down the street from the courthouse.

"I should tell my mom," I said, still admiring the ring.

"She said we have to have a reception," Barclay said with a small grin. "She wants to come to that."

"She wants to plan it. She just hasn't told you yet."

"Let her have her way." He waved his hand in the air dismissively. "I have the only thing that counts. How did *you* want to celebrate?"

An unexpected laugh bubbled out of me, and I had to cover my face with my hands to stop it from getting loud enough to draw too much attention. The events of the morning, of the whole weekend, were absolutely absurd. If we had been anyone besides ourselves, things could have gone so differently. They probably would have. I didn't know many men who would have been as patient as I'd been, and even fewer who would have survived that wedding unscathed. But I'd always seen past Barclay's defenses, whether he liked it or not. It had taken me more than three years to get through them, but I knew the prize was waiting on the other side. And I found it over and over again in the way he smiled at me as we said our vows, and in the promise of his kiss when we sealed them in front of the clerk.

"I suppose we should tell your friends," I said.

"Our friends."

"And Jason."

"Like I said." He shrugged. "Our friends."

I smiled at my lap, dropping my hands down so I could spend some more time admiring my ring without looking lovesick about the whole thing. From the corner of my eye, I saw Barclay pull his phone out and tap at the screen.

"Should I send them the picture?" he asked, showing me the screen and the picture the clerk's assistant had taken of us at the makeshift altar in the middle of the utilitarian carpeted ceremony room.

"Why not?"

I pulled my own phone out of my pocket to thumb over to the picture so I could see it myself. Even though we had tuxes still ready enough from the wedding on Saturday, we'd opted for something more casual. I wore the plaid pants he seemed to be so obsessed with, paired with a white button-up and brown oxfords, and he'd worn black slacks, a black blazer, and a black button-up, the top couple of buttons undone. In the picture, he looked at me like I hung the moon, and my chest felt weak with the intensity of it. Like breathing was hard, doing anything besides *being* loved by him was unnecessary.

I opened my messages from Jason and sent him the picture along with a message that read, *SURPRISE!*

His response came quickly.

Jason: That's the least surprising thing about the two of you.

Jason: But congratulations just the same.

Me: Barclay says we should celebrate soon.

Jason: Just tell me when and where.

Me: Would you be okay to meet some of our other friends?

Thinking about Jason at Rapture or Cunningham's, or any of the places we normally went was almost a culture shock. But he was a good man, a great friend, and I knew that he would have a lot of fun with us…if he wanted to.

Jason: I'd love to.
Jason: And I'd love to take the two of you out for a celebratory drink too. Privately.

I swallowed, heat flooding my face.

Me: We'd like that.
Me: Text you soon.

I sat my phone on the table, laughing under my breath and the positively frustrated expression on his otherwise handsome face.

"What's wrong?"

"I hate this group chat" he grumbled. "Are you sure you don't want to get new friends? Jason's nice. We can start with him."

"He sends his congratulations," I said. "He's happy to go wherever we invite him, but he also said he wants to celebrate a little more privately at some point."

"I'm sure you'd like that," Barclay murmured, turning his eyes back toward his phone.

"What do the Trophy Doms have to say?" I asked.

"Varying stages of shock," he said, dropping his phone onto the table. "Dalton says he's surprised we weren't secretly married the whole time."

"That's much more his speed than ours, I think."

"Archie is mad he didn't get to throw me a bachelor party. Flynn and Rob send their love, which feels much more agreeable."

"Expected responses all around, then."

My phone buzzed, and I pulled it toward me, finding a message from Archie on the screen preview.

Archie: It's about time.
Archie: I'm happy for you. You deserve this.

Me: Thank you

"Who was it?" Barclay asked.

"Archie. Of course."

"Is he wanting to throw you a party too?"

My mouth twitched into a smirk and I shook my head. "He sends his love."

"Why is he nice to you and not to me?" Barclay asked with a pout.

"Because I'm clearly your better half."

He reached across the table and grabbed my hand, turning my palm down so my ring sparkled in the late morning sunlight.

"That's so true," he said softly.

"I need to get you a ring," I said, flipping his hand so it was on top. It was the wrong hand, but the sentiment was the same.

"I need to get you a key."

"Yeah," I said happily, "you do."

CHAPTER 35
BARCLAY

BY THE TIME VAL AND I ARRIVED AT RAPTURE, ALL OF OUR FRIENDS were already there. Our friends, and their boyfriends, and some new additions to the mix as well. We were running late because I'd had too much fun dressing him up in his tux and then edging him until he cried and screamed at me. It was more Archie's speed than mine. I'd always been in the market of giving Val everything he wanted and then some, but it was fun to put him on edge for once. Especially knowing what he was walking into.

When we reached the landing in the loft, a whoop of cheers went up so loud that I was sure it drowned out the music on the dance floor. I had Val's hand in mine and he gave them a triumphant little shake, even as he shied back behind me a step.

"It's the same people who've always been in your corner," I assured him. "The only thing different is you've proven them all right."

He smiled, cheeks flushing under the dim neon of the loft.

He could disagree all he wanted with the statement, but I'd spent years with my friends in my ears accusing me of being in love with the man I'd just made my husband. Spent years denying it and fighting them over it when the truth was right in front of all of our faces. Val had probably seen it first, then them, and I was the last to catch on. But better late than never.

The noise didn't die down, and then all our friends were on their feet. It was crowded and overwhelming, even for me, but Val and I were hugged and kissed and given drinks. I lost my hold on his hand, watching reluctantly as Grayson hauled him to the far end of the loft toward Rose and Rose's friend, Drake. Owen was over there and so was Flynn, which meant it was Rob's arm that came around my shoulders as Dalton's hand slid into mine.

"Does it feel right?" Rob asked.

"Like it should have been this way all along," I admitted.

"I know that feeling," Dalton said, letting go of my hand.

There was room on the couch next to Royce, and I collapsed down against the cushions with a rough breath.

"You look happy," Royce said in greeting. "Congratulations."

"Thank you."

"So, what are your plans for tonight?" Rob asked, eyeing the other group of them over my shoulder.

"I was hoping to play it by ear."

I felt a familiar warmth behind me and then Val's lips pressed against my ear softly.

"Jason is here." He kissed my temple.

"Do you want me to go get him?"

"Archie's already…" he trailed off.

I hadn't even seen Archie sneak off, but I found Jason and Archie in front of me at the top of the stairs. Archie looked like he was in some serious kind of conversation with the man, and Jason, for his part, looked receptive to whatever he was being told.

"I'll go save him," Val said. "Don't want Archie to scare him off."

"Love you."

Val grinned, heading for Jason and Archie. Jason's eyes sparkled when Val approached them, and he gave Val a hug that to most would have looked friendly, but I knew our friendship was different than most. I didn't expect our group of friends to understand the complexities of our relationship with Jason, but they didn't have to. They'd never understood the whole of Val and me, and that was fine.

Our relationship was ours.

"Who's that?" Dalton asked, jerking his chin toward the trio who'd rejoined the larger group.

"Our friend Jason."

"Friend."

"Friend," I confirmed. "With benefits."

"Is he a steady thing?" Rob asked.

"He's not the only, but…"

"I don't know how you do it," Rob muttered.

"That's fine. You don't have to."

"I think I would murder someone who put their cock into Ivey," Dalton said, using the ridiculous nickname he favored for his husband.

"You tried to put Kale into a wall and he's never even thought about me that way," Royce teased. "You possessive brute."

"Kale?" Grayson dropped down on the arm of Rob's chair. "Why are you throwing decorative trash lettuce around?"

"His best friend," Dalton patiently explained, "is named Kale."

"Do people like him more than they like his namesake?"

Rob elbowed Grayson in the ribs. "What did you want?"

"I came to see if you wanted a drink. I was going to run downstairs and get a refill." Grayson gave his empty glass a shake.

"Sure. Get one for Barclay while you're down there."

"Yes, Sir," Grayson gave Rob a mock salute as he stood, but Rob's nostrils flared at the honorific just the same. After he left, I turned to answer Dalton's question.

"Val's different," I said. "I enjoy seeing other people get a taste of what's mine."

"But then they come back for more?" Rob arched a brow. "That Jason man?"

"It's not like that."

"You've said that before," he said. "About Val specifically."

I sighed, knowing there was no easy way to explain why Jason wasn't a threat. If anything, he was a supplement. And I knew we brought a steadiness and satisfaction to his nights that he enjoyed as much as we did. If things changed, they would change, but Val and I never would.

"Don't worry about Jason," I said, holding up my hands. "I don't."

"Then neither will we," Dalton assured me. "Anyway, plans for the night?"

"Hadn't set anything in stone," I said, leaning back and stretching out my legs. "We just wanted to spend some time with our friends."

"Unfortunately, even though half of us have fucked Val at some point, I don't think that's in the cards tonight," Rob said.

"I'm not worried about it. Jason is here, so is Drake. They're plenty of fun."

"Now or later, then?"

I dragged my tongue across the front of my teeth, unsure. Looking up, I waited until Val's attention drifted in my direction. I raised an eyebrow in question, angling my head toward the hallway that held the private playrooms. He grinned, giving me a lopsided shrug.

"Maybe both," I said, pushing up off the couch and dusting myself off.

"You're far too old for that," Rob teased.

I smacked him on the back of his head, then pointed at Val, Jason, and then Drake. The closest playroom was open, and I caught Grayson on the top of the stairs with three drinks balanced unsteadily in his hands. I took one for myself, thanked him, and pushed the playroom door open.

"Leaving so soon?" he whined.

"We'll be back. Don't you worry."

Val, Jason, and Drake filed in behind me, but when I tried to close the door, Flynn's massive body stopped me in my tracks.

"We just want to watch," he said, Rose tucked halfway behind him with wide and very aroused eyes. "If that's okay with you."

"It's okay," Val answered. "As long as it's okay with Jason and Drake."

"Not the first time Rose has seen me naked," Drake answered with a laugh.

"No pictures or anything," Jason said.

"Of course not."

"Then it's fine."

"Everything we do is always private," I assured Jason. "At least, as private as we want it to be. Even if it's public, it's ours. Not for anyone else. And that goes for *all* of my friends."

I emphasized the word, hoping he understood what I was trying to tell him. Our entire friend group played it loose sometimes, but we respected boundaries and limits across the board.

"Alright." He licked his lips and nodded. "I don't want to overstep, but I've been dying to get my cock into your husband for what feels like forever."

"Patience is a virtue," I said with a smirk. "Isn't it, Val?"

"I think you used it all up in the last three years." He palmed himself between his legs, and I closed the door behind me.

Val was a fucking sight.

He was beautiful. Always. Constantly. Consistently.

With a crook of my finger, I beckoned him toward me and he was quick to close the space between us. I reached up and tugged at the knot on his bowtie, groaning happily as it came untied around his throat. His breath smelled like toothpaste and whiskey, and I opened his shirt, one button at a time.

I undressed Val like it was my honor because it very much was. Stripping him bare for my own pleasure, for the observation of our friends…it made me hard as fuck.

Flynn had taken a seat on the couch and propped Rose on his lap, their size difference on full display as Flynn leaned close and said something undoubtedly indecent in Rose's ear.

A few feet away from them, Drake was like a puppy with

barely contained energy ready to pounce. He shifted his weight from one leg to the other, stare flickering from the way Flynn moved his hands over Rose's body to the way I did the same with Val. Jason leaned casually against the wall, belt already undone and his cock visibly hardening behind his fly.

"I'm going to strip you naked," I said softly, only for Val to hear. "I'm going to bend you over the bed in here and pump you full of cum."

He whined, back arching as he leaned desperately into me.

I got his jacket and shirt off, then his shoes and pants, his underwear, and finally his socks.

"I'm going to make sure it's my cock that gets you off the first time." I took his face into my hands and stroked my thumbs across his cheeks and down. "And only after I'm satisfied with how hard you've come, will I let anyone else touch you."

"You do have a possessive streak after all," he murmured.

"You are my husband."

"I am your husband," Val rasped, lashes fluttering.

"Go bend over the bed."

He went and did as I'd told him to do.

Pulling down my fly, I went to the armoire against the far wall and grabbed the lube and some condoms. Jason and Drake knew the rules.

"You can have your way with him after I get him off," I told the both of them.

Drake moved closer to Jason, all that energy rolling off of him in waves. He said something to Jason that I couldn't quite hear, and then he was on his knees with his face pressed against Jason's bulge.

"Look at that," I said to Val, fisting his hair and turning his head toward the side so he could see. "They're so horny for you they can't wait. Almost everyone in this room is desperate to fuck my husband. How does that make you feel?"

A primal and needy sound fell out of Val's mouth, and I knew the edging earlier in the night had already done its job. He was beyond words.

"How does it make you feel?" Flynn asked from the couch.

I chuckled, pouring some lube over my fingers and teasing them up the crack of Val's ass.

"Powerful," I said, glancing back over my shoulder. "Like I've won a prize that everyone covets."

"A trophy, indeed," Flynn murmured, chin propped on Rose's shoulder.

"Do you hear that?" I asked Val, pushing one of my fingers into him all the way to the last knuckle. "You're my trophy."

His hips bucked against the bed and I added a second finger. Pressing my other hand against the small of his back with my fingers splayed wide, I held him down, knowing his cock was smashed between the sheets and his stomach. I imagined it hurt, but only in the way that felt good. He would have told me if it was otherwise.

"Please fuck me," he whimpered.

"I'm going to."

I fucked him with my fingers until sweat beaded in the dips at the small of his back, and then I pulled my cock out of my pants and covered my length with lube. Bending my knees to get down to his level, I notched my cock against his hole and pushed inside. Lifting his hips to get a better downward angle, I situated myself fully inside of him. Val's cock pointed toward the bed, hard and shiny with strings of precum leaking down to the sheets. Across the room, Jason groaned, threading his fingers into Drake's hot pink hair.

Although we had an audience, it was impossible for me to not get lost in Val. Even before he'd become the man who'd given me everything I never allowed myself to believe I wanted, he'd been the one person who understood enough of me—and himself—to wait and to try. It was more than the way our bodies communicated, it was the way his heart had known mine from the start. I'd never admit that in front of other people, but he knew. Because I told him as much with every stroke of my fingers and pump of my hips.

"I'm coming," he blurted the warning just in time for me to watch cum jet from his cock and splatter against the bedding beneath him. His cock pulsed and jumped, every muscle in his body going taut as he finished. Angling one of my knees onto the bed, I hauled him half upright, pressing his back against my chest so I could get a deeper angle as my own orgasm came closer.

Val thrashed in my arms, oversensitive from the teasing earlier and the force of his orgasm, and I curled my hand around his cock and stroked. He dropped his head back onto my shoulder, hair damp with sweat as it stuck to my cheek and the side of my neck.

"Do you want me to stop?" I whispered the question, even though I already knew the answer.

"I want more."

Even frantic with his arousal, Val was predictable. He always wanted more, and I'd spend the rest of my life making sure he had it.

"Make me come and it's yours."

He spread himself open, one hand coming around the back of my head and the other grasping at my thigh. The move pushed his chest out and lessened the depth of my thrusts, but it was such a bare and vulnerable position, it was impossible to not give him what he needed. My pace stuttered when I thought about how much I loved him, when I reflected on how good he made me feel, and my dick pulsed inside of him, spurting as deep as the position allowed. I thought about how whoever else fucked him the rest of the night would have to wear a condom, using my cum as lube, which milked another jet of cum from my balls. I shivered, taking both of our bodies down to the bed until I'd finished entirely inside of him.

Untangling Val's arms, I arranged him neatly on the mattress. He was sweaty and sticky, nearly boneless. His favorite way to be, my second favorite way to have him. I was slow to pull out, leaning down and brushing his hair away from his face to kiss his cheek.

"Are you good?" I asked.

"So good," he murmured. "More."

"Greedy." Standing, I gave a sharp slap against his ass. He moaned and lifted up, wiggling his ass, so I spanked him a second time.

I tucked my cock back into my pants and zipped up, stepping back and glancing over at Jason and Drake.

"You remember the rules?" I asked them both.

"Condoms, yes," Drake said, pulling his slobbery mouth away from Jason's cock.

"Kissing, no," Jason added.

"Good." I bent down and dropped a kiss against the middle of Val's back. "I'm going to get a fresh drink and come back. You okay?"

"So okay," he said with a tired smile.

"I love you."

His smile flashed wider before his entire expression softened again. "I love you."

"Be good and have fun," I told the three of them, trying to figure out where I'd set down the drink Grayson had got me before we'd come into the playroom. "I'll be back."

I passed Flynn on the couch, his hand curled around Rose's cock, dragging up his surprisingly substantial length with lazy and loose strokes. Rose looked like he wanted to crawl out of his skin, and Flynn looked like he sat on top of the world.

"Do you want a drink?" I asked.

"Rose will need one soon," he said with a smile. "Won't you, baby?"

"Please," Rose whimpered.

I chuckled, shaking my head at the fantasy that had become my life.

I'd secretly fought against my friends coupling up the way they had because I didn't want things between us to change. Even though I hadn't always been the most welcoming or forthcoming, they were all important to me and I worried that as they fell in love and found happiness, our friendship would be less important to them or less of a priority. Time had proven, though, that was far from the truth.

Things were different, but they'd settled into a new kind of normalcy that worked for us and it was honestly better than it had been before. Because, at the end of the day, I had my friends and I had my husband. It was more than I'd ever believed a man like me deserved, and yet...It was a whole lifetime of lessons come together to bring me to the present moment, and it was all a dream come true. Even if I'd never even been brave enough to have a dream like this one.

When I reached the door, I found my whiskey on a cocktail table, the ice long melted. I took a sip anyway, turning around in time to watch Val go to his knees taking Jason's cock into his hand and Drake's into his mouth. My own dick gave another valiant twitch, nowhere near being done, even if I was ready for a break.

I'd thought that I would leave Val to it, but listening to him choke and gag around Drake's dick was a sight to behold, so I committed myself to getting back quickly. Slipping out of the room, the air in the hallway smelled decidedly not like sex, which I bemoaned. I left the door to the playroom open, and headed downstairs to the bar to get a drink for myself and something for Rose. There was water in the room, which was the only thing Val would need when he was finished or, rather, after he'd finished everyone else.

Reaching the loft in record time, I stepped onto the landing just in time to see Archie and Owen slip into the playroom. Dalton and Royce were in the far corner of the public loft space, with Royce against the cross, his pants around his knees with eggplant-colored stripes across the back of his ass and thighs. Rob and Grayson sat on the couch we'd all previously occupied, Rob saying something in Grayson's ear while they both watched the cross with rapt attention.

Stepping back into the playroom, I pulled the door closed behind me and took stock of the scene. Rose and Flynn were still on the couch and Rose looked as flushed as his namesake, his now soft cock in Flynn's massive hand. Archie and Owen stood in the corner. Archie whispered something in his ear and Owen's hand moved quickly up and down his shaft. On the far side of the room, Val still had Drake's cock in his mouth, but he now had Jason's cock up his ass. He moaned and writhed, and I'd never loved him more. Jason threw a look over his shoulder, nostrils flaring when he saw I'd returned. I took a sip of my drink and arched a brow.

"There's room for one more," he said.

I laughed, tearing open my belt and fly with my free hand. Val let out a garbled wail, and Drake threw his head back, coming in Val's mouth with a grunt.

"There's room for more than one," I said with a choked-off laugh.

"You're a lucky man, Barclay," Archie said under his breath, and I nodded, heading across the room to the man who'd patiently and tenderly taken the care to show me I deserved all the things he wanted to share with me…

And more.

TROPHY DOMS NEW YORK

All In
Trophy Doms New York #1

Christian is a prince on the run and Kale is a millionaire who hates the word no. Together, the two of them are about to go all in on a love neither saw coming.

Christian

My entire life is nothing but people telling me what to do, where to go, and what to say. I've made it my job to fight back against the rules of the crown, but everything changes when I lock lips with a stranger in a last ditch attempt to dodge my security detail. I'm an expert at giving people the slip, but getting away from Kale is the last thing I want. From the first kiss, I think I've finally found where I belong. But with my trip to New York coming to an end and my royal family breathing down my neck about duty and my responsibility, I know our time is limited.

I might be good at getting away for a night here and there, but one night with Kale will *never* be enough.

Kale

I may have humble beginnings on a farm in central California, but I've always wanted more. More chances at life, more money to live it, and more opportunities to choose from. Thanks for wealthy grandparents, I've been allowed all of those things, and I'm no longer in the habit of accepting when someone tells me *no,* whether it's in the boardroom or the bedroom. But then Christian falls into my lap, and he's everything I've ever wanted, except he's telling me we won't last. We can't work. It's out of our control.

I refuse to accept that from the man whose stolen my heart.

I've been handed a lot of things in my life, but Christian can't be one of them. From the start, everything is against us, but that only keeps me more focused on how to make him mine. I've never been in love before, never wanted to share my life with another person, but something about this bratty, submissive little Prince makes me ready to throw my old life out the window and go all in so I can find out what it's like to truly have someone to call my own.

ALSO BY KATE HAWTHORNE

Trophy Doms Social Club

Humbled

Edged

Praised

Bound

Shared

Trophy Doms New York

All In

Tied Down

Giving Consent

Worth the Risk

Worth the Wait

Worth the Fight

Worth the Chance

All in Good Time

Necessary Space

Necessary Time

Duality

Dual Destruction

Dual Surrender

Dual Defiance

Two Truths and a Lie

A Real Good Lie

A Cold Hard Truth

A Matter of Fact

Room for Love

Reckless

Heartless

Faultless

Fearless

Limitless

A Very Messy Motel Brothers Wedding

Relentless

Secrets in Edgewood

A Taste of Sin

The Cost of Desire

A Love Made Whole

Secrets in Edgewood: The Complete Series

The Lonely Hearts Stories

His Kind of Love

The Colors Between Us

Love Comes After

Until You Say Otherwise

<u>STANDALONES</u>

Rebound

One for the Road

Daybreak - Vino & Veritas

Unfettered

Dreams

A Thousand Lifetimes

<u>COLLABORATIONS</u>

With E.M. Denning

Irreplaceable

Future Fake Husband

Future Gay Boyfriend

Future Ex Enemy

With J.R. Gray

May the Best Man Win

ABOUT KATE HAWTHORNE

Kate Hawthorne is a writer and author educator with over three dozen published romance novels spread across two successful and award winning pen names.

Known for stories that pack a figurative (and sometimes literal) punch, Kate has built a recognizable brand that consistently delivers emotionally charged and character driven happy endings for everyone.

Visit her website
http://www.katehawthornebooks.com

Sign up for Kate's newsletter
http://www.katehawthornebooks.com/extra

facebook.com/authorkatehawthorne
x.com/katewriteswords
instagram.com/kate.hawthorne
patreon.com/katehawthorne

www.ingramcontent.com/pod-product-compliance
Lightning Source LLC
Chambersburg PA
CBHW030124010826
48973CB00002B/404